Wildfire

and other stories

BANAPHOOL

Wildfire

and Other Stories

Translated by
SOMNATH ZUTSHI

With an introduction by
NABANEETA DEV SEN

LONDON NEW YORK CALCUTTA

 Seagull Books, 2018

First published in English translation by Seagull Books, 1999
Translation and Introduction © Seagull Books, 1999

ISBN   978 0 8574 2 497 6

British Library Cataloguing-in-Publication Data
A catalogue record for this book is available
from the British Library.

Typeset by Seagull Books, Calcutta, India
Printed and bound by Maple Press, York, Pennsylvania, USA

Contents

Wildflower

Banaphool means wildflower. Dr Balaichand Mukhopadhyay chose this as the name for a writer who wished to blossom outside the formal garden of Bengali literature. It was the pen-name for this Bengali doctor who lived and worked in Bhagalpur, Bihar, met new people every hour, learnt about the human condition as a detached professional and commented on it as a sensitive human being.

He had started writing short stories while studying medicine in Calcutta, and he found the huge, empty lecture theatres ideally suited for his creative activities. 'Chokh Gelo', generally regarded as his first published story (1922), came out when he was a third-year student at Calcutta Medical College. 'I used to sit alone in the huge, empty galleries,' recalls the author in his memoirs, 'I cannot write except in quiet, peaceful surroundings. The empty classrooms of Calcutta Medical College offered the ideal space for my creative efforts. One fine day, I produced four or five short stories all at one go, and wondered whether they were stories at all.' To make sure, he sent them off to *Prabasi*, the most prestigious literary journal in Bengali at the time. The editor promptly wrote back, accepting all the stories for publication. On his very first appearance, Banaphool was recognized as a unique, refreshing and powerful presence in Bengali literature.

Although he had begun to write quite early, Banaphool's first collection of stories was not available until 1936. Thirty-four books of short stories were published by 1967, bringing the total number of his stories to 578. Typically, in a brief introduction to his collected volumes of short stories, the author had written only a few lines: 'Those who love my writing need no introduction to it. Those who do not, need it even less. As for those who are unfamiliar with my writing, they will recognize my nature as soon as they read my stories. I have nothing in particular to say to them either.'

In other words, Banaphool was confident that the stories speak for themselves. Which they do, and to the Bengali reader his introduction is good enough. But this particular collection is meant for those not familiar with Banaphool's literary work, or even his name. I, too, believe that the   stories are strong enough to introduce their author to the reader. 'Too many unnecessary words spoil the beauty of art,' wrote Banaphool. But two decades after his death, the uninitiated reader may expect a few words by way of introduction.

Banaphool's stories are stark and short, often much too short, some even cryptic, almost like notes for a story. He states the bare minimum. The reader is treated with utmost respect, and most of the narrative is left to our imagination. Many stories do not stretch beyond a page, and most not beyond three. He has a distinct literary style, not descriptive but suggestive, sometimes lyrical, sometimes satirical. There is a wide variety of plots. And an equal variety of characters. The stories introduce us to a wide cross-section of the Indian people.

Then again, some stories do not use a plot but are lyrical and impressionistic. They speak through images. Banaphool's love of precision and economy of words, his eye for the apparently insignificant detail, give us a sudden glimpse of the human condition. His strong sense of irony, as well as his deep empathy, lend a sharp edge and an

unsuspected emotional depth to his stories. He can deal with senti-
mental themes with enormous sensitivity but without sentimentality,
using terse, dispassionate language as his tool to carve out images
from the heart. For this, his wry humour is a great asset.

In these short stories, the 'moment' in time is central, the author
uses very few words to introduce the plot, he comes directly to the cli-
max. Sometimes a dramatic tension is built up through the story and
there is a sudden revelation at the end. Whatever may be the style of
the particular story, it is always short and succinct.

About his own creative process, Banaphool says:

> How I write the stories I do not know myself. The way clouds
> come floating in the sky and flowers bloom in the trees, sto-
> ries sprout in my mind. How and when a plot comes to me
> is hard to tell. I have a feeling that the real storyteller hides
> in the wings somewhere, and when he wishes to tell a story,
> he makes me write it down. Plots come to me all of a sudden
> and someone within forces me to express it in words . . . I
> meet all kinds of people—they leave a permanent mark upon
> my mind, remain stored inside and mix with my imagina-
> tion. When the hidden storyteller wishes to tell a story, he
> borrows the images from the stored material . . . I do not
> know who this story-teller is but I have to depend on his
> moods. You could call it the creative genius, or divine grace.

Banaphool recalls how Tagore had asked him whether he knew
Chekhov and O'Henry, as Banaphool's short stories had reminded
the poet of them. Our author had not had a chance to read either of
them till then, but soon after this meeting he sought out O'Henry and
Chekhov and greatly admired them both. But he found the British
English translation of Chekhov closer to his heart than the unfamiliar
American English originals of O'Henry. (Incidentally, that Chekhov,
too, had a medical degree, although he never practised, might have
had something to do with his literary preference!) Tagore also pointed
out, in a letter, that Banaphool's training in science had been of service

to him—it had moulded his vision of the world, given him an eye for detail, linguistic precision and an analytical mind. It had initiated Banaphool's 'search for the neglected and the rejected in society', for the 'ever-unseen'. His scientific curiosity and keen power of observation had him seek them out and lend them human worth and literary value, thus 'stretching the limits of our vision'. The wild flower, Tagore had told him, has no place in the porcelain vase, nor in the temple; it blossoms by the roadside, unnoticed, except by the creative vision. Banaphool, identifying with it, has brought to our notice the worth of the marginal in society.

Right from the beginning Banaphool has been experimenting with literary forms and succeeded in creating his own literary style. Today his works form an integral part of Bengali literary classics. This volume is the first attempt to take his work out of Bengal. Admittedly, many of his finer nuances are lost in translation. Take, for example, his first published short story, 'Chokh Gelo'. In the first place, that is the name of a bird with romantic associations in Bengal. Second, literally it means 'the eyes are gone'. Third, in idiomatic usage it signifies 'the eyes hurt'. And finally, it also hides the verb 'to gouge' in it. All this is extremely significant for the complex plot of the story, whereas in English translation it has become merely 'Blind Love' which is more explanatory and lacks the suggestive richness. Such risks are always involved in the adventurous task of literary translation, yet are unavoidable in an effort to introduce Banaphool to readers outside Bengal who might enjoy getting to know him. Let us hope the translated stories will offer a taste of the lively, conversational, apparently simple style of stating deep matters, that has charmed the Bengali reader for over seventy years.

This is Banaphool's birth centenary, and time the rest of the world got acquainted with his work. Banaphool is a truly Indian author; he wrote in Bengali about people from all over the country while living and working in Bihar. And this Indianness comes through quite clearly in the translations. The sociocultural experiences depicted in these stories are not exclusive to Bengal but shared by us all. The characters are familiar, as are the situations. It is a pity that in India we are so poor when it comes to knowing our own literary heritage. We are far more familiar with the literatures of the Western world, thanks to our colonial training and the lack of translated material in the Indian regional languages. But happily for us, the scene is changing. Today there is a lot more interest in publishing translations from regional literatures, with a growing readership. We are beginning to get curious about our Indian identity; we want to explore the different faces of India reflected in the regional languages. This book is a part of such an effort. It tries to introduce to our readers an author admired in Bengal but unknown in the rest of the country, including Bihar, which was his home and frequently the backdrop for his stories.

We hope it will give the reader a refreshing whiff of the wildflower.

Nabaneeta Dev Sen
20 December 1998

Preface

Those who love my writing need no introduction to it. Those who do not, need it even less. As for those who are unfamiliar with my writing, they will recognize my nature as soon as they read my stories. I have nothing in particular to say to them, either.

There is something that I consider important to acknowledge, however. I am indebted to my dear friend, Mr Parimal Goswami, the editor of *Shanibarer Chithi*. Without his enthusiasm and constant urging, I would not have written the majority of my stories.

These stories were published through the efforts of the respected literateur Mr Kedarnath Bannerjee and with the help of Mr Haridas Chatterjee.

I extend my heartfelt thanks to both these individuals.

Bhagalpur, Bihar

Wildfire
and Other Stories

Necessity

For two whole months I suffered from malaria. The spleen bloated and painful, the body wrecked and ruined. The doctor had warned that another major illness would be the end of me. The spleen would never recover.

I had sat the matric exams before falling ill—after recovering, I learnt that I had failed. There was a girl in our neighbourhood I was secretly in love with. She got married the other day. Her husband is a healthier, better-educated man. So, from every angle, my life appeared hopeless. Should one, under such circumstances, commit suicide?— I thought about that too, once or twice. But I've always been a bit of a coward, so I couldn't bring myself to do it, after all.

I'd heard that the world held nothing unnecessary, nothing worthless. But me? Was there any necessity for me? There was.

Despite my weak health, I'd come to Calcutta in search of a job. Lived in a Hindu hotel. That afternoon, on my way to meet a saheb at a mercantile firm, I got run over by a car. I can't remember very much after that.

Now I see that medical students are using me to further their knowledge of anatomical science. They are cutting my worn body into pieces and going over it inch by inch, seeing what goes where. At last I've been useful for something. My happiness knows no bounds!

It goes without saying that I am now dead.

Creator

The rolled-up sheet of paper had been in the cupboard for days. Enjoying the peace and quiet. Suddenly, one day, the Artist took it out. Removed the rubber band holding it together and spread the sheet out on the table.

What do you think you're doing? screamed the paper. But that scream did not reach the Artist's ears. The language of paper remains unknown to humans. The Artist picked up the paper, placed it on a piece of black cardboard and pinned its four corners with tacks. Then!

The paper continued to scream!

The Artist paid it no attention.

Dipping his brush into black paint, he smeared it across the paper.

The paper protested: Why are you turning my white into black?

The Artist remained deaf to its protests.

He picked up another brush and splashed some beige onto it.

What's this? What's going on?—shrieks the paper.

The Artist is unmoved.

He starts applying yellow, blue, green, orange, pink, one after the other.

The paper's screams of torment never reach his ears. For two hours, he continues to paint. The paper's wails, pleas, prayers—nothing disturbs the Creator. Once the painting is finished, he stands at a distance and looks at it. He doesn't like it. Taking it off the board, he rips the picture into pieces and throws it away.

Then, he brings out another sheet of paper.

Jogen Pandit

Jogen Pandit, of Haripur Lower Primary School, is mortified in his old age. He just cannot get along with the new ways of the new generation. He still makes his students memorize their lessons and still punishes them if they fail. Ear-tweaking, smacking, standing on their benches or kneeling on the floor while holding their ears, even caning. The stubborn ones are caned so hard they are almost half-dead.

And he does something else. Something he has always done. He sleeps for an hour or two as soon as he comes to school.

He lives some miles away, in a gold merchant's house. There, he has to stay up late into the night, doing the accounts. In return, he gets a rent-free room and provisions. He cooks his own meals. A man of great gravitas. He is feared by everyone. Aside, the students call him Buffalo Pandit. A dark-skinned man, a large-built man. With bloodshot eyes. No one wants to upset him in a hurry.

By the time he gets to school every day, walking the miles-long path from his house, it is almost twelve in the afternoon and his legs are covered with dust up to his knees. No shoes, of course, nor umbrella. Only a small bundle. Containing a small towel, a few books, his spectacles and a small container of moshla. As he walks in, he shouts, 'Water, someone.' The students fetch him a pail of water from the nearby pond. Jogen Pandit then ceremoniously washes his feet. Extracts the towel from his bundle and dries them carefully. Then, with the help of a few students, shifts a few benches close together. Pops a clove or a small cardamom into his mouth and carefully re-ties his bundle. Then turns to the students again, 'Go—memorize your lessons. I'll see what you've learnt after I wake up. No mistakes, mind. Make even one, and I'll not spare you.'

The students leave. And Jogen Pandit, placing his head on his bundle, lies down to sleep.

Outside the schoolhouse is a huge banyan tree. The students sit under it and study. After a few hours, Jogen Pandit wakes up. Again the students fetch him a pail of water and he washes his face, his eyes, his nose, his ears, especially his nose and ears. His nose and ears are both rather large. Not just large but also full of hair.

Drying his face and hands, Jogen Pandit breaks off a branch from the banyan tree and starts his lesson. By the time his lesson is done and the class is over, the branch may be found split into pieces . . .

Thus, every day . . .

But no student from Jogen Pandit's school has ever failed his exams. Every year a few win scholarships. Not one boy has gone bad. Because it was not only in school but also outside that his presence made itself felt. A student who wasn't performing despite the beatings, who wasn't responding to instruction—Jogen Pandit pursued him all the way home, even scolded the parents. How could a boy go bad? Jogen Pandit could not rest in peace until every student had been thoroughly disciplined.

He beat the students but he loved them too. His salary was meagre, yet he managed to reward the good students, buy books for the poor ones. If a child fell ill, he visited regularly and asked after his health. If necessary, he would nurse him too.

He has no family. He had been married once, in Bankura. Where he was teaching then, early in his life. But his wife died. And he couldn't bear to live there any longer. He saw an advertisement in the paper and came away to this village. It's been twenty-five years. These students are all he has. So his hold on them must not loosen, all the more.

But times have changed. People are no longer able to tolerate his old-fashioned ways. No one dared say a word until then, but the day Jogen Pandit thrashed the son of the new police inspector for insolence was the day the conspiracy against him began. The six-foot-tall man was such a towering presence that the inspector couldn't say anything to his face. But he wasn't going to let go. Describing Jogen Pandit's evil ways, he got the villagers to sign a long petition and sent it off to the head of the Education Department. Jogen Pandit knew absolutely nothing of all this.

Some days later, as the leader of the petitioners, the inspector was informed by the Education Department that the District Inspector of Schools would be visiting soon in order to investigate the matter. The inspector was pleased.

On the appointed day, Inspector Bhutnath Bhoumick arrived and took the inspector with him to the school. Jogen Pandit had just finished his siesta and was busy teaching in his usual red-eyed fashion. But what Bhutnath did as soon as he reached the school left the inspector completely astonished. Such a huge, ferocious man Jogen Pandit was that Bhutnath felt like a worm. He greeted Jogen Pandit with a pranam, then stood to one side, wringing his hands. The inspector had not known that Bhutnath Bhoumick was an ex-student of Jogen Pandit. Taught by him during his Bankura days. Jogen Pandit was no less astonished at the sight of him, though he recognized him immediately.

'Arrey, it's Bhuto, isn't it? What're you doing here?'

'I'm an inspector of schools these days, Pandit-moshai.'

'Are you? Good, good. But why are you here? Oh, I see, you're visiting my school, aren't you?'

Jogen Pandit's smile spread from ear to ear. His eyes overflowed with affection and pride.

'Er, no. I'm here on some other business,' an embarrassed Bhutnath mumbled. 'I'm here to see you.'

'What about?'

'Let your lesson finish, then I'll tell you.'

'I can finish the lesson right now. All of you—go home! In honour of the inspector's visit, I'm declaring a holiday! Do you know, he's my student too? Come on, do pranam.'

The students did their pranams and went home.

Seeing which way the wind was blowing, the policeman scuttled off as well. Jogen Pandit did not exchange a single word with him.

'Now tell me about you. Have you married? How many children?'

'Two boys.'

'Good, good.'

After talking of many things, and hesitating for many minutes, Bhutnath finally got to the point. Showed Jogen Pandit the petition. And said, 'Of course, since I'm the one who's here, there'll be no adverse report, but . . .'

Then, glancing at Jogen Pandit's face, Bhutnath Bhoumick fell silent.

Jogen Pandit was staring at the petition, speechless and stunned. As if he couldn't believe his eyes. The very people whose sons he had slaved over for these so many years, those people had written a petition against him! He knew every signature. Many among them he had taught too.

After a few moment, Jogen Pandit finally spoke. 'I'm not staying here any longer, Bhutnath. I'll leave—tomorrow itself.'

'Where?'

'Anywhere!'

Bhutnath knew Jogen Pandit well. He knew the man would not change his mind. He stayed quiet for a minute. Then: 'There's something I'd like to say, if you allow me . . .'

'What?'

'If you're determined to leave, why not come and live with me? I will be honoured to have you home. Take charge of my two boys—I'll be so relieved if you do so. I'm always out, touring . . .'

After a moment's thought, Jogen Pandit said, 'So be it.'

Just before dawn the next day, Jogen Pandit stopped at the village boundary and looked at the village for a long, long time.

Then he went away.

Nawab Sahib

I

I saw the Nawab Sahib three times. Once face to face, and twice in my imagination. Face to face was not for long, either; perhaps five minutes, no more. That's the story I'll tell you.

I was the doctor there. One day I heard that a few of the local notables wanted to invite the Nawab to tea. So that he had company, some of the local gentry were being invited too. Myself included. The person who came to invite me, he said, 'Your house is lying empty, Doctor. When is your family coming?'

'A month or two still, before they come.'

'In that case, if we could use it to prepare the tea for the Nawab's visit, we'd be most grateful. None of us have so much room to spare. Also, given what I've heard—'

The man stopped.

'What've you heard?'

'If we were inviting ordinary folk like ourselves, there'd be none-such trouble. But the Nawab Sahib's a different matter. His own people will come to do the cooking. Three assistant chefs, one head chef. They'll come and tell us what they need. Then, a day earlier, they'll come and see the place, supervise the outdoor oven-building and so on. Then, on the day itself, they'll come by daybreak and start the actual cooking. It's a load of bother, I tell you. Now you've got a large house, lots of room. That's why we were wondering if you'd let us—'

I wasn't at all keen that all this bother take place at home, but I couldn't turn down the request. I said, 'All right, I've no objections.

But tell me, why've you people suddenly invited the Nawab Sahib to tea?'

The gentleman's eyebrows shot up a few inches and he stared at me in amazement.

'Do you know what a great honour it is to have the Nawab Sahib to tea? He doesn't accept invitations from anyone. Why, we've been inviting him for four years. For some reason, he's agreed this time . . .'

I was silent for a few moments.

Then I asked, 'You people know him well, do you?'

'He's one of our biggest debtors.'

'What d'you mean?'

'I mean that we give him thousands of rupees in loans. Whenever he needs money, he informs us and we hand over the sum required.'

I was amazed. I had always been given to believe that the person who borrowed money remained grateful to the person who loaned it to him. But this seemed to be the opposite.

'He borrows a lot, does he?'

'A vast amount.'

'And pays back on time?'

'He does, but not on time. We don't ask him for an IOU or anything like that. We just let him have the money. Then when we hear that he has some money, we visit him to offer our respects. Then we tell him that on such and such a date, we'd had the honour of making a certain sum available for him. It would now be exceedingly helpful if we might have it back.

'He promptly gives his khazanchi an order. We're given whatever sum we ask for. If we ask for ten thousand, having loaned him only five, we get that. He'd certainly never ask. He's a real Nawab Sahib, d'you see?'

What could I say? I just kept quiet. And became curious to see the man.

Even I had heard of the Nawab Sahib, though I had not been fortunate enough to have cast eyes on him yet. I had started my practice in the area very recently.

'When is he supposed to come to tea?'

'In about four days from now. Next Wednesday, at 5 p. m. His chefs will come tomorrow.'

At the appointed hour, the chefs arrived. I did not know what the real Nawab Sahib would be like, but these certainly were mini Nawabs. One had a hennaed beard; another had on velvet slippers and a muslin kurta with a velvet waistcoat and the stone on the third one's finger seemed to be a real diamond. The head chef was dressed in an immaculately cut suit and spoke flawless English. I was told that he had trained as a chef in Europe. French, Italian, Mughal, Afghan, English, Goan, Chinese, Japanese—he could cook any kind of cuisine. His salary was five hundred rupees a month.

I was taken aback by the sight of them but managed to welcome them and asked them to sit down. In turn, they greeted me respectfully. Only the head chef sat; the other three remained standing. One of the notables who had invited the Nawab Sahib had also come along. He sat in another chair. The head chef asked him in English, 'What did you intend to serve the Nawab Sahib?'

'Well, it's an invitation to tea. But we can't just serve the Nawab Sahib only tea, can we? Some pulao, a few meat dishes and whatever else you think would be appropriate. We've ordered bread, cakes, biscuits, jam, etc., from Firpo's. They'll be sending a man along with the linen and the service. They've taken the responsibility for the tea service and . . .'

'But will they be able to provide a gold service?' asked the head chef. 'Since you're inviting the Nawab Sahib to tea . . .'

The head chef was looking at the gentleman with a placid expression on his face. But I could see the notable breaking into sweat inside.

'How many people have you invited?'

'About ten.'

'Oh, just ten? I'll bring the gold service, then.'

'Shall I cancel the order with Firpo's?'

'No, let them come. We'll need the tea cups and things . . . Now, can you get me some paper? I'll make a list.'

I gave him a notepad. Once again, the head chef asked, 'Ten people, eh?'

'Yes.'

The head chef closed his eyes for a minute. 'I don't think we ought to overdo things. Just two kinds of pulao, plain and zarda. And four kinds of kebabs. I don't think curry goes well with tea, do you? I'm making the list accordingly. You could perhaps organize some shingaras, nimkis, kochuris and so on. Oh, by the way, can you get decent ghee in these parts? Because if you can't I'll get it, along with some good quality flour, from my kitchen. It's specially sent over from Kashmir for the Nawab Sahib. The flour comes from the Punjab.'

The rich man said, 'Fine, you get the ghee and the flour. We'll pay whatever it costs.'

'Costs? We're not grocers, sir.'

'No, no, of course not. I'm sorry. I meant no offence,' said the gentleman rather quickly.

The head chef said, 'Please, keep the items on the list ready. I'll be back the day after tomorrow morning. Tuesday, that is. But tomorrow we'll need a couple of servants to clean the courtyard properly. We'll also need a bricklayer, to build the oven. Ramzan Ali, make sure that you supervise the building of the oven . . .'

'Yes, sir.'

The diamond-beringed Ramzan Ali acknowledged his instructions with a salaam.

Then the head chef gave Ghafoor Khan his instructions, 'You'll decorate the kitchen area. Flowerpots, carpets, vases, chairs—whatever your requirements are, please let this gentleman know. He'll organize them for you.'

Ghafoor Khan turned towards the gentleman with an adaab. 'A couple of dozen flower pots, at least one nice flower vase, a carpet and an easy chair. We'll need these at a minimum. Also, two small tea-tables, one for each side of the chair, an ashtray and a pomander. Oh, a decent marquee . . .'

The mind boggled at this recitation.

Did they really need to decorate the kitchen area? With all this?

'You'll need all this for the cooking area, will you?' I blurted out.

The head chef smiled and answered in impeccable English, 'Of course. How will the chefs cook if their ambience isn't pleasant? Or if they're not in a good mood? Moreover, the area where we cook for the Nawab Sahib has to be kept looking nice, doesn't it?'

'Oh yes, indeed. Definitely,' the notable said. But again, I got the feeling that he was sweating inside.

The head chef frowned in thought for a few seconds. 'I'll go home and send you the list in a little while. I might forget a few items if I drew it up here. My man will come a little later and give you the list . . . I'll be going now. But do please organize the items as quickly as you can . . . Abid Miyan, tomorrow you'll come and decorate the room in which the Nawab Sahib will be taking tea. By the way, d'you have chandeliers?'

'We do,' answered the notable. 'How many would you require?'

'About a dozen, if they're large ones.'

'Fine. We'll get them.'

The third chef, Abid Miyan, stood aside after a salaam. The head chef did his courteous adaab and left. The other three followed him. Before leaving, however, they announced that they would return the following day. The notable wiped his face, forehead and neck with a handkerchief, then said, 'We'd imagined that a couple of hundred would do the trick. But I get the feeling that it's going to cost a lot more. Well, so it should, so it should. It's no ordinary matter, you know. Inviting the Nawab Sahib to tea . . . Well, I'm off as well. Please have the list sent across as soon as it's delivered.'

'All right.'

The man left.

A couple of hours later, someone came and handed over a list. I was astounded. Were these people insane? For a group of ten people—seven khaasis (each seven to ten kilos in weight). For the plain pulao, fine long grain rice (twenty kilos). For the zarda pulao, rice from Peshawar (twenty kilos). Plus, twenty different kinds of spices for the pulaos, five kilos each, ten kilos of onions, ten kilos of garlic, five kilos of ginger. Raisins, pistachios and almonds, all five kilos each. Extraordinary! Nevertheless, I sent the list to the gentleman. It was the headache of the people who had invited the Nawab Sahib. I wasn't going to worry myself about it. I intended to arrive at the right time, eat and see this Nawab Sahib. So I sent the list across. And went out to visit my patients.

Ramzan Ali, Ghafoor Khan and Abid Miyan arrived the next morning. Along with a bricklayer, two coolies, some bricks and mortar. I pointed out the empty space at the back and left on my rounds. When I returned, which was around two in the afternoon, I noticed that they had completely altered the appearance of the place. The area had been scrubbed clean, a neat brick oven had come up, there were flower pots scattered all over. They had even covered the area with a small marquee, the material beautifully embroidered. Even the poles were covered with some sort of tinselled stuff. A comfortable canvas deck-chair had been placed nearby, with a small table on each side. The flower vase, pomander and ashtray were all present and accounted for. And a carpet neatly rolled up, on one side.

Ramzan Ali explained politely, 'The carpet, teapoys and chair will be required on Wednesday morning. And that's when we'll need the pomander, flower vase and so on. I'll leave them in one of your empty rooms for the time being . . .'

'But what on earth will you do with all these things?' I asked.

'Mr Noor Mohammed, the head chef I mean, will use them. We'll spread the carpet and put the chair on it, the teapoys will go on either side of the chair. One's for the pomander and the vase, the other for the ashtray.'

Good Lord!! However, I made no comment except to tell them to put the things inside. The next day, the various other items on the list began to arrive, one by one. Seven fat khaasis, bleating in front of my house. The rice and spices. A little later, Mr Noor Mohammed himself, along with his flour from the Punjab and the ghee from Kashmir. I noticed that the notable had come too.

I was due another surprise now. Mr Noor Mohammed circled the animals, carefully examining them. Then he asked Abid Miyan to pick one up by its haunches. Abid did so.

Noor Mohammed looked it over carefully until he was satisfied. 'Keep this one. The others can be sent back. We won't need all the meat from this one either. I'll select about three kilos personally . . .'

He looked at Ramzan Ali next, and said, 'The three of you had better get started. I want two kilos of each type of rice. But I want each grain to be whole and fat. That's why I asked for so much extra. Two of you should clean the rice. Then get to work on the spices. I want two hundred and fifty grammes of each, but make sure they're the choicest bits. Be particularly careful while you select the cloves, cardamom, peppercorns, etc. I don't want to see a single bad peppercorn. The same applies for the raisins and dry fruits. They often have a lot of rubbish mixed in with them. Make sure there are no spoilt raisins and so on . . .'

'Yes, sir.'

Ramzan Ali proceeded towards the rice. The head chef left after delivering his instructions. Before leaving, he informed me that his three assistants would be doing the initial cleaning, etc., of the ingredients, and he would return the next day. After he left, the three men got to work and by nine in the evening had finished everything. Most of the rice, spices and dry fruits were rejected. Only the flawless portions were retained.

Early the next morning, Mr Noor Mohammed arrived. Ramzan, Ghafoor and Abid began to carry out his orders while he sat in comfort on the deck-chair, smoked expensive cigarettes and issued instructions. The entire area soon filled with the aroma of cooking. Mr Noor Mohammed exerted himself only occasionally, while the pulao was cooking. The rice was carefully mixed with the ghee and spices, measured amounts of stock were added, lids put on top of the pots and the edges sealed with dough. From time to time, Mr Noor Mohammed would get up and, with the aid of a stethoscope, listen to the sounds emanating from the pots. Much in the way of a physician examining the chest of a patient, Mr Noor Mohammed was deciding on the condition of the boiling pulao by the sounds from within.

By now, I was simply stunned into submission.

At precisely 5 p. m. the Nawab Sahib alighted from his limousine. He had come dressed in a snowy white kurta and churidaar. On his head was a white Muslim cap. A strange simile came to my mind when I saw him—he was not a man but a shining sword blade! Bright blue eyes and a faint smile on his lips, he greeted us individually and then sat down. The individuals who had invited him said various effusive things. He listened with his head tilted to one side and a smile on his lips. Occasionally, he nodded gently.

The food arrived, on the gold service, followed by the tea. The Nawab Sahib took a few sips from a cup. He did not touch any of the food. After drinking half a cup of tea, he got up. 'You must forgive me but I have another appointment,' he said, with great courtesy.

He left after saying adaab to everyone.

II

I next heard of the Nawab Sahib from a very different source. I was treating a paanwala's son for some illness or other. The man was dirt poor and couldn't pay my fee in full. His only possessions were a ramshackle hut and his paan shop. The man had become destitute paying for medicines. Some months later, he called me once again. This time, his wife had fallen ill. I noticed, then, that he was much better off—he now possessed a two-storey house. However, he again gave me only a part of my fees.

'You seem to be doing well now,' I told him, 'Your two-storey house . . .'

'I'm just as poor as I ever was, Doctor,' the man said. 'The Nawab Sahib had this house built.'

'The Nawab Sahib?'

'Yes, Doctor. I was fortunate that his car had a flat tyre right in front of my house. I helped his chauffeur to change the tyre. And did a qurnish to the Nawab Sahib. He smiled at me and asked, "Is this where you live?"

'I answered, "Yes Master, this is my house."

'He looked at my shack and then left. The next day an architect arrived and said that the Nawab Sahib had ordered a house built for me. The work started the same day and before you knew it, my hut had been replaced by this two-storey house.'

It was as though I could see the Nawab Sahib. Fair, blue-eyed and with a faint smile on his face . . .

III

A few days ago I was told that the Nawab Sahib had died. Not from illness but by drowning. Many people were saying that he had walked into the sea. Apparently because of the bizarre will he had left behind. It said, 'I hereby bequeath my entire property to the poor, for their benefit. But now, I no longer have a penny. What will I survive on for the rest of my life.'

I had gone to Puri recently. I was on the beach when I felt that I could see the Nawab Sahib's face in the waves. He was gazing at the starry skies; the same blue eyes, that familiar faint smile on his face.

Blind Love

I imagine that most people would not have considered her attractive.

It is not as though I thought her very beautiful—but I loved her. There was something about her eyes, I don't know what. I have never seen such beautiful, dreamy eyes. She also had a reputation for being a tomboy.

That plain and fickle creature had won my heart. I had fallen in love with her eyes.

I remember, one day, after kissing her in secret, I said, 'I wish I could steal your eyes away.'

'Why?'

'They're driving me mad. They're what I love the most.'

I loved her passionately. But she was not to be mine.

A stranger arrived and took her away, to the sound of a wedding band.

The sound of it broke my heart.

But the pain might have faded if another heart-rending incident had not taken place.

When she came home for a visit, I noticed she was blind. It was said that she had mistakenly put some medicine in her eyes, thinking it to be rose water.

We met in secret one day.

I said, 'Carelessness made you blind.'

'If you don't realize what made me blind, perhaps you're better off not knowing,' she retorted.

Insects

I

Nikhilranjan was the sworn enemy of all insects. He would kill an insect as soon as he spotted it. This was a habit of his since childhood. Once he had seen an insect, he could not rest until he had killed it. As a child, he would wander about his house, looking for insects. Butterflies or other flying insects being difficult to catch, he would look for insects that crawled or remained still. There is a kind of round, reddish-coloured insect found on cucumber or marrow vines. Nikhil used to be the implacable enemy of those creatures. But then he started a campaign against another kind of insect. These were ash-coloured, their bodies covered with a hard shell. They had cruel eyes. A friend gave Nikhil some information about them.

'Very nasty things, these. They're called earwigs. They enter through the ear whenever they get the opportunity. Very wicked.' Nikhil promptly squashed it to death. And after that, he would squash them whenever he set eyes on them. God only knows how many he killed. Actually, killing insects had been his only hobby during his childhood and his youth.

II

When Nikhilranjan went to university, his hobby suffered an interruption. Mainly because Calcutta is not as infested with insects as a village is. In Calcutta, it's the humans that crawl about like insects. Nevertheless, Nikhilranjan could occasionally be observed at night, staring up at the street lamps. The lamps were covered with insects. But they were out of reach, of course. Nikhilranjan would gaze at them awhile and return to his lodgings. One day, he suddenly felt as though an insect had crept in beneath his shirt and was crawling up and down his back. He quickly took off the shirt and saw that it was indeed an insect—an ash-coloured earwig. He immediately crushed it. But what happened a month later was rather strange. Nikhilranjan was a rather fussily clean person. He would wash his towel himself, make his bed neatly, dust his mosquito net before hanging it up and so on. One night, he was just about to drop off to sleep, when he felt as though something was crawling about on his neck. He quickly got up and switched on the light. At first, he couldn't see a thing. Then he turned the pillow over and saw an insect rapidly crawling away. One of those ash-coloured insects. It was almost behaving like a spy, the way it was hiding in one spot and then another. But Nikhil was not the sort to give up easily. He finally caught it and crushed it between his thumb and forefinger. The insect made a strange sound as it died, 'scrreenchh'. The sound pierced his head like a needle.

Immediately after, Nikhil raised his eyes and saw that another was clinging to the roof of the mosquito net. As if it was waiting in ambush. As he reached for it, the insect flew at him and bit him on his forehead; then sat elsewhere within the net. Nikhil was convinced that the insect had attacked him. He stood up in rage. But every time he tried to catch the thing, it would fly away. Nevertheless, how long can an insect avoid a man? Nikhil caught it in a while and crushed it between his fingers. This one made the same noise, 'scrreenchh'.

Then Nikhil saw that a few more were crawling about near the ceiling. By now, he was berserk with rage. He got hold of a broom and clambered up on a table. As soon as the insects fell off, he jumped from the table and crushed them underfoot. Each one died with a scream: 'scrreenchh'. But Nikhil was not able to kill them all. One flew away through the window.

It was after this that Nikhil noticed he was being shadowed by those ash-coloured insects. Every day he would notice one sitting somewhere in the room—perhaps near a corner, or on a bookshelf, or somewhere else. It goes without saying that he killed them as soon as he saw them. He also realized that one or two were getting away. Then one night, two were found inside the mosquito net. They didn't survive, of course, but Nikhil began to worry. He began to feel as though they had an ulterior motive of some kind. And that strange sound they made before dying, 'scrreenchh'. Did it float through the ether, warning the others? Nikhil became very watchful indeed. On one occasion he discovered with considerable amazement that two of were sitting on top of his desk. Though he killed them on the spot, he felt uncomfortable somehow . . .

One night he woke in terrible pain. He had a terrible earache, as though someone was turning a screwdriver in his ear. He poured some of the methylated spirit which he kept for lighting a spirit lamp, into his ear. But the pain didn't ease a bit. The poor fellow started sobbing in agony.

The next morning, the doctor took out a large insect from his ear—an ash-coloured insect.

Following this incident, Nikhil's expenses went up. He started buying cottonwool, to stuff into his ears. Not just at night before going to bed but sometimes during the day as well. He started buying all the insect repellents that he could find. He put insecticides everywhere; on his bed, the book-shelves, on the chairs and in every corner of the room. But the insects were still there, waiting quietly or slowly crawling about, outside the range of the chemicals. It is understood that Nikhil never spared them; he crushed them as soon as he caught them. It was not possible to keep count, of course, but it would be no exaggeration to say that he killed them in their thousands. But the insects kept coming. Nikhil could gain no respite from them.

III

Years have passed. Nikhil has started working. He was unable to get a job after graduating and has finally started a wholesale grain business, with money borrowed from his father-in-law. He was travelling to Guskhara that day and had, through sheer good fortune, managed to find an empty Third Class compartment. He promptly raised all the windows as soon as he got on. It was raining outside anyway. These days he rarely took the cottonwool out of his ears. Both his ears were stuffed. Seeing that there was no one else in the compartment, Nikhil sprayed insecticide everywhere. Then he unrolled his bedding, dusted it off carefully and spread it on one of the benches. He sprayed the insecticide once again and looked around carefully—no, not an insect in sight. Nikhil was as careful about insects as ever. He had noticed that any slackness on his part resulted in the earwigs trying to surround him. Before lying down, Nikhil examined the windows once again. Yes, everything was all right, not a gap anywhere. He lay down.

'Scrreenchh', 'scrreenchh', 'scrreenchh'.

Nikhil had fallen asleep. He woke with a start. Didn't it sound like those earwigs? He looked around carefully but again, not an insect anywhere. The screeching sound began to increase, however. It was as though the death screams of millions of insects could be heard at once. It soon turned into a terrible tumult. A little while later, Nikhil felt as though his face and his eyes were being struck by pellets, not one but thousands. He covered his face with his hands. He now felt his hands being struck; the pain was unbearable; he had to remove his hands. He started groping in front of him blindly, to see what was happening. He could feel nothing. The compartment was empty.

'Scrreenchh', 'scrreenchh', 'Scrreenchh'.

The death screams seemed to change into a shout of joy. His face felt as though it was being ripped to shreds. Two pellets seemed to strike his eyes suddenly. He fell down, then he felt as though someone was removing the cottonwool from his ears. He felt as though something was entering through his ears. He lost his senses.

Everyone was baffled when the body was found the next morning. The doctor said that the man had been shocked to death.

A Puja Story

You want to hear a story, do you? Then listen to this one.

On that occasion, I was returning from Simla, just a couple of days before the Pujas. I'm an insurance agent and I get to all sorts of places because of my job. I had not been able to get the 'life' I had gone for. Someone else had bagged it. Therefore, I was depressed.

The compartment I boarded contained not one but three extraordinarily beautiful women. I had never seen such beauty before; my eyes were dazzled. There was a young man with them and he looked like a demigod. I felt quite embarrassed to sit next to them, I can tell you. I am fat and ugly. But I did. A little while was spent in silence, then I addressed the young man hesitantly, 'Going far?' I had noticed that he was concentrating on a film magazine—the picture of a scantily clad starlet obviously had him mesmerized.

'Going far?'

The youth turned with a start, 'I beg your pardon. Were you saying something?'

'Nothing of consequence, really. Just asking whether you were going far.'

'To the land of Bengal.'

'That's where I'm going as well. At least we can keep each other company.' But the young man had gone back to his magazine.

I noticed that my firm had placed an advertisement in the magazine. Hoping to attract the youth's attention to it, I said, 'My firm placed that ad, you know. The bonus and . . .'

With his eyes still riveted on the pin-up, the youth said, 'I don't understand all that stuff.'

'What d'you mean? You are insured, aren't you?'

'Didn't I say that I don't understand all that stuff? I'm looking at what I do understand.' He immediately turned back to his starlet. But I'm Bishnucharan Barma, not a man to be discouraged easily. 'A smart man like you,' I began, 'can't understand life insurance? I don't believe it for a second. For a few rupees each month, your life . . .'

He interrupted me sharply, 'Don't bother with all that chat about rupees. If you want to discuss worldly matters, talk to my mother.'

I greeted the mother with my best smile and said, 'Your son doesn't want to discuss the matter. But I'm sure that you'll agree with me, madam, when I say that insuring one's life is everyone's duty.'

The lady's face suffused with a smile, 'I'm afraid that I don't know too much about it, either. Perhaps you wouldn't mind explaining in greater detail.'

'Not at all,' said I, and promptly started my incantation of the standard magic phrases. Strangely, the lady seemed totally unaffected. Both the other women listened to my speech with due care yet seemed as unenthusiastic.

I stopped to draw my breath. 'I do hope that I've been able to make myself clear?'

'Oh, absolutely,' the lady replied. 'But I'm afraid I don't need any life insurance.'

'You might not, madam. But what about your son? Or your husband for that matter?'

'My husband is immortal. He won't need any either.'

Just then, the Lord Ganesh stuck his elephant head out from the top bunk and said in his deep bronze voice, 'Really, Mother, I do wish you'd stop making this unholy row! You know we won't get a moment's rest for the next four days. Get some sleep.'

My eyes popped out in wonder. I realized my mistake. It was the Mother of All, Durga herself, travelling to Bengal with her four children, Lakshmi, Saraswati, Kartik and Ganesh. I fell on my knees and humbly touched her feet. 'Forgive me, Mother, I'm a fool.'

Smiling, she replied, 'You've done nothing wrong, my son. Give me one of your forms. I'll insure the Pujas in Bengal. I'm quite bowled over by your speech.'

Inner and Outer

Our mind is normally divided into two parts. One part belongs to the outer world; the other, to the inner. The part which is outside is polite; it is social and civilized. The inner mind is not always so, however—its ways and thoughts are strange. Sometimes it laughs at the doings of the outer mind, occasionally it weeps for it and very, very rarely, it encourages it. The two quarrel frequently.

Ramkishore-babu's inner mind has been moribund for a long time; it has reached its last gasp because of the torture inflicted upon it by the outer. Ramkishore is a lawyer. Producing a false witness to get murderers acquitted, or appearing on the behalf of rich land-lords in order to ensure the destitution of impoverished peasants or creating fake wills—these were the sort of tasks for which he had taken the help of the outer mind. The inner mind had initially protested very sharply indeed. Of late, it has said very little.

That particular morning, Ramkishore-babu was walking in his garden, absentmindedly rubbing his hairless pate. The litigation over a widow's will has been bothering him for some days. The case is coming to court today; he is worried, to say nothing of being tense.

Just then, a middle-aged man turned up and greeted him politely, and said he needed an urgent consultation. Since he did not know the man, Ramkishore said without a trace of embarrassment, 'Do you have any idea of what I charge as consultation fees?'

'How much do you charge, sir?'

'Thirty-two rupees.'

'Fine.'

The two of them entered the drawing room.

'I have a relative. His only son has been married for ten years. But there're no children. Very few chances of there being any, either.'

'Have you consulted any specialists?'

'Yes, we have. They have all confirmed that it's very unlikely that the couple will ever have any.'

'The husband's healthy, is he?'

'No illnesses, as far as we know.'

'So what did you want to consult me about?' asked Ramkishore, taking a pinch of snuff from his snuff box.

'Who stands to inherit if the couple remains childless.'

Ramkishore drew the snuff into his nose and said, 'Since the husband's healthy, he can marry again. There're no restrictions against it, according to Hindu law.'

'Perhaps there aren't. But should we do something simply because it isn't expressly forbidden by the law?'

'This world doesn't run on sentiment, you know. It's this sentimentalism that's ruining us.' Ramkishore smiled. And then delivered a modest lecture on the varied ill-effects of sentiment. The outer mind provided both the words as well as the logic. The inner mind remained mute.

The visitor asked, 'Just in case the husband decides against remarriage, who would stand to inherit?'

Ramkishore listed the relatives who stood to inherit in the eyes of the law.

But he couldn't help adding, 'If you take my advice, you'll marry him off again. How can any man live happily with a sterile wife? After all, without children a marriage isn't a marriage. I'm only telling you what I think is right. You must forgive me if it hurts your sentiments.'

The visitor said, 'No, no, not at all. We'd heard that you were a plain-speaking man as well as one who's devoted to his client's welfare. That's why we came to you.'

The man parted with the thirty-two rupees and left.

About a week or so later, a car stopped in front of Ramkishore's house. A young woman got out.

Ramkishore is a widower. The house is run by servants. But there are few of them around in the afternoon; just a houseboy. Ramkishore himself is at court. The houseboy picked up the woman's various pieces of luggage and took them into the house. A large trunk had a name printed on it—Sarojini Devi.

From the houseboy's behaviour, it was quite obvious that he didn't have a clue as to who Sarojini Devi might be. Moreover, he was astounded at the young woman's behaviour.

After overseeing the removal of her luggage, Sarojini asked the houseboy, 'Where's your master?'

'At the assizes.'

'When is he expected to return?'

'I don't know.'

She sat on a trunk which was still lying in the verandah—a picture of desolation.

On his return, Ramkishore was astonished. 'Good God, Sari. Why didn't you let me know you were coming?'

'It's not possible to live there any longer.'

'What d'you mean, not possible to live there?'

'They're arranging their son's second marriage. And you've given your consent, haven't you?'

'What on earth does that mean, given my consent?'

'Apparently, they sent a stranger to find out your views. At least, that was what I was told. And you said that it was rational to marry again . . .'

By now, Ramkishore's well-buried inner mind had taken his outer mind by the throat.

A speechless Ramkishore stared helplessly at his daughter.

'Tell me the truth, Father,' Sarojini said, 'Did you really say that?'

The Human Mind

Naresh and Paresh. Two brothers, but not the least bit like two peas in a pod. Both in looks as well as temperament, their differences far outweigh their similarities. Naresh might be described thus—dark, large, with unruly hair that rarely sees a comb and a round face dominated by a pair of piercing bright eyes. A hooked nose and a thick moustache.

Paresh is tall and gaunt, with a head of well-barbered wavy hair. His face is long and his nose blunt. His eyes are always dreamy, his face cleanshaven. He wears a sandalwood rosary round his neck and a sandalwood mark on his forehead.

As for their temperaments, both may be called devout. One is devoted to science while the other is devoted to religion. Naresh had chosen science with the same careful dedication as Paresh had done religion.

Whilst Naresh's 'combined hand' is cooking a fowl cutlet for Naresh and Naresh is delighting over the Theory of Relativity, Paresh may be seen cooking a vegetarian meal for himself and, seated in the lotus posture, reading the Ramayana. Quite commonplace really, such occurrences.

But please; don't for a moment think that they are quarrelling all the time. Not at all. They have no major differences with each other, as a matter of fact. The principal reason for this may be that neither is dependent on the other. Both have MA degrees. Naresh in Chemistry and Paresh in Sanskrit. Both earn reasonable salaries as professors in their chosen subjects. Their father had left them equal amounts of money. The house they lived in was ancestral property;

moreover, it was a large house. Large enough to house at least two or three families in some comfort. But the brothers were both without families. Naresh's wife had died within a short while of their marriage. Her departure from this vale of tears had reminded both brothers of the impermanence of this mortal world so strongly that neither married. Paresh pondered on *Ka Tava Kanta*—it seemed so very true. Naresh, with his head full of Relativity, thought—Is Nirmala really dead? It's just that I cannot perceive her any longer, that's all.

Thus, despite being brothers, Naresh and Paresh are very different creatures and, despite being very different, they live peacefully in the same house.

There was something on which they were united, however.

Both loved Poltu. Poltu was Tapesh's son; Tapesh, the younger brother of Naresh and Paresh. Tapesh was working in Allahabad when he and his wife Manorama died suddenly of cholera. Naresh and Paresh, summoned by telegram, arrived just in time to hear their last words, the gist of which was, 'We're off! Take care of Poltu.' Naresh and Paresh returned to Calcutta with Poltu. Tapesh too had been willed some money by their father. To make Paresh happy, Naresh suggested that half the money be donated to the Ramakrishna Mission. Paresh promptly suggested that the other half be donated towards the advancement of science in India. That is what was done. As for Poltu, they thought, 'Since we don't have families, he'll inherit our shares.'

Poltu grew up to be the apple of their eyes. Neither attempted to impose his opinions on the boy. He grew up doing what he pleased. If he got tired of eating meat with Naresh, he could simply walk across to his other uncle for a vegetarian meal. And after a period of unmitigated vegetarianism, when his carnivorous inclinations raised their head, why, he could simply return to Uncle Naresh.

Neither Naresh nor Paresh ever entertained the notion of tying Poltu down—though each secretly hoped that the boy would follow in his footsteps.

Poltu is sixteen years old and about to sit the matric exams. He is a strapping, good-looking youth. Both Naresh and Paresh love the boy over everything else. Indeed, on this one issue, their identity of interests is quite extraordinary.

But one day Poltu fell ill.

Both the brothers were worried. As a man of scientific temper, Naresh naturally called an allopath. Paresh did not object to begin with; but when an entire week had passed without any improvement in the boy's condition, he could not restrain himself. He told Naresh, 'I think we ought to call a kaviraj.'

The kaviraj was duly summoned and treated the boy for seven days. The fever did not remit; in fact, it became worse. Poltu became delirious. A distraught Paresh said, 'Listen, why don't we consult an astrologer and get his horoscope read? Well, what d'you think?'

'If you wish. But the fever won't remit until the twenty-first day, whatever you do. The doctor said it was typhoid fever.'

Paresh ran to the astrologer with Poltu's horoscope. The man said, 'The Lord of Destruction, Mars, is angry.' He then proceeded to detail what needed to be done in order to pacify that deity. Paresh returned to tie a talisman of coral on Poltu's arm and organize the rites for the pacification of Mars.

But the fever continued to rise. Naresh said, 'The kaviraj's potions don't seem to be achieving very much. Hadn't I better call the doctor once again?'

'I suppose you should, really . . .'

Naresh departed to fetch the doctor. Paresh sat next to Poltu and applied cold-water poultices to his forehead. Poltu was babbling in his delirium, 'Ma, Ma, I want to go home. Where is Baba?'

Paresh shuddered with dread. Suddenly he remembered having heard that people sought miracle cures at Tarakeshwar. Right!

The moment Naresh returned, Paresh announced, 'I'm off to Tarakeshwar. I shouldn't be more than a couple of days.'

'Why Tarakeshwar, all of a sudden?'

'Oh, I thought I'd go to the temple as a supplicant . . .'

Naresh made no further comment. An agitated Paresh rushed off. The doctor examined Poltu and said, 'It's taken a turn for the worse.'

The physician's treatment continued.

Paresh returned two days later, carrying an earthenware pot and said with a beaming smile, 'Shiva gave me his instructions. He said the boy was not to be given any injections. Only some of this holy water each day. Poltu will soon get well.'

The doctor immediately objected. So did Naresh. They were not going to permit a typhoid patient to be given some filthy water with rotting flowers and who-knows-what-else in it!

A stunned Paresh stood there, holding his pot of holy water.

But, later, the whole affair took a different turn. The doctor kept giving Poltu his injections during Paresh's absence, and Paresh kept feeding the boy holy water when their backs were turned.

This continued for a few days. Still no improvement.

Late one night, Naresh wakes his brother, 'We'd better call the doctor. I don't like the look of Poltu.'

'Good Lord! What's wrong?'

Poltu was gasping for breath.

Paresh runs down the stairs like a man possessed and phones the doctor. His voice can be heard clearly.

'Hello doctor, can you hear me . . . Yes, yes, I've got no objections to your giving him injections . . . hello . . . d'you understand, no objections whatever . . . Please come immediately with your injections, please . . . I don't have any objections . . . do you understand . . .'

Meanwhile Naresh is trying to spoon some holy water into Poltu's mouth, imploring him all the while, 'Please Poltu, drink some of this, please, just a drop . . .'

His hand is shaking uncontrollably.

The holy water drips off the little spoon.

A Moment's Glory

I

Gurgan Khan started flexing his arms in front of the mirror. His real name is not Gurgan Khan, of course; it is Kalikanta. But he is known as Gurgan Khan—a few years ago he had played the role of Gurgan Khan in *Chandra Sekhar*, causing many a female heart to miss a beat or two.

Gurgan Khan is a little over twenty-five.

A chin covered with a pointy beard.

A moustache to match.

A fair complexion.

A hairy chest.

But these only constitute his external identity.

His real identity: Gurgan is wealthy, powerful, educated.

A zamindar.

Unmarried.

Carnivorous.

II

The young woman known as Srimati has recently attracted his attention.

Unfortunately, Srimati is in love with someone else.

A poor and rather skinny sort of a fellow.

Gurgan finds that intolerable.

Prefer that liverish-looking bag of bones to him?

His muscular body tenses with disgust.

Why, he could knock the fellow's head off with just one thump.

Though, to be fair, Gurgan has made no attempts to do so.

Instead, he has tried to behave in a gallant manner.

That is, sung romantic songs in his tuneless heavy voice.

Dressed with elegance and style.

Applied creams on his face.

Even grown sideburns.

But the imperturbable Srimati remains steadfast to her skinny young man.

Gurgan Khan is in a raging fury.

III

Srimati had visited earlier in the afternoon.

She was with him for quite a while, at that. But she might as well not have been there.

Gurgan could see that her thoughts were entirely with that skinny lout. She had come because Gurgan had ordered her to appear. It was not possible to defy him and continue to live in this village.

He exploded in a rage.

Pulling out a revolver from one of the drawers of his writing desk with a flourish, Gurgan declaimed—

He wanted Srimati.

Today.

This very minute.

Otherwise: this revolver.

He was in a murderous mood.

Srimati stared at him with her bright, laughing eyes.

Then softly said, 'Please don't shout like that. There's something I wanted to ask you. What will you do if you don't get me?'

'I'll kill that damned Tinu,' roared Gurgan Khan.

Tinu was the skinny one.

Srimati said, 'I see. Let me think about it for a while. I'd like to be alone. Please wait in the other room, and close the door behind you when you leave.'

In a voice quivering with emotion, Gurgan said, 'For how long?'

'Ten minutes.'

'Very well, then.'

Gurgan stumbled out of the room.

'Right. Let us see what she does now.'

A swollen-muscled Gurgan thought as he stood in front of the mirror.

After ten minutes of thought, Srimati announced that she would come to him that night. He was to send his coach precisely at ten o'clock.

Gurgan glanced at the clock—only nine. An hour to go.

Ohh!

No, he has not been bitten by red ants.

Merely the sigh of a self-important lovelorn Gurgan Khan.

Suddenly he laughs—an uproarious laugh.

Whatever will old Skinny think? Poor chap!

Poor chap? Poor chap?

There should have been a limit to the little ape's impudence.

Gurgan looks at the image of his muscular body in the mirror, once again.

His face is covered with a bland smile.

IV

It is past ten o'clock.

The coach has left.

An expectant Gurgan Khan is pouring cologne on his kerchief while he waits.

His mental state?

Metaphorically speaking—much like water boiling in a kettle.

The sound of an approaching coach can be heard.

It is as if the eight hooves are beating a furious tattoo on his breast.

It stops.

Someone is coming up the stairs.

The someone stops for a moment behind the drapes, then pushes them aside and enters.

Srimati!

But Gurgan's fires of passion are doused after one look at her face.

In a shamed voice she says, 'I came because I trusted your word.'

'Word? What word?'

'You promised never to breathe a word to Tinu. You won't tell Tinu, will you?'

'No.'

The two of them stand face to face.

For a few moments only.

A few sharp and bitter moments.

Who can say what happened during those moments?

Gurgan abruptly breaks the silence, 'Well, you can leave now.'

Srimati stares at him in amazement.

Then she leaves.

Immediately after her departure, Gurgan Khan thinks, 'Why did I say that? I had her and I let her go.'

Who was it that used his voice? Who?

Strange!

He listens eagerly to the faint sound of the departing horses.

Vidyasagar

I

Just before leaving, the gentleman said in a polite manner, 'I've set myself up in practice and started a dispensary near that corner . . . I do hope you'll . . .'

'Yes, I will . . .'

. . . Certain incidents come to mind vividly.

II

I used to give private tuition in those days.

It may have been because I had 'failed' the BA exams several times, or it may have been the influence of Swami Chinmayananda. Whatever. I had developed a taste for religion. I spent a great deal of time at the swami's feet, plumbing the intricate depths of Hinduism. I had come to realize that, despite their occasional failings in the material world, the Hindus were the unquestioned leaders in the world of religion. The various issues that the swami discussed, day in and day out, are quite irrelevant for the purposes of this story. I shall therefore restrain myself only to the relevant.

On one occasion, he delivered a profound lecture on the subject of reincarnation, the likes of which I had never heard before. It was quite extraordinary. I was totally bowled over. I buttonholed the swami as soon as the lecture was over—he had to reveal the mysteries of reincarnation to me.

He refused, to start with.

I persisted.

In the end, he told me.

I started meditating according to his instructions.

The mysteries of reincarnation had to be penetrated.

III

I was teaching a student.

'What's the fourth person plural form of sadhu?'

No answer.

'What is the second person plural form of muni?'

After scratching his head for a while, he provided me with an answer. The wrong answer. I cuffed him across the ear and threw the grammar book away.

. . . And so on each day.

One day I suddenly wanted to know what the lad had been in his previous life. My suspicion was that he had been born an ass, or perhaps a buffalo. The swami's technique would allow me to find out very easily.

I sat in meditation late that night in order to discover who or what he had been. I was stunned.

He had been Vidyasagar.

The one and only *Ishwarchandra Vidyasagar*.

The writer of the grammar book was not able to define the word nara. Such were the mysteries of reincarnation!

This was truly astonishing.

The boy was no better at declension the next day.

But I was not inclined to punish him.

Instead, I wanted to bow to him—

To wash his feet for him!

That Vidyasagar was reduced to this state!

From then on I never punished him for as long as I taught him—I treated him respectfully.

As a result, he never got beyond the fourth grade.

Consequently, I lost my job. Through sheer good fortune, I found a clerical post elsewhere. I left.

IV

About five years later, I ran into Vidyasagar one day. He brought me up to date. He had given up his studies and joined an amateur theatrical group. He was doing female impersonations. He had won prizes.

But these days he was an insurance agent—would I kindly consider . . .

Tears came to my eyes.

I insured myself for the largest sum I could possibly afford.

He was here again today.

He had become rather grave and dignified-looking. I learnt that he had not been able to make a successful career as an insurance agent. He had therefore studied homoeopathy privately and decided to start a practice in town. He hoped that I would come to him if I needed medical attention.

I promised that I would—whenever I needed to.

There were two things that I did not tell him, as I felt that they were irrelevant. They were—

1. Swami Chinmayananda was serving a prison sentence for theft.

2. I had converted to Christianity.

The Pebble and the Palm Tree

A vast plain. In the middle stands a huge palm tree. No one knows how long it's been there. There are no other trees nearby; only field after field, all the way to the distant horizon.

Just underneath the palm tree lies a small pebble. Again, no one knows for how long. Around it are small blades of grass. For as long as it can remember, the pebble has seen nothing else but this grass. It grows during the monsoons, and shrivels during the hot summers; then, when the monsoon comes again, embraces it once more in green affection. This is all that the pebble has seen—the grass growing on the earth, shrivelling and then growing once again. This is the sum of its experiences. But from time to time it thinks to itself: There must be other things happening, things which I cannot perceive.

One day, the pebble became aware of the palm tree.

What was this thick black object that rose upward? As far as it could remember, the thing had always been like this—erect, powerful, upward-looking.

'Excuse me?'

The palm tree remains silent.

'Excuse me, can you hear me?'

The pebble is small but persistent. It finally manages to disturb the palm tree after much shouting and calling out.

'Who is it? What do you want?'

'I'm the pebble lying underneath you. Who are you?'

'I am the palm tree.'

'Oh!'

Though it has been lying beneath the palm tree for so long, the pebble has not known the palm tree's name. It is surprised—the palm rises to such a great height! Suddenly, it occurs to the pebble that perhaps the tree's experiences might be novel, different from its own.

Hesitantly it asks: 'Will you tell me what you see from that great height?'

'The sun rising and setting in the sky.'

'And then?'

'Rising once again . . .'

A Two-Toned Tale

I

One is pale, the other dark. Both are plump, vivacious and juicy. The folks who had come to select a bride had examined both. After they left, the pale one said, 'They'll choose me, you know.'

'Oh! And how did you arrive at that conclusion, pray?'

'Didn't you notice the way they looked at me?'

'They looked at me as well.'

'I know. But you only noticed their glances, not the way their lips curled at you.'

They continued to argue.

Those selecting the bride had left, saying that they would get back once they had decided on their choice.

II

A similar incident was taking place next door. There too—one pale and the other dark. Again, the people selecting the bride had made very careful examinations indeed but failed to make a choice. They too had left saying they would get back after deciding.

But the second pale and dark pair did not argue. They kept their opinions hidden within themselves.

Pale thought: They'll have to choose me, of course. Who'd choose that horrid black creature?

Dark said to herself: I might be dark, but what about my eyes, my face, my features? Don't they count for anything? She's pallid, I suppose, but she's got button eyes, a squashed nose and a mouth like a hippopotamus. Who could choose her?

III

In the first house, Dark was chosen, because it is traditional to sacrifice a black goat during Kali Puja.

In the second, it was Pale. Because a widower remarrying for the third time cannot bear to look at a dark woman.

Life in the Pond

SNAIL. It's my opinion that there's something very wrong with him.

MUSSEL. Of course there is. He wouldn't shun his own community otherwise, would he?

SILT. The moment I noticed his antics, I realized that things were in a bad way.

SPAWN. You should've punished him then and there. After all, you're our leader.

SMALL FRY. It's a moot point whether he's our leader, or Scum is. Anyway, we digress. The point is, Silt should've disciplined him. He brought the fellow up, after all.

SILT. Believe me, I did everything possible. I tried to reason with him, I even scolded him. But I'm not made of stone, you know. I can't become hard!

MUSSEL. We wouldn't survive for long if you were stone. We aren't asking you to be hard. Just rein the fellow in.

FLAT FISH. There's nothing to be done now.

SNAIL. But we must do something. There's something very wrong with him.

LARVA. I know what's wrong with him. I keep coming up from the bottom, so I know what's wrong . . .

SILT. Well? Tell us what it is, then.

LARVA. He's become friendly with some low-class flies, that's what it is. They're always buzzing and hanging around him . . .

MUSSEL. Is that what it is? Frankly, I was wondering whether he'd gone crazy. I mean, have you noticed how he's always gazing upwards? And swaying . . . ?

SPAWN. Very bad signs, these!

SMALL FRY. We're not going to put up with this. If Silt can't do anything, we'll go to Scum. This sort of dissolute behaviour is quite intolerable. (*To Mussel*) You're quite wrong, you know. He's not in the least bit crazy, or anything like that. It's all an act.

The flat fish said nothing, merely smiled.

2ND LARVA (*in a whisper*). I've been told that he's been seen with some trollop or the other.

SNAIL. Well, now!

MUSSEL. Really? Are you sure?

2ND LARVA. Oh, yes. Her name's Light, apparently.

SNAIL. Lord! I said that something's wrong.

POND WATERS. What rubbish! I've been listening to you all without saying a word but you don't know a thing, do you? Let me tell you what's going on. He's neither gone crazy nor fallen in love. He's neither a lover nor a lunatic—he's a traitor. That's right, a traitor. He's involved in a plot. And do you know who with? With the Sun, that's who. The same Sun that's sucking us dry every minute . . .

Everyone is stunned by the horrible news.

SPAWN. But what can we do?

SMALL FRY. Agitate! All we've got to do is to launch an agitation and he'll be sorted out, in no time . . .

EVERYONE. Yes . . . that's right . . . let's launch an agitation.

The agitation starts.

The waters grow murky.

The lotus in bloom remains unaffected.

Remarkable Learning

I woke with a start.

A fire had broken out in the neighbourhood. My God! All our houses had thatched roofs. I came out of my room at a run, then realized we were being raided by dacoits. They were the ones who had started the fire. But where was everyone? Nothing could be heard but the crackling of the fire and the sound of bamboo exploding in the heat. As I ran down the verandah, someone punched me violently in the nose. I fell in a daze. Some people rushed up and tied me hand and foot but one of the dacoits peered at me and said, 'It's the doctor. Untie him immediately.' I couldn't recognize the good Samaritan because he was masked. They were all masked. I was untied and left there, stunned by their swiftness and stealth. I realized that every man, woman and child had been tied and gagged. That was why there was no noise at all.

I managed to stagger up. It was difficult to decide what to do. What, in fact, could I do against this small but heavily armed force? Suddenly, a woman's scream rent the air. I walked a few paces to see that not only looting but rape too was in progress. Something had to be done, some protest registered. I screamed at them to stop but no one paid the slightest attention. Casting about for some kind of a weapon, I saw a brick lying nearby. I picked it up in a frenzy and was about to attempt to brain one of them when someone grabbed my arm.

'What d'you think you're doing? Throw that away and come with me.'

I turned around to see Apurba-babu, my neighbour, a revered and wise scientist. A man I had always respected. I threw the brick away.

'Come with me.'

There was an overgrown stretch of woods behind my house. I followed Apurba-babu deep inside the woods. I saw that my family and Apurba-babu's were already there—presumably as a direct result of Apurba-babu's wisdom.

Apurba-babu said, 'You must keep a steady head. We have to understand what the problem is. The real problem is the absence of unity. Do you really think that the dacoits would've dared raid the neighbourhood if we were united? What could you have achieved by throwing a brick? You must consider the root problem. Take Russia, for instance . . .'

Apurba-babu continued his lecture in a low voice. The whole of history, geography, politics and much else was at his fingertips. Wiping my bleeding nose and desperately trying to concentrate on the learned Apurba-babu's fingertips, I attempted to understand the real problem.

The looting continued.

Yesterday's Rai-Bahadur

The Rai-Bahadur is busy discharging his duties.

He has hardly eaten or slept during the last few days. In an attempt to crush the uprising, he has had to travel from village to village, accompanied by a force of soldiers. The dutiful Rai-Bahadur has been busily maintaining peace and order by showering the disobedient public with bullets, arresting the leaders of the uprising and issuing summons against the absconding criminals. An educated gentleman, he is unused to such jobs. But in these dark days he is having to undertake such tasks, even if much against his inclination. He is fully aware that indiscriminate firing at the public tends to result in the death of the odd innocent person. Moreover, it is not entirely impossible that the police dragnets pick up a number of quite blameless individuals. But what can one do under the circumstances? Nobody seems willing to respect the law. Indeed, everyone seems determined to disobey it. At such times, making subtle moral judgements would hinder the job of quelling the unrest. In fact, creating a climate of terror was essential in order to instil some fear in the minds of the rebels. The country had to be saved at any cost from this unexpected danger. It was the duty of every right-thinking individual. The Rai-Bahadur is incapable of neglecting his duties.

The Rai-Bahadur is engrossed in writing.

He is no traitor. The Rai-Bahadur is a well-wisher of his country. He is not unaware of what is good or bad for his country's welfare. A brilliant student, he got a first in his MA in history. During his long years in administration, he has really been serving the motherland. Furthermore, he has come to realize, with every fibre of his being, that it is only by faithfully serving the British government that we might acquire the capacity to be worthy of self-government some time in the future. This is the only way.

And those who, out of stupidity or mischievousness, were inciting the excitable population away from the paths of righteousness—why, they were lunatics. The asylum was the best place for them!

The Rai-Bahadur stops his writing with a slight frown. The sound of a distant tumult can be heard. No time to waste, though; the report must be completed today. He concentrates on his work.

Is looting going to give us independence? Are we meant to gain swaraj by burning railway stations and post offices? Would the British government really be crippled because some telegraph lines were cut? Were these people raving mad, or merely drunk?

If independence were to become a reality, it would be through the indulgence of the British government. The Rai-Bahadur could demonstrate with great ease (and apt historical examples) how we were advancing step by step towards the stage of a self-conscious nation; as well as how, in the future, we would mature successfully into a state of unmitigated independence. That we did not deserve our independence at the moment was not to be doubted. It was pointless giving these weak-kneed, divided, quarrelsome and self-seeking people independence. The British people would not hesitate to grant us independence as soon as we earned it! This was something the Rai-Bahadur is quite convinced of. The British people never hesitate to recognize the deserving—he is the best proof of this. The only son of a poor widow from an obscure family, he has educated himself through enormous effort. The ever-appreciative British had rewarded his Herculean labours appropriately.

Vande Mataram, Inquilab Zindabad—the tumult is louder and closer.

Vande Mataram, Inquilab Zindabad.
Vande Mataram, Inquilab Zindabad.
Vande Mataram, Inquilab Zindabad.

The shouts are more loud, more fierce.

Blamm—blamm—blammmmmm . . .

The firing starts. Then, everything is silent. The Rai-Bahadur rises and steps outside. He notices that the cowards have all fled; only one man is lying on the road. Dead, most likely. Still clutching a Congress flag. The Rai-Bahadur walks up to the body. And his heart stops beating for a few moments as he looks at the blood-spattered corpse. It is his eldest son. For a moment he stares at the body, stunned. But only for a moment.

The next moment he rushes off in his car towards the Commissioner's residence.

He must apologize for the foolish boy's treachery.

As It Happened

'You're late once again, Mrs Mitra. It's past eleven-thirty . . .' Mrs Mitra looked embarrassed for a few seconds. Then smiled her radiant smile and replied, 'I'm terribly sorry, Mr Lahiri, but my mother-in-law's been rather ill for the past few days. The doctor is invariably late. That's why I'm so . . .'

Mr Lahiri, an unbending bureaucrat and an IAS officer, made a faint face and said, 'I see. I'm sorry to hear that. Nevertheless, I have to tell you that things can't go on like this. The office will come to a standstill if the staff don't turn up on time. The files are . . .'

'I'll make sure they're done today.'

'Fine. By the way, why do you need to wait for the doctor? Is there no one else at home?'

'No, there isn't. My husband's been transferred to Siliguri. There's only a maid and me. The doctor said my mother-in-law has typhoid fever.'

'In that case, shouldn't you think of engaging a nurse?'

'We couldn't afford one, I'm afraid. It would cost another twenty-five rupees a day. As it is, the doctor's fees and the medicines cost about fifteen rupees a day.'

'Then why don't you admit her to a hospital?'

'It's not easy getting admission to a hospital. And in any case, she doesn't want to go to a hospital.'

'I see . . . Well, I suppose you'd better start clearing your files.'

Manoranjan arrived as soon as Mrs Mitra sat down at her desk. Manoranjan used to be Mrs Mitra's fellow student during their university days. They had taken their MA degrees in the same year. But there is something else that might be worth mentioning at this stage. Manoranjan is in love with Mrs Mitra. He has been suffering from this affliction since his student days. And he is yet to be cured of it. The tall, good-looking Manoranjan really has no need for a job. He is the son of a rich father. But no sooner had he heard that Mrs Mitra had got employment in this particular department than he pulled various strings to get himself a job in the same office. He is employed as a clerk, and on a very meagre pay indeed. The authorities had hardly expected to get a First Cass MA in English Literature for a mere hundred rupees a month. He was therefore appointed on the spot.

Manoranjan had proposed during their student days. Indeed, he had fulfilled every criterion save one: he had not been able to change his caste to a higher one.

The offspring of orthodox parents, Mrs Sushila Mitra was an obedient child. She had dutifully followed her parents' instructions and changed from a Miss Ghosh to a Mrs Mitra. Not so very long ago—a mere six months ago, as a matter of fact. She had started her job before her marriage; she continued after as well. Baladeb Mitra, her husband, had asked her to stop working. But Sushila had not. She had realized that it would not be possible to run an entire household on what her husband earned. Two hundred and fifty rupees were nowhere near enough to make ends meet these days, not when things were so dear. No, she had not given up her job. Baladeb kept on nagging, of course. Then he was suddenly transferred. The fact that Sushila was not going with him made him even more irritated. His mother declared, 'I'm going to stay with Bouma. I shan't leave my home for anywhere else.' But she has had a fever for these past few days. Though Sushila feels she ought to stay with her, there is no leave available. Her being even a bit late is enough to make her boss irate.

But Sushila's biggest problem is Manoranjan. Had he been a bad person, she could have got rid of him with ease. But she knows that he is an absolute jewel. And if she has been unable to make this jewel hers, the jewel has been unwilling to give her up as well. In fact, it has repeatedly said that whether you want me or not, I am forever yours. Not perhaps in those very words, though it sometimes does seem like it.

On that particular day, Manoranjan said, 'We'll sort out the files that're in arrears. They'll get done today itself. Don't worry your head about it. In fact, I wanted to talk about something entirely different. I feel you ought to engage a nurse to look after your mother-in-law. Don't worry about the expenses.'

'But I must. We haven't got a nurse because we can't afford one.'

'But I have the money to pay for the . . .'

'And why should I take your money?'

'But you would have if we'd been married. You're not going to shun me because we aren't married, are you? Do you really not know how I feel about you?'

Sushila was somewhat embarrassed. She turned her head away to hide her blushes. Then she said, 'There's another side to it as well. What'll he think, if I accept your money?'

'What is there to think about? Friends helping each other!'

'Quite a lot really, if the friend's as attractive as you are,' replied Sushila smiling.

Deep within Manoranjan lay an extremely obstinate and stubborn person. This person had driven him to accept all manner of dares in the past. He had swum the Padma from bank to bank, once even eaten a huge bowl of rice pudding after a full meal. This hidden being suddenly raised his head.

Manoranjan said, 'I'm going to help you, no matter what.'

'You won't, you know. I shan't take your money.'

'Oh yes, you will.'

Sushila was a bit late home that evening. But what she discovered when she got there left her in a very agitated state of mind indeed.

Her mother-in-law had fallen out of bed in her delirium, and was now unconscious. The local GP examined her and said, 'She's concussed.'

The next day the lady died.

After the funeral rites, etc., Baladeb said to Sushila, 'My mother lay in agony while you were busy with your office work . . . Well, what's done is done, I suppose. But now, I want to make something clear to you. You can either give up your job, or you can leave me . . . Talk of riding two horses at the same time . . . !'

What happened after this?

Various things could have happened, such as:

(1) Sushila says, 'I'm not giving up my job! I'd rather leave you instead . . .'

(2) Sushila leaves her job. But they can only make ends meet with great difficulty. Then something very dramatic happens. One day, a letter arrives by registered post. Sushila opens it—and finds a will. Manoranjan has left her his entire property (which fetches an income of Rs 250,000 annually) and committed suicide. But Sushila does not accept the money. Instead, she uses it to open a school named after Manoranjan.

(3) Sushila does not leave her job. A few days later, her husband Baladeb feels relieved that she has not done so. He has injured both his arms in an accident and the doctors have had to amputate them.

But none of this happened.

Things carried on as they were. Sushila and Baladeb continue to row frequently over the subject of her job. But Sushila refuses to give it up. Nor has she left her husband. Neither has Manoranjan left Sushila. He circles her like the very embodiment of platonic love. This out-of-key harmony was what personified their lives.

Nothing very dramatic happened.

A Pearl of Wisdom

How beautiful it looks. Exactly like a molten pearl. And inside the pearl another tiny drop; even that looks like a tiny bead.

From within the pearl comes an arm-like protrusion, then the entire body vanishes silently within the arm. The arm protrudes yet again, again the body advances in the same direction. Then, two arms protrude, and grasp the food particle. It swallows the food. Again it moves forward. The body twists and turns and crumples. But it does not stop. Its constant movement never stops. Though impediments appear occasionally, they cannot stop its progress; it wriggles past all barriers. Indefatigable worker, it takes not a moment's rest. Food, it wants food, more food. Then, after a while, everything stops. Immobile, it gives the impression of being in a trance. At the beginning of creation, God is supposed to have said, 'I am one, I shall become many.' I don't know if they say such things, but out of their one body are born many. This is not a god but an amoeba. It lives neither in heaven nor in fantasy, but in the bowels . . . If they had been human beings, what sort of society would they have built? At present they have no sexual desires, but would they have them? What would their politics be like? Would they have their pots? And scientists? Would their scientists want to reach the moon? Would they have films? Or black markets? What about murder? Or embezzlement? But have we achieved peace through any of this? Where is there any peace? I have been starving in front of the microscope since I got my medical degree. What have I gained? Where is peace? . . . Where is peace? . . .

When microbiologist Dr Chintamoni Dhar was removed to a lunatic asylum, the above piece of paper was found on his desk.

He spends his time in the asylum screaming, 'I want to be an amoeba, I want to be an amoeba,' and slithering about on the floor, practising amoeboid movements.

Dr Chintamoni Dhar is the scion of an illustrious, educated family.

Under the Same Verandah

There is a small verandah adjacent to my surgery. It collects dust during the day; at night the coolies and rickshaw-pullers use it to sleep on. I have heard that it even finds use as an impromptu gambling den late at nights. I was in my surgery one day when yet another possibility for the verandah suddenly manifested itself.

A nineteen- or twenty-year-old lad entered the surgery, greeted me with a namaskar and then stood there in an embarrassed manner. Obviously not a patient but someone seeking help. A refugee from East Bengal. He spoke in a hesitant manner and with a thick East Bengal accent, 'I'm in great difficulty. Please help me.' I had given such 'help' many times before. A couple of rupees would have done the trick. But for some obscure reason, a strange idea came to me.

I said, 'A couple of rupees are hardly going to make much difference to your condition. And in any case, how long are you going to keep on begging?'

'Please help me find a job.'

'Have you got any qualifications?'

'I've taken the matric exams.'

'Not much chance of getting a decent job with a matric. Why don't you open a small shop or something?'

'But who will advance me the capital?'

'Look, you don't want a lot of capital to start with. First, get something going with a small amount of capital. You want to gain some experience in shopkeeping. After that, you can do something that requires lots of capital.'

'But what should I . . .'

'There's this wide thoroughfare running outside the surgery. Think of all the people who use it. Why don't you keep bundles of biris and boxes of matches? Besides, loads of children pass by on the way to school and back. You could keep pencils, exercise books, ink . . . There's a verandah next to my surgery. Start from tomorrow.'

'But I can't even afford to buy all this.'

'Here. I'll advance you ten rupees.'

I gave him the ten rupees. He purchased the necessary items. I gave him a mat; he spread this on the floor of the verandah and started his shop. He had purchased an assortment of sweets, so the children started dropping in. But the first problem was language. The local Bihari children were unable to understand Harshakumar, and vice versa. Then I noticed that Harshakumar did not—how should I put it?—have the most urbane ways of speaking nor the most benign of expressions. In the main, he tended to bark at people. For a man sitting on a reed mattress and with a working capital of ten rupees, he had the temperament of an oriental despot. He was obviously unaware of the honorific form—aap. The moment he noticed a child touching any of his wares, he would scream in his mother tongue, 'Oi you, watchadoon?' To start with, the children used to laugh. Then, in the eternal way of children, they began to tease him. They would stand outside the shop every day, screaming 'Mr Watchadoon, Mr Watchadoon.'

Finally, even I got fed up. Not that he didn't make some sales every day, but in the end Harshakumar was unable to keep his shop going. One fine day he informed me that he was a zamindar's son, and hence unable to continue doing what amounted to menial work. He hoped I would find it in me to forgive him. The very next day he left the verandah and, a few days after that, he even returned my ten rupees. There it ended—or at least, so I thought at the time. In fact, however, it ended some three months later. Harshakumar arrived once again, looking a proper dandy. Hair beautifully styled, a new wristwatch, a brand-new jacket and trousers. 'I have a job,' he told me. I asked him how much he was being paid. 'Forty rupees a month,' he said. There would be increments later. I noticed that he seemed very happy.

Six months after this incident, a pleasant-looking youth arrived at my doorstep. Another refugee. From the Punjab. I was charmed by his appearance. As soon as he saw me, he greeted me politely and came forward. In Hindi, he said he had a small request.

'What sort of a request?'

He said he wanted to open a small teashop in my verandah. As a poor refugee, he could pay me only a rent of five rupees a month. He would remain eternally grateful, however, if I gave my permission.

'Yes, well, go ahead. I don't want any rent.'

He seemed quite overwhelmed by this gesture.

Yagna Dutt started his teashop the very next day. His only possessions: a coal stove, a bucket, water, milk, tea and sugar. He used to light the stove well away from the house. I was, therefore, never bothered by the smoke.

Moreover, he made himself useful in innumerable ways. He would supply me and my friends free cups of tea. Early each morning, he would sweep my surgery clean, dust the table and chairs and fetch my drinking water. 'Your shoes haven't been polished for a long time. If you let me, I could polish them for you.' I felt embarrassed looking at my shoes. They had remained unpolished for an awfully long time.

'Never mind. I'll ask Bhutua to do it for me.'

'Let me do it. I can do it a lot better. Please . . .'

He virtually removed the shoes from my feet. And when he brought them back, they gleamed with polish. Even a professional cobbler could not have done a better job.

I was overjoyed by all this. So was my wife. Her main problem was the shopping every morning. My servant Bhutua would go shopping for fresh food but only after finishing his work in the surgery. Since Yagna Dutt was doing much of his work, his mornings were free. This meant that he could do the shopping the first thing in the morning.

In the meanwhile, his teashop started prospering. Most people were attracted by his courtesy and good looks. They would stand by the roadside and drink his tea. He soon started keeping biscuits and cakes. The shop did better and better.

A while later, a room became available on the opposite side of the road. Yagna Dutt shifted his shop there. Tables and chairs made their appearance. One day I noticed that the menu had expanded to include cutlets and such like.

Though Yagna Dutt's establishment ultimately shifted elsewhere, our relationship remained the same. The dusting, sweeping, fetching water and the occasional shoe-polishing—all continued as before. Yagna Dutt became a reliable member of the family.

One day he came and handed me a letter, and said, 'I'm afraid I can't read English. Could you please tell me what this letter says?' I noticed that the letter was from New Delhi. I was dumbstruck by what I read. The letter said that his property in West Pakistan had been sold and that his share of the property came to a 150,000 rupees. Yagna Dutt was to take all legal measures to assume control of his money. I explained the gist of the letter to Yagna Dutt.

'And what sort of property did you possess?'

'I was a zamindar, Doctor. I also had a jewellery business. We used to keep an elephant tied outside our house . . .'

I felt like bowing to Yagna Dutt. But somehow, I couldn't bring myself to do it.

Wildfire

I have to tell a story each night at my four-year-old granddaughter's behest.

One night she told me, 'Grandpa, tell me a story about a king.' I am now telling you the tale I told her that night.

Once upon a time there was a king. His name was Bhunath. He was an exceedingly kind-hearted and nice-natured man. He was quite unable to get cross with or scold anyone. His kingdom was governed by his minister. The king had a Shiva temple in which there was a snowy white marble idol of Shiva. The king used to worship this particular idol.

The king had two queens, an older (senior) queen and a younger (junior) queen. The king was very unhappy with them. Even though they were queens, they were very envious of each other and quarrelled like fishwives. Shout and scream like a couple of shrews, abuse each other, occasionally even pull each other's hair or scratch and pinch. The palace would ring with their screams. Even crows avoided the palace. And the servants lived in a state of fear.

If the older queen wore a pair of nice earrings, the younger would rush across and give them a yank: 'How dare you wear that, that's mine.' Immediately a tremendous fight would start, complete with screams and punches. If the younger wore a nice necklace, the older one would try to rip it off her.

'Who told you to wear my necklace, you . . .'

One more fight would start.

So they carried on each day.

Every day a tremendous quarrel for some petty reason or the other. King Bhunath was too kind to be able to scold his wives. He was also too embarrassed to ask his ministers for help. After all, one can hardly tell others about one's private affairs. So he poured out his woes to Lord Shiva.

'Please, please do something about this, O Lord Shiva. Please, please help me . . .'

The idol remained silent. The god never answered. One day, the king rested his head on the feet of the idol and wept. And after a very long time, Lord Shiva finally spoke.

'Look here, Bhunath, all this is your own fault, really. You've made a rod for your own back by marrying twice, but never mind that for now. I've finally thought up a solution to your problem. There's a devotee of mine called Wildfire. Chap has extraordinary powers, does a couple of impossible things each day, if you know what I mean. I'll send him over to you. You know, there was a time when he had quite a reputation as a wizard. Of course, these days he's stopped all that. Spends his time meditating. Indeed, he's become a great adept at that too. I think he'll be able to sort out your problems for you. He's a rather irritable sort of chap, but very powerful indeed. I should let him do whatever's necessary.'

Soon enough, the king could hear someone shouting in a thunderous voice, just outside the palace's main gate, 'Bom Mahadev.'

The king peered out of his window and saw a huge, near-naked mendicant, with a head of wild, unkempt hair. He was carrying a gigantic trident. His face was covered with a beard, his eyes were like burning coals. He seemed more a living flame than a man.

Bhunath came to the door in order to greet the great personage.

'Are you Bhunath, the king?'

'Indeed I am, sir.'

'What've you been bothering the Lord Shiva every day for? What the devil have you got yourself into?'

'Please, I'll tell you everything. Won't you come . . . ?'

'Get a meal organized for me first. Usually I eat only once a week. Today was to be my day for eating. But of course, the Lord said, "Off you go." And so, here I am. For now, I want to eat. I'll listen to your squalid little stories after that.'

'Whatever you say, sir. But please, come in . . .'

The king took him to the throne room and ushered him towards the throne.

'No, I shan't sit there, I don't sit on thrones. I'll sit on the floor instead,' said he and promptly squatted on the floor.

'Now get me something to eat . . .'

'What would you like to eat, sir?'

'I want two dozen ripe plantains as well as a large bowl of kheer.'

The plantains and the bowl of kheer soon arrived.

A servant also brought along a velvet mat for him to sit on.

'I am not used to sitting on velvet,' said Wildfire. 'Fetch me a pitcher of water, and a gamchha.'

Then Wildfire took his time dipping the plantains in the kheer and then eating them. It took a long time. And it also left his beard covered with cream.

Then he said, 'I live all alone in the forest. Vishwakarma has planted lots of plantains all around my ashram. And Kaamdhenu sends me a bowl of kheer once a week. These were nice too. I enjoyed my meal.'

Then he washed his face and dried himself off with the gamchha.

'Now tell me what's been happening. Why've you been bothering Lord Shiva?'

Bhunath told him everything. And Wildfire promptly scolded him. 'What on earth made you marry twice? People can barely cope with one marriage, and you have the gall to marry twice! You're an utter imbecile! You should've expected your wives to quarrel. Isn't that the usual way . . . ?'

Bhunath folded his hands in supplication. 'Please help me, sir. Do something.'

'Where are they?'

'In the women's quarters.'

'Well, come on then . . .'

As soon as they entered, a horrendous screech was heard. The younger queen was biting the arm of the older queen who was pulling out the younger one's hair by the handful. The mystic stood outside the doorway and commanded in a ringing voice, 'Quiet, you two.'

Neither queen paid the slightest bit of attention.

'You've still got time. I'm telling you to be quiet.'

The two queens did not shut up. On the contrary, they shouted even louder.

The sage's eyes began to glow like fire.

He raised his trident high, 'Be quiet, or I will curse you.'

But the queens took no notice at all. They carried on shouting at the top of their voices. Wildfire cursed in a loud voice, 'Turn into dolls, both of you.' Immediately, the two queens turned into dolls, and the screeching stopped abruptly.

Wildfire looked at the king and said, 'They're never going to shout again, nor quarrel, for that matter. Dolls don't quarrel. Let's go.'

Outside, Bhunath asked, 'Are they going to remain dolls for ever?'

'For ever. You can store them on shelves, if you want to.'

'But what about me? Are you saying I'll have to spend my entire life with a pair of dolls?'

'So you will. But at least you'll have some peace. Weren't you pestering Lord Shiva every day because you married two shrews?'

Bhunath fell at the sage's feet. 'Please make them human again. I don't care what happens. Oh please, have mercy,' he sobbed.

Wildfire gazed at him with burning eyes, then exclaimed, 'My word, you really are a pest, aren't you?'

'I know that you can sort this out. Please be merciful.'

'Well, all right then. Let's go inside. And get me a sheet.'

Again, they entered the women's quarters.

'Get me a sheet . . .'

Bhunath produced a gigantic shawl.

Wildfire entered the room in which the dolls were standing. Again he raised his trident and said, 'Become human, become human, become human.'

Immediately, the two dolls turned back into the queens.

Then Wildfire asked, 'Are you two going to fight again?'

The queens said, 'No, we'll never quarrel again. Never ever again.'

'Right then, you two. Go and lie on that bed there and hold each other tight.'

The two queens did as they were told.

Wildfire covered them with the shawl. Then he raised his trident and said, 'Become one, become one, become one . . .'

The shawl was then removed. The two queens had disappeared— a single person had taken their place. Half the face was the older queen's and the other half like the younger one's. The two bodies had merged into one.

'My God, what've you done?'

'I've left both your queens intact—but in one body. They'll never quarrel again.'

Wildfire strode off at great speed and soon disappeared from sight.

Two Kinds of Freedom

I was sitting in my garden because I was feeling out of sorts. I had become poor, therefore the garden was no longer looking as pretty as it once did. But I was sitting there anyway, when I suddenly noticed that a single Lady Hillingdon had bloomed. I was astonished. I'd had to let the gardener go long ago. The shrub had not been cared for at all—indeed, it had rarely been watered. Yet, despite the weeds growing around it, a solitary flower had bloomed. Even more astonishing, it spoke to me.

'Good morning, I haven't seen you for a long time . . .'

I stared, dumbfounded.

'Are you feeling unwell? You look quite ill.'

I came out of my daze, and my bitterness spilt out.

'How am I supposed to look well when I can hardly get one square meal a day?'

'Why is that?'

'Because I've got my freedom.'

The Lady Hillingdon stared at me in some surprise.

'I notice that your clothes look terrible as well.'

'Same thing again—freedom.'

'Freedom, you say? This is most extraordinary! I'm free as well but I'm not in your state. I won't deny that I was better off when I was being looked after by your gardener, but I'm doing quite well even now. You must've noticed the flower. It might not be too large but it is a flower . . .'

I remained silent.

The Lady Hillingdon continued, 'I feel bad seeing you reduced to this state. But tell me, what've you done to sort things out?'

'Well, I've written to the papers, addressed public meetings . . .' I don't think that the Lady Hillingdon understood me. After a brief silence, she said, 'I don't understand how freedom can turn into a problem. I'm free and I don't suffer because of it . . .'

'You're just a flowering plant—I'm a human being. For my kind, freedom means . . .'

Somehow, everything became confused. All the books I had read— history, economics, sociology—all got muddled. I couldn't remember a thing from any of them. I looked at her for a while and then said, 'You won't understand my difficulties. You've no idea what I'm going through.'

'I know how you feel.'

A near-dead chrysanthemum in a pot next to me spoke up.

'You see, the Lady Hillingdon draws her strength from the soil. Even when she's not watered, her roots draw sustenance from the earth. But look at me. I'm in a pot. If I'm not watered, I would die. My roots cannot go beyond the boundaries of the pot, they can't reach the soil. And you, my friend, are in the same situation—you're stuck in an invisible pot. You can only survive if you get your food from outside. We're the same kind, the both of us! That's why I understand you. We can only flower if we get our sustenance from outside. Without that, we can only languish and die. Our freedom and the Lady Hillingdon's freedom are not the same thing at all.'

I remained silent for a while. Then I broke the chrysanthemum's pot and re-planted it in the soil.

The Lady Hillingdon smiled, 'And when will your pot break, do you think?'

'I don't know.'

Transformation

The sight of the genie did not frighten me in the least; indeed, I was quite pleased to lay eyes on it. The genie smiled at me for a little while and said, 'I am all-powerful. Name your wish.'

'A job.'

'What sort of a job?'

'A really nice job.'

'Right. You wait here. I'll be back in a jiffy.'

The gargantuan being strode off with vast strides. I sat there quietly, waiting. Seeing its towering size, its palm-tree-sized eyes and so on had filled me with hope. An individual of such tremendous power ought easily to be able to get me a brilliant job.

The genie returned in a short while. It had a ream of paper tucked under one arm and a pen clutched in its other hand.

'Start writing applications.'

'Applications? To whom?'

'I have the names and addresses here.'

It threw loads of newspapers at me: 'These papers are full of job advertisements. Apply to each and every one of them. I'll have them typed up and then I'll deliver them personally.'

I wrote thirty-five applications and handed them over to the genie. It left. When it returned in a little while, I was shocked to see that the giant was no longer its original size—it had been transformed into a dwarf. It stood in front of me with a faint grin.

'Goodness, what happened to you?'

It did not reply but pointed its thumbs downwards.

'How did you diminish so much in size?'

'Out of sheer humiliation. I hadn't realized this before, but now I understand that those who are able to provide jobs are even more powerful than I am.'

'But what am I going to do?'

'Don't worry, I've taken care of that.'

The genie looked over his shoulders and made a gesture. A gentleman materialized out of thin air.

'This man has a beautiful daughter. Marry her immediately. He'll loan you a sum of five thousand rupees. You can start a small business with it.'

With this, the genie vanished. The person whose head had been touching the sky only a short while ago dwindled to nothingness.

I did not disobey the dwarf. This large grocery store that you see was started with my father-in-law's money.

I am sure you don't believe all this genie–dwarf nonsense. You no doubt think that I'm either a drunk or a nut of some kind.

But it's really nothing like that. The net that I had cast in the ocean of knowledge had brought up a bottle, and inside that bottle was that genie. The bottle was a degree, and that genie's name is Arrogance. The tale no longer remains in its familiar *Arabian Nights* form. How can it? After all, I am not an Arab.

And in any case, this is not Arabia—this is India.

Sunanda

It was not yet five minutes to ten when Sunanda stood in front of the lift. The lift operator greeted her respectfully and then took her up to her floor. In a few minutes she had reached her room where the office-boy greeted her with equal respect and then politely held the door open for her. He looked at the wall clock briefly and switched on the fan. A few of the documents on the desk are blown away. The office-boy runs about, picks them up, arranges them on the table and then places a paperweight on them. Sunanda looks at the paperweight, made out of beautifully carved white marble, in some surprise. This did not belong here; she used to have a dull old disc of lead. How did this get here?

'Where did the paperweight come from?'

'Chandra-babu changed it . . .'

Mr Chandrakanta Ghosh is Sunanda's private secretary.

The wall clock rings ten.

'Call Chandra-babu, will you?'

The office-boy leaves. Sunanda bites her lower lip for a few moments.

Sunanda is very dark, has small eyes and very thin brows, and her face is as round as a pumpkin. But she is a highly educated woman— an MA, PhD, in fact. She has done a great deal of research in various American and British universities. She has, therefore, not had any trouble finding a job after returning to India. She holds a senior post entirely through her own merit. She is the daughter of a mere clerk; there are ten children in all. Had she not been a scholarship girl, she would never have been able to complete her studies. Indeed, she basks entirely in her own glory. Moreover, she has taken over all her father's responsibilities.

There are a few files on her desk. She starts looking through them. Then she glances up at the clock again. It's nearly ten thirty, still no sign of Chandra-babu. Most exasperating. Finally, at ten thirty, an abashed Chandrakanta enters her room.

'Look at the clock and tell me what time it is . . .'

'I'm terribly sorry I'm late yet again. My wife's not been very well. I had to fetch the doctor.'

Sunanda replies in a sharp tone, 'You're lying, because I know that you're not married. I know that your father's looking for a beautiful bride for you. He wants a fairy princess and half the kingdom for his son, the petty clerk. Yes, I know everything.'

Chandrakanta is mortified with embarrassment. His face looks like wet dough, his eyes downward.

'Where did the paperweight come from?'

'It was my paperweight. I left it for you to use. Yours was so ugly that I thought you might like . . .'

'Please remove your paperweight. I'm happy with the one that the office provides. What's that you're holding?'

Chandrakanta is silent for a few seconds. Then, in a virtually inaudible voice, exclaims, 'Cashew nuts . . .'

'Cashew nuts . . . ! Are you telling me you spend your time in the office chewing cashew nuts?'

'I got them for you. I'd heard that you like cashew nuts . . .'

After a few seconds, Sunanda's nostrils flare; her eyes glitter with rage.

'What the hell do you think you're up to? Get out of this room! I'm going to suspend you. What're you waiting for, go on . . .'

Chandrakanta Ghosh starts sobbing loudly. Then falls at Sunanda's feet in a dramatic manner, 'Please, I'm helpless. Forgive me this once, please . . .'

It is not possible to tell whether Sunanda forgave Chandrakanta or not, because about then she was woken by the bite of a bedbug. Her horrendous existence was suddenly reflected in front of her: the smelly bed, her half-naked brothers and sisters sleeping all around her, the grimy walls, the smell of the open sewer next to the house. Her mother was calling her, 'Suni, wake up, love. Come on, you've got to light the stove quickly. It's Monday, we've got to cook a meal for your father before he leaves for office.'

She remembers that Chandrakanta Ghosh had visited their house, with about ten people in tow. He had come to view her as a prospective bride. She remembers how her father had flattered him. She remembers how they had spent nearly ten rupees on the high tea. But Chandrakanta had not considered her suitable. She remembers everything.

From the other room, her father's voice can be heard: 'Dear, do make sure Suni's dressed up properly in the evening. Ramtaran Mitra from my office is coming to see her . . .'

Sunanda used to be rather good at her studies. She had always been at the top of her class and passed the matric exams with a first division. But her father had not allowed her to continue her education.

Sunanda rises and walks out of the front door. And never returns. You might have seen her photograph in the 'Missing' columns.

Then again, you might not have.

Kenaaram the Enlightened and K

Bidhubhushan had warned Kenaaram. He had said, 'Why is that K fellow sitting in your balcony every day? Don't encourage him so much. They're a dangerous lot.'

Everyone is aware that Kenaaram is a liberal and broadminded individual. He said with a superior smile on his face, 'Why bring up his race? After all, there're god-knows-how-many dangerous people in our race.'

Bidhubhushan folded his hands: 'My dear man, I know that you're an enlightened being! But I also know K—which is why I'm warning you, as a friend. You're newly married, and your wife is beautiful.'

Hearing this, Kenaaram screwed up his nose and started shaking with rage. He had never imagined that someone like Bidhubhushan could be so obscene. No words came out of his mouth. Only his flared nostrils expressed his rage.

Bidhubhushan left with a faint grin.

A fortnight later, Bidhubhushan noticed that K had forsaken the balcony—he was now ensconced in the drawing room. Sitting on Kenaaram's expensive settee, he was stroking his beard and engaging in what can be described in polite language as serious flirtation. He thought to himself; Good Lord!

Bidhubhushan entered the drawing room. K was chewing paan and saying, 'I'd never imagined that your wife could make such exquisite paan. Truly magnificent. This is not paan—it's a ghazal.'

Bidhubhushan again said to himself: Good Lord!

Kenaaram pointed towards Bidhubhushan and said, 'My friend Bidhu's concerned about your presence. He's such a nasty-minded fellow that he's always full of suspicions.'

Bidhubhushan said with a smile, 'I'm neither enlightened, nor made of stone. Which is why I'm not only full of fears but suspicions as well. I come complete with anger and sorrow and so on, I'm afraid.'

K said, laughing, 'Love, that's the thing. Once you have love in your heart, everything becomes all right. Heh . . . heh . . . love's the only thing there is.'

Hearing this, Kenaaram Kundu's face started resembling a heavily buttered slice of bread. Bidhubhushan said to himself yet again: Good Lord!

Bidhubhushan ran into Kenaaram about ten days later, at the corner of the road. Kenaaram was carrying a leg of mutton.

Kenaaram: 'Bidhubhushan, I'm glad I ran into you. Would you like to come to dinner at my place this evening? My wife's making a korma, and K is making shammi kebabs.'

Bidhubhushan: 'Oh really. What's all this for?'

Kenaaram: 'My dear fellow, I can't tell you what a fine chap K is. Why, he's just presented my wife with such an expensive shawl. I kept telling him not to bother, but would he listen? If you came this evening, you'd see what a magnificent shawl it is. He said I was not to forbid him because it was a token of the love he had for my wife. Naturally, I hadn't the heart to forbid him after that.'

Bidhubhushan: 'You know, Kenaaram, I'd always known that you were enlightened but I'd never realized you were an eunuch as well. Are you telling me that you're not aware that K is a rapist and a thug? All you've got to do is to enquire at the local police station. They'd have arrested him on the spot but there was never enough evidence. But they have grave suspicions that . . .'

Kenaaram: 'Now look, Bidhu. My second cousin's third brother-in-law was a rapist as well. But that wasn't sufficient reason for me to cut off relations with him. And it won't ever be. I mean, listen—the moon has blemishes, the sun has spots . . . Don't worry your head about such things. Look at the good side of—'

Bidhubhushan: 'No, you look at their good side. I'm going.'

Kenaaram: 'Aren't you coming to dinner?'

Bidhubhushan: 'No!'

A month later.

Kenaaram had been away from home. He returned to find that K was visiting. The cane that K carried was leaning against the wall of the drawing room but K was not to be seen. What greeted Kenaaram's eyes as he entered his bedroom, however, was a shattering sight: K was sitting on the bed, caressing his wife's cheeks. Anyone else would have created a scene, started a brawl, taken a whip to the man. But Kenaaram was an enlightened soul. He merely protested in a voice quivering with emotion.

'My dear fellow,' said Kenaaram, 'I really must condemn your behaviour. Putibala is my lawfully wedded wife. It's illegal to fondle her in this manner. I don't want you to repeat this again. Just think, is this appropriate?'

What K said in return totally flabbergasted the enlightened soul.

K said, 'Friend Kenaaram, I accept that you recited some Sanskrit mumbo-jumbo and married Putibala. But that this ritual gives you a right to monopolize Puntibala for ever, that I do not accept. Indeed, not one of the enlightened men and women of our contemporary civilization would accept such a contention. You, too, are an enlightened person. Therefore, I ask you to consider the matter most carefully. You must accept Putibala's opinions in this affair. After all, this is the age of individual freedom.'

Saying this, K left in a rather dramatic manner. Putibala stood with her back turned, her eyes lowered, a malicious smile on her face. Despite repeated questions, she refused to express any feelings.

Another person might have whipped her to an inch of her life. But since Kenaaram was an enlightened soul, his only option was to frown quizzically. That is what he did.

Another two months later.

Kenaaram had been away that day as well. He returned to discover that K was at his home. In fact K was in the habit of coming every day, despite repeated admonitions. The cane was in its usual place in the drawing room. But when Kenaaram entered the bedroom that day, he was truly flustered. He saw that K was not only in his bedroom and on his bed but also that Putibala's state was what might be described as the indescribable.

Kenaaram said, 'My dear fellow, I had trusted you. I had taken you close to my heart. Was this the way to repay me?'

Kenaaram felt that K was quite stricken with guilt at hearing these words. He felt as though the dark rain clouds of repentance were gathering in the man's soul. What looked like a smile to the naked eyes was, in reality, shame.

Immediately upon this realization, of course, his anger evaporated. In his enlightened joy, he reached a land that is not described in the geography books.

Putibala disappeared the very next day.

Nor was there any trace of K.

I heard the rest from Bidhubhushan.

Bidhubhushan said, 'Kenaaram's sold all his property and bought a plot of land near the crossroads. He intends to build a high marble podium there. And the gist of the sermon that he intends to scream in three languages each morning and evening is, "Cast the beam from your own eyes before you look for the mote in the other's. K might be a characterless thug, but can I forget that my second cousin's third brother-in-law was exactly the same? The moon has blemishes and the sun has spots, roses have thorns and the lotus blooms in muck. If you see someone behaving in a disgusting manner, remind yourself that you, too, are disgusting. Not only will you be at peace, you will also have resolved the problem. If people accuse you of ruining your own home to help others, pay no attention. Take refuge in the truth."

And this, precisely, is what he is doing these days. Mysterious are the ways of the enlightened ones.'

Many years later, a diary of Kenaaram's came into my possession. There was a strange entry in it. Kenaaram had written: I am an enlightened soul. The tragedy is, however, that no one seems to recognize this. But I'm not the type to give up. I will prove to everyone that I am enlightened. Let us see whether people recognize me.

Kenaaram has remained outside the lunatic asylum till today.

Two Disciples

It was some fifty years ago. The road went past Lachhmanjhula towards Kedar–Badri. Some miles down the road, those days, one could see a number of poplar trees arranged in rows on the lower slopes of the Himalayas. The Himalayas are full of poplar trees, but these trees were rather distinctive. They looked as though they were surrounding something in order to protect it from prying eyes. On one side of the trees was a ravine with a stream flowing through it and on the other, a small hill. During the monsoons, the ravine would be filled by a rushing torrent; in the summers, however, strange-looking boulders would be revealed. On top of the hillock was a small cabin, made of stone. No one knew when it had been built, or indeed, who had built it. Its two sides were of stone, the roof was a single large slab of stone, the front was entirely open. A single person could live there with ease. Beyond the hill was a beautiful lake, where the lotus flower bloomed. On the other side of the lake was a poplar forest, beyond that the open sky and, against the horizon, the Himalayas, with their ever-changing beauty. It was this hill that the poplars seemed to be trying to shield. A sage used to live there. Occasionally, the hill people would leave him offerings of fruit and milk. He used to dig out a certain root from the hillsides. The root apparently had the effect of diminishing hunger. The other thing that sustained him was the lake. He used to meditate in that lonely but beautiful spot. Hidden from the public gaze, he was attempting to advance towards enlightenment.

II

To avoid the public gaze for any great length of time, however, is a difficult task. One day, two young men could be seen crossing the boulders at the bottom of the ravine, on their way towards the poplar trees. One of them was named Paresh and the other Sudhir. At one stage, they had joined a terrorist group. They had sworn that they would lay down their lives if necessary to free their country from the bonds of servitude. Aurobindo Ghosh's writings in the journal *Vande Mataram* had particularly affected them. Aurobindo had become their ideal. When the same Aurobindo Ghosh suddenly left politics to journey in the metaphysical planes, they started to despair. They even went and met Aurobindo. He told them, 'Spiritual strength will have to be India's salvation. The spiritual way is India's way. We have become materialistic. In this state, we won't be able to retain independence even if we achieve it. You should try to gain spiritual strength.'

A former terrorist had taken the name Niralamba Swami and become a sannyasi. They wanted to be his disciples but he refused. He told them that he had not yet become worthy of being anyone's guru. But he also told them that on top of a hill on the way to Kedar–Badri lived a person who was truly a worthy guru. It would benefit them greatly if they could become his disciples.

As Paresh and Sudhir arrived at the hill, the sage returned from a swim. He looked at the two young strangers in some surprise. The surprise was considerably increased upon hearing their proposition.

'I'm still searching for the way myself—it's eluded me so far. How am I supposed to show you the way?'

He stopped for a while and then continued, 'At the beginning, you have to search for the way yourself. That search is the sadhana. If you're truly dedicated, the way will reveal itself.'

Paresh said, 'Please tell us how.'

The sage said, 'You must meditate. There are millions of gods and goddesses in our pantheon. Keep the image of any one of them in front of you and meditate. You don't have to be ordained for this. Be your own gurus to start with. In due course your real guru will reveal himself to you.'

'But what if we can't concentrate on any god or goddess?' asked Sudhir.

'The image is only the means, it's the meditation that is the end. If you can't concentrate on God, think of some noble ideal. If you can't even do that, meditate on some question: Where have I come from, who am I, where am I going? Concentrate on the question and meditate. Your mind will not settle to start with. But don't worry about that. Simply start again after each distraction. If you're strong and have a pure spirit, you will get results.'

Paresh immediately became curious, 'What sort of results are you talking about?'

'That depends on the nature of your meditation. If you meditate according to the rule of Tantra, you might gain occult or supernatural powers. But it's best not to boast too much about such things.' He stopped for a while, then said, 'You two'd better leave now. I want to meditate.'

They had taken a room in a little inn near Lacchmanjhula. They returned there for the night. When they came back the next day, the sage had disappeared. A long wait produced no results.

'How long are you planning to wait for him?' asked Paresh.

'Until he makes an appearance,' replied Sudhir.

'Well, I'm not waiting that long. My father was rather ill when I left. I've got to return home.'

'You had better leave then. I'll wait.'

III

A quarter of a century passes before they meet again, on that holiest of pilgrimages, to the city of Benaras. Paresh is no longer Paresh; he has been transformed into Swami Kaivalyananda—a quivering obese figure, his face covered with salt-and-pepper whiskers. On his way back after a purifying dip in the Ganges, he is carrying a large copper kamandal. His feet are adorned in elegant clogs. He is accompanied by a man holding a huge red umbrella. The passers-by move out of his way in dread and respect. A scrawny-looking individual is walking a few paces behind him. His face is also covered in a salt-and-pepper beard but his clothes are in tatters. His feet are bare, their soles cracked and filthy. But he has the smile of a child, and his eyes blaze with a fantastic light, as though someone has bathed his face in the glow of an unearthly joy. The man suddenly comes close and says, 'Good Lord! It's Paresh, isn't it?'

Swami Kaivalyananda comes to an abrupt halt.

'And who might you be?'

'It's me, Sudhir. Well, you've certainly changed a lot. But I managed to recognize you all right. Do you live here, then?'

Kaivalyananda stares for a few moments in blank surprise, before he recognizes Sudhir.

'Sudhir! What an extraordinary thing . . . Yes, I live close by. I've got an ashram hereabouts. Come along . . .'

Sudhir stands with a faintly mischievous grin on his face.

'So you want me to come to your ashram, do you?'

'Yes, why don't you?'

'Just hang on for a moment then while I get some pakoras. I don't get to eat them very often . . . Would you like some?'

Kaivalyananda seems rather offended.

'We sannyasis are not meant to eat things from street vendors.'

'Well, I'm going to, anyway. Tailanga Swami would support me, even if you don't.'

Munching on a pakora, Sudhir follows Kaivalyananda Swami. Kaivalyananda is grave; Sudhir's face is covered with a beatific smile. Suddenly he asks, 'Why've you got a red umbrella? Aren't black ones good enough . . . ?'

Kaivalyananda does not answer.

In a little while, they arrive in front of a modestly sized palace. A servant comes rushing out and pours a bucket of holy Ganges water on Kaivalyananda's clog-adorned feet.

'You wash your feet as well, Sudhir. It's not appropriate to enter the ashram with dirty feet.'

'Wash my feet . . . ? Well, if you say so.'

Another bucket of water duly arrives but Sudhir takes it from the servant and washes his own feet.

'Now we can enter.'

A huge paved courtyard.

Kaivalyananda halts as soon as he enters. Then he starts shouting, 'Keshav, Keshav . . .!'

A lad who looks like a purohit emerges.

'I can't smell any incense. Haven't you lit any today?'

'We've run out. I was just about to send out for some.'

'Well why didn't you tell me about it? What's inside that rusty pail in the corner . . . ?'

'The builders were at work. I think they left some sand in it.'

'Well, fetch it, man.'

Keshav runs and fetches the pail. Kaivalyananda picks up a handful of sand from the pail.

'Put the bucket down and hold out your hand.'

The sand has turned into incense.

'Go and light this in the drawing room. Make sure that you mix some chandan and guggul with it.'

'As you wish, sir.'

An awestruck Keshav departs. As soon as he leaves, Sudhir bursts into peals of laughter, his eyes streaming. At last, he wipes his eyes and says, 'It's finally come to incense, has it?'

With a faint smile, Kaivalyananda says proudly, 'Yes, I can convert sand into incense.'

'Yes, so I noticed. But I was under the impression that we'd been seeking enlightenment, not incense. Incense one can buy from the shops. And you . . .' he bursts into gales of laughter.

Kaivalyananda is somewhat irritated. 'Who says I haven't gained enlightenment?' he asks. 'But one is forced into such things out of deference to public taste, you know.'

'Is that what it is? Well, let's see whether I can do it or not.'

Sudhir puts his hand inside the bucket and pulls out a handful of sand.

'I don't seem to have managed it. Could you do it once again, I'd like to observe it.'

Kaivalyananda proudly puts his hand inside the bucket and says, 'It's nothing, really . . .'

But his face turns ashen as soon as he withdraws his hand. The sand has not changed into incense—it remains plain old sand. Sudhir is laughing mischievously.

'Well, I must be off now . . .'

'You can't leave so soon. We've met after such a long time. Where are you now . . . ?'

'Oh, roaming round that mountain lake, you know.'

'Have you found anything?'

'Not a thing—I'm still looking.'

'And the gurudev? Is he still there?'

'No, he never returned. He's moved on to a higher plane. Goodbye . . .'

Sudhir leaves . . .

During the Riots

Even the air had stopped moving in terror of the Hindu–Muslim riots. The days passed somehow but the nights seemed to last for ever. The blare of the conch shell from one direction, shouts of 'Vande Mataram' from another! At the slightest hint of disturbance, we scrambled up to the terrace. Not a lot happened, generally; things quietened down in a couple of minutes. Moreover, the bitter cold made it impossible to stay on the terrace for long. My wife spent her time checking to see that the various doors and windows were bolted and secured. We took turns staying awake. Even 'Sunri' the maid had taken shelter in our house with her entire family. Faizu, her lanky, pug-nosed drunk of a husband was our only hope of succour. Because, apart from me, he was the only other man at home. The third 'man' of the household was my ten-year-old son. My only support was a staff, though it could be better described as a cane. Faizu had managed to get hold of a blunt spear. A large number of bricks had been piled on the terrace. This was the extent of the war materials that we had been able to gather. But given the stories that one was hearing about the murderous ferocity, ungovernable strength and Hitlerite behaviour of the Muslims, I was not convinced that these meagre preparations would be sufficient to do battle with them. I had a gun, but no cartridges. Every one of the few officers that I knew had been requested to provide me with a few. Each had faithfully promised of course, but in practice I was reminded each evening of that old truth: promises are meant to be broken. Meanwhile the Muslims were tormenting us. If they attacked, we would have to defend ourselves with that slender stick and the blunt spear.

The rumours doing the rounds were truly hair-raising. It was said that the Muslims were suddenly going to descend on us via the river. They had apparently collected a lot of boats. And they were well armed—not just with rifles and grenades but also the occasional small artillery piece. My house was on the river; which meant that we would have to bear the brunt of the attack. But the thought of withstanding anything with a stick and a blunt spear was turning my blood cold. Faizu, on the other hand, was quite unafraid. 'Not to worry, master, we'll be fine. There's a huge village of Gwalas in Daryapur . . . ,' and so on and so forth.

The terror seemed to abate somewhat during the day. Therefore, I indulged in rationalizations, used instances from history to reassure myself, and so on. Indeed, the light of day even gave me the courage to examine my own experiences. Whatever the recent turn of events, I had many friends and acquaintances among the Muslims until recently. Indeed, I had been very close to some of them.

The other day, I was suddenly reminded of Rahim's mother. How could Rahim or his mother become my enemies? Rahim's father, Abdul, had been an employee of ours; he used to look after our farm. What was to be sown and when, how many ploughs would be needed, which field was to be harvested when, how many labourers would be required, which crop fetched the best prices in which market—all this and more besides had been his responsibility. Another way of putting it would be that Abdul was the real owner; he certainly took care of everything. Nor had there ever been any reason to doubt his honesty.

Something else came to mind . . . I had even suckled at Rahim's mother's breast. Rahim and I are the same age; we were born in the same month of the same year. About two months after I was born, my mother fell very ill. Rahim's mother had breastfed me then. She had a lot of milk; I had suckled at her breast for a long time. Until I was a few years old, I mean. I remember Rahim's mother taking me to the fields. Rahim and I would play under the huge ashwattha tree; his mother would be working in the field. She would feed us when she had a moment or two to spare . . . Abdul had died; had he been alive, he would undoubtedly have been living with me. Rahim had been my classmate. After completing his matric, he had found a job in Patna. His mother had joined him a couple of years ago. Who knows where he was living nowadays.

The fading light of the afternoon was falling on one corner of the verandah. There was not a soul in sight; a bird was calling incessantly. The ruddy sunlight seemed to touch the landscape with magic. I had completely forgotten about the riots for a moment. I can't remember how long I had been sitting mesmerized, but my trance was broken by the sound of my neighbour Haren-babu's voice.

'Heard the latest news?'

'What, what?'

'The Hindu village on the other bank—Daryapur. Massacred, wiped out completely.'

My heart began to thud in my chest.

'Good God, what're you saying? The Gwalas of Daryapur were our only hope!'

'Like I said, not a soul left alive.'

There was no adequate response to this. We stared at each other for a while. Then Haren-babu broke the silence to give me the second bit of news.

'According to Bishu, they're planning to cross the Ganges and attack us tonight. They've got a lot of boats.'

'Do you really think that they'll dare go that far?'

'Absolutely! They're capable of anything, you know. You'd better keep your gun handy!'

'Oh, the gun's handy enough. It's the cartridges that're missing.'

'No cartridges? Used them up shooting ducks, have you? Well, you've had it now.'

Haren-babu generally had a schoolmaster-ish attitude; I did not bother to reply. After a minute, he said, 'I'll ask Basudeo-babu. He often has a fair stock.'

'I asked him already . . .'

'Let's see.'

Haren-babu set off for Basudeo-babu's house. The Bihari zamin-dar, Basudeo Mishra, was a famous big-game hunter in this area. It was entirely possible that he would have spare cartridges.

My wife made her appearance as soon as Haren-babu departed. The news she brought from next door was, if anything, even more terrifying. Our neighbour worked for the railways. And he had apparently observed about two hundred and fifty huge Pathans alighting from the afternoon train.

'If the Kabulis manage to enter our house, they'll massacre everyone. I've given up reminding you to repair the wall. Locking the gate won't do much good, will it, when there's such a large gap in the wall itself!'

The boundary wall around my property did have a rather large gap, as a result of subsidence during the last rains. I had managed to put off repairing it time after time. Now I stared at the gap goggle-eyed. In any case, there was no way of repairing it for the time being. The masons were all Muslims.

. . . The sun finally set. The neighbours started dropping in one by one—well-wishers all. Each repeated the same warning, 'Be careful, be very, very careful. There's bound to be trouble tonight.' One took me aside and whispered, 'The local Muslim SDO's distributed arms to the Muslims of Sajangi. They mean to attack us en masse after ten o'clock.'

Another said, 'The military units that've arrived are Muslims to a man . . .'

I was in a state of total confusion. Faizu had in the meanwhile managed to procure two more spears. He said that if it was necessary 'the Mistress' could use one and Sunri the other. Apparently, that emaciated bag of skin and bones, Sunri, was an expert in spear-fighting. I, for one, was unaware of this.

'Don't you worry about anything, master,' he kept reassuring me.

But I felt as though I was hopelessly adrift.

Two hundred and fifty Kabulis, fifty boatloads from Daryapur, mad butchers and the armed Pathans of Sajangi! And the man intended to stop them with three spears? Was he insane? But in a little while, a slender lifeline was thrown to me: Haren-babu delivered four bullets. Four bullets!

The local lads had undertaken the task of patrolling the neighbourhood. At every street corner and lane, groups of youths had gathered, armed with whistles which they were to blow at the first sign of any trouble. At the sound of the whistles, everyone was to go to their terrace and blow conch shells. Bamboo scaffolds had been put outside those houses that did not possess stairways to the terrace. Those who lived in thatch-and-mud cottages were to take shelter in the nearest brick-built house. The arrangements were quite complete.

It was a moonless night. The atmosphere was tense, there was no sound of any human activity. Only the chirping of cicadas filled the air. The children had fallen asleep; there was no sound from Faizu either. My wife and I were lying side by side, reading—I, an English novel, she, a Bengali one. In reality, we were tensely waiting for the slightest sound. Seconds, minutes, hours were passing . . . I was not sure when we fell asleep but I was jarred awake by a dig in my ribs.

'Wake up, will you . . . I can hear the sound of whistles.'

My wife was sitting up in a dishevelled state. Yes, the sound of whistles could indeed be heard. A conch shell blared from next door. I woke the sleeping child and we rushed to the terrace. My wife started blowing her conch. The air reverberated in every direction with the sound of conch shells. 'Jai Hind' . . . 'Vande Mataram' . . . the darkness resonated with cries.

Suddenly Haren-babu screamed from next door, 'There're two people crawling past your wall . . . Can you see them? . . . Quickly man, fire . . . fire!'

I had left my gun downstairs. I rushed down to fetch it and returned to see my wife having hysterics.

'Someone's entered through the gap in the wall. Oh my God, what're we going to do now . . . Oh Lord, save us, please help us.' I used the torch and saw that someone was indeed crawling through the gap.

I asked Faizu to shine the torch and fired, not once but twice. The blaring sound of conch shells rent the skies. 'Jai Hind' . . . 'Vande Mataram' . . . 'Jai Hind' . . . 'Vande Mataram'—I felt as though the night skies were being torn apart by the sounds. The next moment, a military jeep arrived.

All of us crowded near the gap in the wall. Suddenly, someone screamed from behind the dark bushes across the road, 'Paresh, it's Rahim. I've run away from Patna with mother. I thought you'd shelter us. Please, help us. The gate's locked and Mother's trying to crawl through the gap.'

The blood-soaked corpse was dragged out.

The bullet had pierced the left breast.

Discovered the Next Day

Finally, he came to meet God himself. God asked, 'And who might you be?'

'I'm Divakar.'

'Divakar? My creation Divakar is bright with a million rays, immortal in his power. You're a shrunken sort, aren't you? And dark! Who gave you this name?'

'Grandpa . . .'

'Well, what do you want . . . ?'

'A job.'

'And what qualifications have you acquired?'

'I've got a BA degree.'

'Oh! And what've you learnt?'

Divakar was a little flustered. He thought to himself: You can't bluff God. He is omniscient, after all.

'To be honest, sire, I've not really learnt a thing. Passed all my exams by copying, you see.'

'Now why did you do something like that?'

'Well, Lord, you need a degree, and not learning, to survive in the job market. So I spent my time organizing my degree. And I've spent an awful sum of money getting my degree, let me tell you. But I can't seem to get a job. So I thought you might very kindly arrange one for me.'

'But I don't have an official position. One can't give people jobs without an official position.'

Divakar suddenly saw red.

He quite forgot who he was talking to.

He raised his pipegun and said, 'Get me a job, or you're dead.'

God's smile surpassed all understanding.

He said, 'Why would you want to waste a bullet? I am immortal, after all. I've been alive since time immemorial and I shall stay for all eternity. I came because you were calling me so fervently. But you're asking for a boon that I cannot grant. You cannot give someone a job without an official position.'

'Well, then, do something.'

'What would you want me to do? Since you're a clod, eat and drink and roam about like any other animal.'

'Eat? What d'you want me to eat? My tummy's burning with hunger. I haven't eaten for two days!'

God had a kamandal in his hand.

'All right. Open your mouth. I'll give you something to eat.'

'What's in that thing?'

'It's nectar. It satisfies divine hunger. The gods gain immortality from it.'

Divakar opened his mouth. God poured some nectar into it. But Divakar was not satisfied. He said, 'I couldn't feel a thing. No taste, no smell, I couldn't tell I'd eaten anything.'

'That's nectar for you.'

God disappeared.

The next day it became obvious that Divakar was not divine but, in fact, quite human. Because the nectar had neither satisfied his hunger nor made him immortal.

His body was discovered the next day.

There was a bullet hole in his temple.

Afzal

I

The river on whose bank Moi Choudhury's huge mansion stands has no specific name. Some people call it Aleya, some Maya, some others Kheyali, and some others yet, Begum. The river has many names; it has had different names at different times. People use whichever one they like. During the Pathan days, a famous Muslim jagirdar named Alla-ud-din Khan used to live by the river. He had apparently named the river Raushni, or 'light'. Apparently, the river waters reflected many colours in those days.

Moi Choudhury lives in one corner of a huge tumbledown mansion, a mansion which nowadays resembles a vast ruin, with its near-obliterated minarets and domes, with its marble floors, with its large and small halls which can still create a sense of awe in the visitor. This mansion once belonged to that same Alla-ud-din Khan. Which is why it is still known as Ala Manzil.

There is a large area of open land in front of Ala Manzil. Beyond that is a wide road, lined on both sides by gulmohur trees. Beyond the trees is that river. It could easily be called Shatarupa or Aparupa, for it seems to have no prefixed form. Today it might be mainly sand banks, with a thin stream meandering through it somewhere, and tomorrow, a vast all-inundating sheet of water. Today the water might be quite murky but tomorrow, crystal clear; on some days a shining blue, on others a sullen ochre. On certain occasions, the river resembles a floating forest—trees, large branches, moss and vines, large and small bushes, all can be seen floating past. It arises from a mountain in the Santhal Parganas but no one knows exactly which one. Many people simply call it Hidden Mountain; it is surrounded by three or four mountains whose ogre-ish size conceals it. In short, not a lot is known about it. But because the river occasionally meanders very near Ala Manzil, Moi Choudhury can hear the sound of its waters from his room.

I am a bit of a wanderer, what they would call in English a vagabond. I have no one that I can call my own, nor have I ever settled down anywhere. I spend my time travelling, to places that might be unknown but are beautiful. I had been living on one of the bends of the Jhelum river in the Punjab for a while. Then I spent some time in the forests near Biratnagar in Purnea. I lived in a village named Bagdama, in the Mandar Hills. There were hardly any people in Bagdama in those days. I used to spend my days in the fields, bird-watching. It was there that I spotted my first partridge quail. Hunting and photography, these were my two passions. As for friends, I found them as I went along. It was old Rua Majhi of Bagdam who told me about Moi Choudhury and the Begum river.

I live near Moi Choudhury's beloved Ala Manzil. An elderly, child-less Santhal couple have given me shelter. They have a cow. I buy whatever milk she gives and give a portion to the old couple. She makes thick chapatis for me. And at night, some meat of whatever bird I have managed to bag. On the occasions when I am unsuccess-ful in my hunt, we fall back on the traditional chicken. There is a bird called the shun-chaha in these parts, which is utterly delicious.

I can clearly remember my first meeting with Moi Choudhury. The old majhi had warned me that the very first thing to do would be to make a formal qurnish to Moi Choudhury. Otherwise he would get angry and start roaring, 'Afzal, get rid of this utter barbarian.' And immediately, a servant would arrive to show one out. 'Not Afzal, some other servant. Afzal never turns up, none of us has ever seen Afzal. Nevertheless, he is the major-domo. Otherwise, Choudhury is a very pleasant person, an amusing chap. So off you go.'

When I turned up, Choudhury was smoking from a large hookah. The pipe of the hookah was exquisitely inlaid with silver. The air was redolent with the fragrance of aromatic tobacco. As soon as I had fin-ished making my qurnish, he said, 'And who might you be, sir?'

'I'm camping on your zamindari. I'm just an ordinary person . . .'

'Zamindari? I don't have any zamindari, no zamindari any more. The Government of India is the sole zamindar of Hindustan these days. I've still got Afzal and so I get by. Oh, please, do sit . . .'

I sat.

'Are you hungry? Tell me, what sort of food do you like?'

'I'm really not hungry . . .'

'It is our custom to feed our guests, though I've heard that things have changed somewhat elsewhere. People like to stuff themselves at other peoples' expense but don't like inviting others. I'm afraid I've maintained the old customs. Have a bite to eat with your coffee.' He shouted, 'Afzal, we have a guest. Coffee and something to eat, please.'

In a little while, two dark-skinned boys arrived bearing silver trays. Coffee things and expensive English biscuits on one, black grapes, apples and halwa on the other. The halwa was still oozing ghee. I started eating silently, having come to the conclusion that arguments would prove futile here.

That day, the Maya river was running virtually next to Moi Choudhury's house. Splash, splash, splash went the waters.

Choudhury suddenly burst out, 'The bitch is back again.'

'Who?'

'That river. Can't you hear the waters? It's not a river, it's a bloody messenger. Brings me news of the children and grandchildren whose ashes I've consigned to its depths. And it keeps tempting me, says come along, come along. But I tell you, I'm not going to. I'm meant for the ocean. It can splash all it damn well wants, I'm not to be tempted.'

My only reaction was astonishment. The man had obviously taken leave of his senses.

I used to visit Moi Choudhury regularly.

He used to tell me stories of 'those' days.

Once he told me about his grandfather who used to keep pet tigers. Apparently, they would follow him around like obedient dogs. But they were tigers after all. So, every so often, one or other would become enraged. Not that it ever did it much good. Dikpal Choudhury would simply wrestle it to the ground, then whip it to its senses with a bull whip. Things would immediately return to normal.

Another day he said, 'My father, Prabal-Pratap, was crazy about horses and carriages. All kinds of horses and carriages. He had a special carriage built to his specifications. Almost the size of a small drawing room, it needed four huge dray horses to pull it. Inside, it had carpets, mattresses and cushions, to say nothing of hookahs of various kinds, and even a hand-drawn fan. There was a small box-like affair behind the carriage, where Moti, my father's favourite servant would sit, and pull the fan. Those were the days. They seem like a dream now.'

'What happened to the carriage?'

'Couldn't keep it. Couldn't maintain a thing. Blew my inheritance on horses. Well, a portion anyway. The rest on mynah.'

This 'mynah' business confused me to begin with. I thought that the man was a fellow bird-lover.

'Like keeping mynah birds, do you?'

'Birds, yes, but not quite the sort you mean. Mynah was a baiji. Extraordinary woman . . .'

Moi Choudhury gazed at a portrait on the wall opposite him. The portrait of a beautiful young woman. The painting looked alive, as though it was a figure of light and brightness and not a mere human being.

'Got it done by a famous European portrait painter, you know. He didn't want to do it, saying that no painter could do justice to such beauty. But I persisted.'

I didn't know how to respond. After a few moments of silence, he burst out laughing. 'Strange creatures, women. All they want is to get married. But you can't just marry anyone, can you? I mean, the woman who'd be mother to the descendants of Prabal-Pratap and Dikpal couldn't come from any old rubbish heap, could she? So what if she was beautiful? I tried to explain, but would she listen? Committed suicide one day!'

He was silent for a while, then stroked his moustache and smiled, 'There were a number of descendants, you know. But not one lasted. My fault, really. I'd miscalculated. Only thought of the field, not of the seed.'

More silence, then a smile, and he said, 'Anyway, it's all over now. Have a mango. I've just received some Kohinoor mangoes. Afzal, some mangoes and cream for Biren-babu . . .'

The mangoes and cream duly arrived, carried by the same two lads, in what looked like the finest porcelain.

Later, I learnt that they were named Tinku and Chhatku.

There was one thing that kept mystifying me. That was: How did Moi Choudhury, despite having almost no income, manage to live like a king? He slept in a silver-chased mahogany bed. The house was furnished in a luxurious manner. He tended to eat foods that even the rich could not easily afford. All he would say was that Afzal arranged everything. But who was this Afzal? And how did he manage to arrange things so conveniently? How did all that expensive produce from Calcutta get to these backwoods? He even gave me some priceless Beluga caviar on one occasion! But all he seemed to worry about was: What would happen to him after his death? Would there be sufficient pall-bearers to carry that enormous body? And even if they were found, would he be cremated by the banks of 'that' river? One day, I asked him who Afzal was. He merely smiled.

I was on a bird-shoot with an elderly hunter from those parts, Pingla Majhi. This was during the winter. Someone had told us that 'pink foot' geese were roosting by the Maya river. These birds arrive early, just before the break of day, and fly away at first light. To bag them, one has to get to their roost well before dawn. We had prepared a little lean-to of branches, leaves and grass by the river, the previous day. Pingla and I got there before midnight; there were pallets of straw inside. We had brought a couple of warm blankets with us, and made ourselves comfortable. Time passed. Then, we heard the sound of the birds. Pingla whispered in my ear, 'Let them settle down a bit, then we'll go out.' But the birds did not get an opportunity to settle down. All of a sudden, there was an unholy cackle. We rushed out of the lean-to. I had a torch with me, and tried to see what was going on in its pallid light. To begin with, nothing could be seen. Why were they shrieking so? Then I noticed a giant black shape stepping out of the river, holding the neck of a huge goose in either hand. The man looked neither right nor left; he merely climbed the river bank and disappeared in the darkness. The two of us stared in stunned silence. Finally, Pingla exclaimed in a choked voice, 'Afzal.'

'Afzal? Do you mean you know Afzal?'

'No, I don't. No one knows Afzal. But I've seen him once before. There's a huge jackfruit tree outside my house. Some years ago, there was a gigantic beehive on it. One night, I heard a loud cracking sound. I rushed out of my house and saw a giant black man. He had broken the branch off. and was squeezing the honey out of the hive into a bucket. My father was alive those days. "Get away," he told me, "that's Afzal. Don't get in his way. He's the biggest and darkest man in these parts. Move away if you see him."'

'But who is he?' I asked.

'No one knows,' Pingla said. 'And what my father told me was truly fantastic.'

'Told you? Told you what?'

'Let's go back to the lean-to. I'll tell you there.'

We went back to the little hut.

'One of Moi Choudhury's ancestors was a man named Yogambar,' Pingla said. 'It was rumoured that he made human sacrifices to Kali. Those days, you could buy people for money. One day, a tall, dark-skinned young man arrived and said that he was a Brahmin who had been forcibly converted to Islam by his Muslim zamindar. He had seriously considered suicide but lacked the courage. He wanted to offer himself as a human sacrifice. In return, he promised faithfully to serve the family, if there was life after death. Apparently, Afzal appeared soon afterwards.'

Pingla became quiet. The atmosphere seemed very overcast.

The next morning, I was invited to Moi Choudhury's house. As soon as I arrived he told me, 'Afzal brought two very fine geese yesterday. I've asked him to make a roast. I thought of you because you're a bit of a gourmand.' The 'pink foot' is a rare bird, but the roast that day defies description. I've never eaten better.

II

One morning, I was woken and told that Moi Choudhury had died. I rushed to Ala Manzil immediately, but I never got there. I had only gone a little way when I came to a halt. What I saw was so unexpected that I couldn't move. There was a huge pleasure barge standing at the bend of the Maya river. And outside Moi Choudhury's house, an equally large carriage, drawn by four giant black horses, resplendent in ornate regalia. The carriage was truly the size of a small drawing room, with polished wood, gleaming decorations, and covered with the most remarkable flowers that I have ever seen. In fact, I have never seen such flowers. It was as though white sea foam had taken the shape of flowers. The person holding the reins was no ordinary coachman—it was a stunningly beautiful young woman. I recognized the baiji, Mynah, from her portrait. In a little while, four giant black men came out bearing the mahogany bed. Moi Choudhury was lying on it, covered with an exquisitely embroidered shawl. He looked as though he was sleeping.

The four men opened the door of the carriage, and gently put the bed in. The carriage slowly proceeded towards the barge—the barge that was to carry Moi Choudhury to the sea.

The horses' hooves rang on the road.

I stared in stunned silence.

The Ultimate Dance

My friend Jogen came rushing into my house, then slammed the door shut and barred it. I noticed that his expression was agitated, his hair was dishevelled. His nostrils flaring.

'Good Lord, Jogen! What're you doing here? Why did you bar the door?'

Jogen stared at me for a while, then whispered, 'Chasing me.'

'Chasing you? Who is?'

'That bitch, who else. She's come to tell me how much she loves me.'

'Who on earth are you talking about . . . ?'

'Dulari, for God's sake, Dulari. That lying young whore.'

'How's that? I thought she was in some Nawab's court . . .'

'. . . of course she is. Nawabs have more money, don't they? I raise her, teach her music and dance, make sure she has a roof over her head. And as soon as she's able to, she's off to greener pastures. Now she's come to lie to me.'

He burst out laughing in such an odd manner that I was startled.

Jogen stared at me, bewildered.

'Did you know that she was a gipsy?'

'You'd told me once.'

'They used to work the streets. Her father used to do magic tricks. That's where I'd bought her from, you know, the streets. Now she's showing me magic tricks. Strange magic . . .'

'Magic . . . ?'

'That's right, magic. Witchcraft, sorcery, that sort of thing—the bitch.'

Jogen was grinding his teeth by now.

'Stop being mysterious and tell me everything.'

'You won't believe me if I tell you everything. You won't.'

He was nearly screaming by now.

'Well, just try me, then. Whyever did you bar the door?'

'That slut's chasing me. She's standing near the crossroads. You know, I'd named her Angel. Now the angel's turned into a demon . . .'

'Standing by the crossroads, is she? Let's have a look then . . .'

I went to the door to unbar it. Jogen desperately grabbed my hand: 'No, no, no! Don't open it, for heaven's sake. You won't see a thing, anyway. I'm the only one who can see her. If you open the door, she'll come in. She might come in through the barred doors anyway. They can do anything, that lot—it's the witchcraft, you see. Do you still have your revolver?'

'It's on the shelf behind you.'

Jogen held the revolver firmly: 'Is it loaded? 'I'll shoot her if she enters. I'll shoot that witchiness of her's is what I'll do . . .'

'Why don't you tell me about it, for goodness' sake?'

Jogen brooded for a while. 'But will you believe me? You won't think I'm mad, will you?'

'Why don't you tell me about it first?'

'Oh, all right. I used to correspond with Angel regularly, even though she had joined the Nawab's court. One day I got a letter: "If you go to your place in Giridih, I'll come and dance for you. I've taken the Sunday off, so I'll see you in the evening. I'll dance for you, then return in the morning." Today's Tuesday. I was in Giridih by Sunday evening, waiting for her. She hadn't arrived even past midnight. It was a moonlit night. The lawn in front of the house was flooded with moonlight. As though it was waiting for her, as though it was my heart. Suddenly I heard the mournful cry of a jackal. I noticed that it was one in the morning. I decided to switch off the lights and go to bed. It was then that the incident took place. The magic show started. I saw that something was hopping in through the door. It was a leg, complete up to the thigh. As soon as it entered the room, it straightened up; then it started dancing round me, in circles.'

'Dancing round you?'

'Yes, that's right, dancing. And what a dance it was too! Shiva's dance of destruction! Hopping and circling around me went the leg, and that's when I realized that the slut was using witchcraft. They have all manners of powers, strange powers. They can hex people, or burn someone by burning a little straw figure, or hypnotize someone into doing anything that they want, and who knows what else. A gipsy's daughter, after all. She'd sent a leg along to take her place. And what a leg it was, the size of a small banana tree! Exactly what the Sanskrit poets would call a rambhoru. And it was cavorting all around me. I screamed, "Get away, you slut." And instantly, it whizzed out through the door. By now, I was shaking with rage. I left the house and walked to the station, and took the first train to Calcutta. When I got to Howrah Station, I noticed that she was there among the passengers—Angel—holding her amputated leg over her shoulder. She's been following me ever since. Everywhere I go, she follows, hopping along, her dismembered limb slung over her shoulder. I'd gone to Birinchi's house, but he wasn't in. So I thought I'd come to you. That slut is standing by the crossroads. As soon as I go out, she'll start following me. And of course, no one else can see a thing. Extraordinary thing, witchcraft.'

'And it's witchcraft, is it?'

'Yes, that's right, witchcraft. Gipsy women practise all kinds of witchcraft.'

Someone started banging on the door.

'Who's there?'

'It's me, Birinchi. Is Jogen with you?'

As soon as I opened the door, Birinchi, another dear friend, entered.

Birinchi looked at Jogen and said, 'Have you heard? Your Angel's been killed by the train.'

Jogen exploded, 'Bloody rubbish. Angel can't die, *she is immortal.*'

'For God's sake, man, I saw it with my own eyes. The train had started moving when the woman tried to board it. She slipped and fell underneath. Her leg got cut off at the thigh. Died almost immediately. Apparently her bag contained some money, a pair of ghungroos and a ticket to Giridih . . .'

'I don't believe a word. You're lying . . .'

'But I saw it with my own eyes . . .'

'You're a liar. You heard me, a liar, that's what you are. Angel's not dead, she can't die.'

'But I tell you . . .'

'*Shut up* . . .'

'Why don't you believe me . . .?'

What Jogen did next was quite unbelievable—he raised the gun and shot Birinchi in the chest. Birinchi fell, and I tried to grab Jogen. He shot me as well. I fell down, too.

I assume that he must have shot himself after that.

Because, soon after, I noticed that we were attending a dance soiree in the hereafter.

And that Angel was dancing.

Ramsevak

In the end, Ramsevak Ray achieved something extraordinary, even though he was not an extraordinary man by any stretch of the imagination. The child of an ordinary middle-class Bengali family, his upbringing was quite traditional. There was an old-fashioned brass idol of Narayan in the house which he worshipped daily. Indeed, he was quite a devout man and prayed to the god twice each day. His only error in youth had been his falling in love with Montu. Of course, Montu was a girl from the neighbourhood and belonged to the same caste, so there had been no problems.

Ramsevak had been an academically able boy.

This was during the British Raj. There was a decent job which he had applied for but which he did not get. Not even after making vows to all the gods he worshipped. The European boss appointed the son of one of his sycophants.

After years of clerkship, he ended his working career on a monthly salary of two hundred rupees. Imploring the household deity had not brought about any improvement in his financial condition. He had had eight children, of whom three had died. Not through any fault of his, because he had neither spared any expenses during their treatment nor forgotten to implore Narayan. But they did not survive. One died of tetanus, another of cholera and the third of typhoid fever. The physician was wholly unsuccessful and Narayan remained wholly impervious to any entreaties.

After he retired, Ramsevak discovered he had a new ambition. He wanted to stand for the post of commissioner, in the local municipal council. He stood for the election, and, despite incurring considerable expenditure, including those for the daily Narayan puja, he lost. The drunken and dissolute Golak-babu was duly elected.

Eventually, Ramsevak's final moments arrived. His children sat around his bed and, in the time-honoured manner, started reciting Harinaam.

Ramsevak suddenly shouted, 'Shut up, damn you.'

The children were startled into silence.

Montu was weeping silently by the head of the bed. Ramsevak said, 'Sit in front of me, please . . .'

As soon as Montu came in front of him he held her hand, and breathed his last while looking at her face.

The next day, the local rag of course announced that Ramsevak Ray, while fully conscious, and reciting the name of God, had gone to his well-deserved rest to a world far better than this.

A Century Apart

The year 1872.

An exhausted Dr Nityananda Sen has returned home at ten o'clock at night. He is about to sit down to a well-deserved meal when an anguished voice is heard shouting outside his door—

'Doctor Sen, please, Doctor . . .'

Gopi-babu, from Rampur village, is outside.

'My son is delirious with fever. Please, could you . . . would you . . . ?'

'Yes, of course I'll see him. Give me a moment.'

A country practice in those days meant travelling by bullock cart. Rampur is more than a mile away.

By the time the physician gets there, the patient is dead.

The physician returns without accepting any fees.

The year 1972.

Dr P. Sen, the grandson of Dr Nityananda Sen, is running an extremely successful practice in Calcutta, after having acquired a number of foreign qualifications. One day, the aforementioned Gopi-babu's grandson arrives at his consulting room.

'I wanted to consult you about my wife. She's seriously ill. Could you see her at once? Your grandfather used to be our family physician—he was very close to us. He . . .'

Dr P. Sen looks at his diary and interrupts, 'Can't give you an appointment for the next seven days, I'm afraid.'

'But my wife is dying . . .'

'Sorry, can't help, I'm afraid. You'd better get someone else.'
And Dr Sen shrugged.

Another Day

'What was the blood test like, Doctor?'

'Not very good, I'm afraid. Very low haemoglobin. The RBC count's low as well.'

'What would you suggest? I . . .'

'I'm prescribing some medicines for it. Two sorts of pills, one injection . . .'

'How much do I owe you for the blood tests?'

'I don't want any fees, thanks. If you get the injection, I'll administer it as well. Don't worry about fees.'

'I'm sorry, I didn't understand what you said about my blood . . .'

'Its become a bit thin. All the constituents aren't present in the proper proportions.'

'Is that right! But what makes blood grow thin?'

'Lots of things. It's hard to explain in a quick sentence or two. Look, why don't you just get the stuff!'

'Do you think that is why I'm having these palpitations?'

'Yes, I think it is.'

Atul-babu raised his sunken eyes and stared at me for a few moments.

'Do you know how much the drugs . . . ?'

'No, I don't. I'm not the owner of a pharmacy, you know. Why don't you find out?'

'Oh well, thanks very much then.'

Atul Roy lives in our neighbourhood. An elderly man, nearing retirement, he has a horde of children. The oldest boy is eighteen, he has failed his matric twice.

Atul-babu rationalizes by saying, 'It's not the boy's fault, my dear fellow. There's precious little teaching going on in schools these days. All the teachers spend their time giving private tuitions. In school, they spend their time sleeping. Worse, they teach in Hindi. The boys don't understand half of it. Plus, of course, every Bihari teacher hates them because they're Bengalis. They give them low marks whenever they can. The odd Bengali teacher doesn't dare do anything for fear of upsetting the Bihari masters. How on earth can my boy pass the exams under such circumstances? Personally, I think it's remarkable that he got as far as the matric.'

Atul-babu continues after a moment's pause, 'I'm flattering Mr Singh daily. He's promised me that he'll get the boy a job in his office, provided he passes his exams. But I'm not sure that I ought to do what he suggested . . .'

'Oh? What has he suggested?'

'He advised me to change my son's name by deed poll, from Kanan Kumar to Khublal. Apparently the title won't cause any problems. Rai is a common enough surname among Bhumihars. Indeed there are Kayasthas named Rai as well. Mr Singh says that "upstairs" will reject the application if they spot a Bengali name. I'm not sure what to do. After all, his grandmother had named him . . .'

Atul-babu's oldest child is a daughter; her nickname is Rini. A distant aunt of hers, a student in Santiniketan, was a brilliant exponent of Tagore music and dance. This lady had been advised a change of climate after some illness or other; she had stayed with the Roys for a while. During that time, Rini had learnt music and dancing from her. And just as well, for she is now able to supplement her father's meagre income by a further seventy-five rupees a month. Rini never stopped the training her aunt had initiated. In fact, she is quite a competent dancer. She is in the good books of the local magistrate, and through his efforts has been appointed the dance teacher in the local girls' school. She visits this gentleman's bungalow two or three times each week, so that he is even more favourable towards her. Atul-babu escorts her there.

None of the other children are in good health; they always seem to have one illness or other. I am the local physician. I treat them free of charge, of course. But I hear that from time to time he tries out homoeopathy. He has a little box of homoeopathic medicines as well as a few Bengali books on the subject. He often does the prescribing himself. Indeed, he had been treating himself and was consulting me only because he had got nowhere with his own treatment.

Atul-babu turned up once again in the evening.

'Do you know how much that prescription of yours costs? The two lots of tablets are nine-and-a-half rupees, and each injection is two rupees and eight annas. You want me to have six injections— that's fifteen rupees for the injections alone. Fifteen and nine and a half make twenty-four-and-a-half. Twenty-four and a half rupees, for seven days' worth of treatment! Do you think that I can afford such an expensive cure?'

He just stood there and stared at me with those sunken eyes. I didn't know what to say. How was I going to treat someone who couldn't afford the medicines?

'What about the local hospital? They might give . . .'

'The local hospital, sir? Are you crazy? That's only for the local big-wigs, they're the ones who get the free medicines. The poor people have to pay bribes. They can't get anything done there without money. Or anywhere else, for that matter. That poultry farm that the government's recently started. Do you reckon that even one chicken, or a solitary egg, reaches an outsider? The big shots take the lot . . .'

Atul-babu has the habit of stopping abruptly in the middle of a harangue, and staring at one in an unblinking fashion. That is precisely what he did now.

I said, 'You might consider improving your diet in that case. Milk, fish . . .'

'Do you know how much fish costs these days? Prawn is expensive, much less proper fish! Even looking at it costs money. Meat costs nearly three rupees a seer, milk is five pav to a rupee. Even potatoes and potols are expensive. The other day I wanted to buy a little white pumpkin—the shopkeeper wanted eight annas for it. I tell you, sir, I simply got out of there. Improve my diet? When the government's ration shops can't supply wheat? When everything's being sold on the black market? In the meanwhile, a different minister flies in each day to preach morals. Do you know who our physician is? Death, that's who. I keep "calling" him every day, but he doesn't answer.'

I was pierced once again by the gaze of those sunken eyes.

'I'm off, then. Thank you.'

He never forgot to say 'thank you'.

A new problem raised its ugly head in a week's time—the language problem. Bihar University announced that all candidates would have to sit their exams in Hindi rather than their mother tongues. Tempers rose. How dare they attempt something so unconstitutional? Only the other day in Hyderabad, President Rajendra Prasad said that Hindi was not going to be forced down anyone's throat. Yet this was happening in his own state. Intolerable! I promptly started drafting a petition. Then, I caught hold of a local lad and said, 'Go to every Bengali household, and ask them to sign this petition. After that, you'll have to go to the Muslims. Take this notebook with you, and see if you can start raising contributions as well.'

The lad said, 'OK.'

Having said that, he stood rooted to the spot.

'Well, what're you standing here for?'

'The rear wheel of my bicycle's damaged. I'm not sure that I can make it on foot.'

'Well, get your cycle repaired, immediately.'

The lad looked even more embarrassed. 'It'll cost four or five rupees, sir. I don't think I can afford it.'

My irritation had reached fever pitch by now.

'Never mind all that. Just get it done. I'll pay for it.'

The boy left with the petition, an enthusiastic grin on his face.

Soon after he left, Atul-babu's voice was heard outside.

'Are you there, Doctor? Come and look . . .'

'What is it you want me to see? Please, come inside . . .'

Atul-babu entered my surgery.

'It's laal shaak. Jiten-babu advised me to eat it. It's good for the haemoglobin. But even this is four annas for a seer.'

Atul-babu turned to leave.

I said, 'By the way, I've drafted a petition and had it sent to everyone in the neighbourhood. Sign it, will you? And see if you can donate a bit of money.'

'A petition? What about?'

'You'll find out when you read it.'

Atul-babu returned after about three days or so.

'I'm afraid I haven't signed your petition. I'm aware of how our mother tongue's being treated. Nevertheless, I couldn't sign. Can't upset my bosses, you see. Mr Singh's a Hindi fanatic. If I stay in his good books, I might even get an extension. I'm ruined if I sign one of these petitions, I can tell you. And in any case, will your Bengal and Bengali give me food and shelter? Does one Bengali help another? No, he doesn't. In that case, I've got to keep the people who feed and clothe me happy, haven't I? In the old days, I used to worship the British, nowadays I worship these people. You've got to be alive to worry about language.'

Then he pulled out a four-anna coin and said, 'I'm contributing to the best of my ability. But please make sure that my name doesn't appear anywhere. If you have to record a name, use XYZ.'

He put the coin on the table and fixed me with his sunken eyes.

'I have to go. Anyway, this is good work you're doing, carry on. Thank you.'

Atul-babu left.

It was as though a certain aspect of the condition of the Bengali living outside Bengal, the desperate crisis in their lower-middle-class lives, became illuminated for an instant

I felt overcome, somehow.

I could not find it in me to get angry with Atul-babu for not signing my petition.

A Mere Ten Rupees

I

An embarrassed Bidhu-babu said, 'Oh please, don't worry about it, it's not that important, really. Pay me back when you can. There's no hurry.'

An equally embarrassed Nikhil-babu replied, 'Of course there's a hurry. This is the third time that I've let you down. I really would have paid you back today. In fact, I'd kept the money ready since last night. But Mr Bosja arrived this morning and was quite persistent. Received a telegram, apparently. His son's ill in Benaras; he needed the money desperately and so on . . .'

'No, no, I'm glad you lent him the money,' said Bidhu-babu. 'It's not a problem, truly. Return it to me when he lets you have it back. I'll have a word with Bipin; perhaps he'll give me a loan. It's just that today I needed . . .' Bidhu-babu left. As soon as he departed, Nikhil-babu's expression changed. He said to himself, 'Damned leech! You'd think he was facing destitution because of a mere ten rupees.'

Bidhu-babu's expression changed as soon as he stepped out of the house, and he, too, muttered, 'It'll be like squeezing blood out of a stone, getting that money back.'

II

The days passed by in the ordinary way. A week went by. One fine morning, Bidhu-babu turned up in Nikhil-babu's drawing room once again. About three months ago, he had given Nikhil-babu a loan of ten rupees, and in return, had received a promise of 'return-it-tomorrow-itself'. But such are the inscrutable workings of fate that Mr

Nikhilnath Mitra, the revered head clerk of the office has had to remain a debtor—for a mere ten rupees, and that too to a loafer like Bidhucharan Bose. 'O Fate, thou hast reduced Kings to penury; I am merely a clerk'—was Nikhil-babu's solace. It is said that in his childhood, Nikhil-babu enjoyed listening to stories from the Mahabharata.

When Bidhucharan turned up, Nikhilnath seemed as though he had spent the entire week anxiously awaiting Bidhucharan's arrival. Bidhu- charan's presence seemed to have lifted a great burden from his soul.

'At last, Bidhu-babu! You've turned up. I think about you every day, you know. The Ganesh Opera Company is staging a jatra tonight. Would you like to see it? One likes to attend such things in the right sort of company. Please, why don't you come along?'

Bidhu-babu's entire expression seemed to glow with an inner radiance, as though he had just been handed something infinitely precious. He raised his shining eyes and said, 'You're absolutely right. I'd love to. When should I . . . ?'

'Around eight o'clock, in the evening.'

'I'll be here.'

Just then, Nikhil-babu's six-year-old daughter Mintu arrived to say, 'Ma says we've run out of sugar, Baba.' Bidhu-babu promptly started a long conversation with her. He rarely talks so much with his own daughter.

'That's a nice dress you've got on. What a lovely ribbon that is.' These and similar comments meant that another ten minutes went by.

Bidhucharan had really come for the ten rupees. His problem was that he found it difficult to ask for the money directly. He wasted time on various pretexts, hoping that Nikhilnath would broach the subject himself. Bidhucharan is rather easily embarrassed.

Nikhil-babu's is a Mahabharatian mind. He refused to have anything to do with this delicate subject. Instead he expressed great concern over the freezing weather around Fatehpur Sikri and its effects on the poor inhabitants of that unfortunate city.

The clock loudly struck nine. Nikhil-babu said, 'We mustn't be late for office.'

In sheer desperation, Bidhucharan blurted out, 'Did Mr Bosja return the money he borrowed?' Nikhilnath seemed thunderstruck. 'Oh good lord! Do you know, I'd completely forgotten. I've got your money.' He started rummaging in his pocket.

'My word, I can't seem to find my keys.' He searched all his pockets. He searched under the table. He searched inside the cupboards. The strange thing was that the keys were nowhere to be found. Bidhucharan joined the search, and finally said, 'Never mind, there's no hurry, in any case.'

III

Arriving that evening at the appointed time, Bidhucharan discovered that Nikhil-babu was absent. He enquired and was told that he had left on urgent business, and it was not certain when he would be back. He saw the jatra on his own. He was quite impressed by the actress in the role of Uttara. The deep interrelationship between the body and mind is undeniable. In any case, the proof was soon at hand. He had shed a lot of tears over Uttara's sufferings. The next morning, he woke up to discover that the ache in his heart had travelled to his throat. He was having difficulty swallowing, and his tonsils were swollen. He took his temperature and discovered that he even had a slight fever. The slight fever soon rose, however, and the bed-ridden Bidhucharan concluded that he would under no circumstances have gone to the jatra had he not met Nikhilnath. Moreover, but for the matter of the ten rupees, he would not have sought Nikhil-babu's company under any circumstances. After this well-rounded analysis, Bidhucharan was forced to say to himself, 'It's not enough he owes me money, now the so-and-so wants to kill me off as well.'

Bidhucharan remained bedridden for a week. The costs of treatment amounted to ten rupees and eighty-seven paise.

IV

A month has passed since then. Since the planet is not a Bengali, it turns on its own axis, and night and day follow at regular intervals.

It is the sixth of the month. Nikhil-babu is in the drawing room making mental calculations. Tomorrow, his wages are due: fifty-five rupees and forty-seven paise, after deductions. From this sum, he has to pay fifteen rupees by way of rent, and twenty rupees to the grocer. This leaves the sum of twenty rupees and forty-seven paise. Disregarding the forty-seven paise for the minute, it leaves him twenty rupees in hand. Out of this sum will have to come the entire month's greengroceries, the children's school fees, the monthly milk bill, the kerosene, any clothes that became necessary, and so on. Bidhucharan would simply have to wait for his money.

Nikhilnath's wife has a few rupees saved, of course; the result of putting aside the odd paise from here and there, over many months. But Nikhil-babu neither knows how much money Shobha has, nor is he willing to deprive her of it. Not that he is in any position to do so.

He had borrowed the money to have a flutter at the racetrack. It goes without saying that he lost. This is hardly something he can confess to his wife. Nikhilnath had imagined that he would somehow manage to pay the money back. But each month's mental calculation demonstrates that this is an impossible proposition. In the meanwhile, keeping Bidhucharan at bay by inventing excuses is becoming equally impossible. Everything has a limit. Nikhilnath was pondering what to do, when he heard Bidhucharan's voice in the distance, 'I was just going to visit Nikhil-babu.' Nikhil-babu remained frozen for a few seconds, then bolted into a little priest's hole situated next to the room, and locked the door from the inside.

V

'Nikhil-babu?'

Mintu arrived. 'Father was here a minute ago. I think he must have gone out.'

'When he returns home, tell him I dropped in.'

'Yes I will. Bye.'

Bidhu-babu left. As soon as he departed, an anguished Nikhilnath virtually exploded from the priest's hole—the little room had a bee-hive at one corner. Almost out of his senses because of the stings, Nikhil-babu managed to crawl to a pitcher of water, and started splashing some on his face and eyes. Within minutes his swollen left eyelid covered his eye, and the puffiness on the right side of his face made young Mintu giggle. Nikhil-babu dragged himself upstairs to rest.

Just then, two men arrived, supporting Bidhu-babu between them. Preoccupied with thoughts of how to extract his money from Nikhilnath, Bidhucharan had slipped on a banana skin, and hurt himself badly. He had a broken arm, as well as a nasty wound on his head. He had somehow made his way back to Nikhil-babu's house with the help of two passers-by. He lived too far away to return home.

Nikhilnath was lying down upstairs. Hearing the commotion, he came down and saw—with his one good eye—that Bidhucharan had returned.

The two men looked at one another and exclaimed simultaneously, 'Lord help us.'

A further three months have passed.

Nikhilnath has not returned the money yet.

Bidhucharan continues to visit him regularly.

Paired Dreams

I

Sudhir has arrived. He is carrying a tube-rose on its stem. His face is wreathed in smiles. His heart feels like a bird in flight.

The moment he arrives, Sudhir says, 'I have some good news, Hashi. But you'll have to give me something, or I'm not telling you.'

Hashi replies with a smile, 'What is it? Please, tell me.'

'But what'll you give me . . . ?'

'What can I give you? I'll embroider a pattern on one of your hand- kerchiefs. I've just found a beautiful pattern.'

'I'm not interested in embroidery.'

'How about some chocolate, then?'

'Do you think I'm a child, that I'll be satisfied with chocolates?'

Hashi bursts out laughing. 'Forget it. You don't want me to embroider for you, you don't want my chocolates. If that doesn't satisfy you . . .'

Sudhir says, 'I'm off, then.'

Hashi says, 'Are you sure you don't want to tell me?'

'Only if I get something special. What I'd asked for the other day . . .' Sudhir smiles meaningfully.

Hashi colours in embarrassment. 'I've already told you, you can't have that . . .'

But she feels a little shiver of fear looking at Sudhir's face. She hears him saying, 'I'd thought that I'd be able to joke about it. But I can't. You must forgive me. I've just heard that your marriage has been arranged, with that boy from Santragachhi.'

Sudhir turns and leaves.

Hashi calls out, 'Sudhir, come back.'

II

Alaka has arrived.

The same Alaka who Ajay used to wait all day to catch sight of.

Alaka is saying, 'Do you know if there's a word in English like pate?'

Ajay says, 'Yes, there is. It means head.'

'You're serious.'

'Why don't you look it up in the dictionary? Pate means head.'

'So our "Baruna-di" was right after all?'

Ajay asks, 'Do you know what the English for mundu is?'

Alaka peers at him and says, 'Head.'

'But the word for head is matha.'

'And mundu is the same as matha, isn't it?'

Ajay laughs, 'So much for your knowledge of Bengali. Matha and mundu are hardly the same things, are they?'

'And what might the difference be?'

'So there's no difference between you and Panchi-dhobani, eh? Because you're both women?'

'And who might this Panchi creature be?'

Ajay smiles sardonically, 'That washerman's daughter who lives down your lane. Quite young, about your age, I'd say.'

'I'm pleased to see that you're observing everyone so meticulously, including Panchi-dhobani.'

'Naturally. I've got to compare what is mine to see how good it truly is.'

'Who is this, who's yours?'

'Oh, there is someone, never fear . . .'

Alaka suddenly starts cleaning up the table.

Ajay stares out of the window for no reason at all.

Two people are dreaming these two dreams.

Sleeping side by side, close together.

Hashi's hand is lying on Ajay's chest.

Ajay and Hashi—husband and wife.

Bourgeois–Proletariat

I

Haladhar Haldar, a middle-class family man, realized while making a list of expenditures for his fourth daughter's marriage that once again he was in desperate straits. Despite using up whatever was left of his meagre savings, and borrowing a thousand rupees, he was not making ends meet. The groom's family had clearly indicated the dowry they expected. They were certainly not going to take a paisa less. Haladhar was, therefore, seeking advice from his friend, philosopher and guide, Akhil Mitra, about whether the wedding menu could be cut down. Akhil heard him out carefully, then said, 'You can't possibly pare the cheese any finer. What could you leave out?'

Haladhar frowned at the menu, and noticed that there was not even one item that could be dropped. Only the bare minimum with which to preserve face! Respectability demanded this much at least.

'I've gone grey through all this, my friend,' said Akhil. 'You can't bring it down further. It just cannot be done, that's all.'

He laughed. Meaning thereby: Are you mad? It was obvious Akhil Mitra would remain unmoved. Haladhar, his frown even more pronounced, asked, 'In that case . . .'

'No hope, I'm afraid,' said Akhil.

A disappointed Haladhar returned home to see that Nidhiram Goala was waiting to receive his advance for supplying the yoghurt. Seeing him, Haladhar suddenly had an idea. Haladhar, the petty bourgeois, decided to make some savings with the help of Nidhiram, the proletariat.

'How much would a maund of the best-quality yoghurt cost?'

'Twenty rupees, sir.'

'And not such good quality . . . ?'

'Fifteen, or even ten.'

'Is there nothing cheaper than that?'

'Of course there is, sir. You can get yoghurt that's seven-and-a-half rupees a maund, or even five for that matter. Mind you, it's not very good stuff, that.'

Haladhar calculated that about two maunds of yoghurt would be needed. A saving of at least twenty-five rupees.

'You'd better supply two maunds of that five-rupee stuff. But there's one thing though . . .'

'Yes sir . . . ?'

'If people start blaming me for the quality of the yoghurt . . . ?'

'They're certainly going to do that, sir. It's five rupees a maund after all. It's going to be pretty lethal, you can be sure of that . . .'

'Yes, quite. So if someone starts blaming me, I shall start shouting at you. As though I had asked you to supply me with the best quality stuff but you'd cheated me, do you know what I mean? All you've got to do is stand there looking guilty, that's all.'

Nidhiram ran his fingers through his luxuriant moustache and said, 'That won't be right, will it, sir? I mean, it's cheating . . .'

'I'll pay you a rupee extra for your trouble, but you've got to rescue me from this humiliation. I can't afford the good-quality yoghurt, yet I've got to save face somehow . . .'

After much hesitation, Nidhiram finally agreed.

II

Nidhiram was proved right.

The yoghurt was as sharp as a knife.

The wedding guests were in any case fuming throughout the meal at Haladhar's miserliness. The yoghurt became the spark on a pile of gunpowder; everyone flared up simultaneously, 'No gentleman would dream of feeding people this rubbish.'

People pushed their plantain leaves towards the back of the table and covered their nostrils.

Haladhar arrived with folded hands, 'Is the yoghurt . . . ?'

'Inedible is what it is, inedible . . .'

'Really? But I'd asked him to supply me with the best yoghurt he had.' Suddenly, Haladhar seemed to lose his temper. He started shouting loudly, 'Nidhu, oi you, Nidhiram . . .'

Nidhiram was standing nearby. He soon arrived.

'What sort of yoghurt have you supplied?'

'Why, it's perfectly good yoghurt, master . . .'

'And all these people are liars, are they? You cheating bastard, you had to choose this occasion, did you . . . ?'

Nidhiram looked down in embarrassment. But Haladhar possibly got carried away by his emotions. He rushed over to Nidhiram and slapped him hard, shouting, 'You cheat, miserable scoundrel . . .'

Nidhiram raised his face and said, 'You weren't supposed to slap me! Who gave you the right to slap me? You people here, you decide if this is right . . .'

A desperate Haladhar clapped his palm over Nidhiram's mouth.

Punishment

The evening shadows were darkening steadily, particularly as the skies were heavily overcast. A thin drizzle was falling and the wind quickening—a storm. Birinchilal was walking along a rustic footpath that led across an orchard. Rather a large orchard, and now his property, it had been constructed by his uncle Kundanlal for his pleasure. About fifty acres, the orchard was laden with not only all the local varieties of fruit but also with all manners of exotic ones. Kundanlal, a bit of a hedonist, had even planted sandalwood and other such trees. He had been the scion of a poor family, but possessed of enormous ambition and drive. A lion among men, he had created a huge empire in the area. But there is a special fate reserved for lions in this country. It goes without saying that Kundanlal suffered that fate. A group of scavengers were always after him. His relatives had, to a man, turned against him. In any society, most people enjoy trying to hamstring the successful individual. Failing that, they enjoy slandering him. And indeed, this was precisely what happened to Kundanlal. But he was truly a lion; he never paid the slightest bit of notice to such things. And of course, no one ever dared to say anything to his face.

His wife Kanchanmala once went for a meal to his niece's house. On her return, she fell seriously ill. Two days later, she was dead. The doctor suspected some strong poison as the cause of death. Kundanlal had sent his nephew, Birinchilal, to accompany Kanchanmala. He was meant to have looked after her. In any case, Kundanlal did not remarry. Instead, he employed four troll-sized servants and bought a huge Alsatian. When they died one after the other, within a space of six months, Kundanlal began to feel somewhat concerned. The physician once again suspected poison. 'You have an enemy in your own household,' he said. 'Please, be careful.' Kundanlal frowned, then asked for his nephew and said, 'Please send for Haricharan-babu. I have something I want to discuss with him very urgently.'

Haricharan-babu was Kundanlal's solicitor and lived about twenty miles away. Kundanlal sent an elephant for him. When he arrived, Kundanlal told him, 'I don't want to live here any longer. I'll go on an extended holiday. Tour the country, then visit Europe and America. What I've got in the bank ought to be more than enough for me to live my life out in comfort. As for the rest, I want to donate it to the Ramakrishna Mission. Would you draw up the papers as soon as possible, please.'

Birinchi was eavesdropping on the conversation. Haricharan-babu said, 'You've just been sitting there like a graven Buddha while a number of people have died in this house. You should've asked the police to investigate, carry out autopsies. The local daroga is in awe of you, so he does nothing. But you really should've had the entire affair investigated.'

'Why wash your dirty linen in public?' Kundanlal retorted, 'It wouldn't bring anyone back, would it? Don't you worry about such matters, God will sort them out in due course. Just get the will ready.'

'Aren't you going to leave anything for your nephew?' Haricharan-babu asked.

Kundanlal became grimly silent. His eyes seemed to bulge with rage. Then he said, 'No I shan't, not a single paisa. I'm going to donate everything to the Mission.'

Haricharan-babu left.

Kundanlal died the very next day. Soon after dinner, he developed a terrible griping pain, followed by blood vomiting. The physician suspected arsenic poisoning, but Birinchilal had the body cremated immediately. Large sums of money ensured the doctor's as well as the police's silence.

It was, in fact, the magistrate's court that Birinchilal was returning from. He had gone to confirm that he was the legal heir. Everything had been arranged by Haricharan-babu who told him, 'Since Kundan-lal didn't manage to leave a will behind, you're the legal successor. I don't foresee any problems.' And indeed, there had been none. Birinchilal had attempted to give Haricharan-babu a considerable sum of money in addition to his legal fees, but Haricharan-babu had refused to take it. Looking at Birinchilal coldly, he'd said, 'I'm hardly a waiter in a restaurant. You're not required to give me a tip.'

Birinchi had walked some distance before the drizzle turned into a downpour. The fury of the storm increased as well. He started walking as fast as he could. But then came to an abrupt halt. A branch from a huge mango tree was barring his path, as though the tree had raised a giant arm and said, 'You can't proceed.' Birinchi sidled past, and carried on. He felt as though the entire orchard had gone berserk. A little further, and a large branch from a jackfruit tree came crashing down, missing his head by inches. Birinchilal managed to save himself, and then began to run. The wind was shrieking through the trees—the storm was like a demented thing. He suddenly felt as though he was being pursued by a howling mob. He turned to look. Very little could be seen in the darkness; but the trees in the orchard seemed to be chasing him. All those fruit trees—all pursuing him. Stumbling after him like drunkards, like madmen, like demons. No, he had to get out of this orchard somehow. But then the top of the trellis collapsed, and the vines seemed to wrap themselves around him. But thank heavens for his knife. Birinchilal always kept a knife on him. He pulled it out and started hacking at the vines. They felt as though they were the tentacles of an octopus. As he cut them off and stumbled away, a huge bel fell on his back. Fortunately for him, it did not land on his head. He kept running. And burning with rage. He had asked for a horse to be sent to the railway station; a horse, or failing that, the sedan chair. He would sack the major-domo first thing in the morning. It was no joke walking the five miles from the station. No transport, despite instructions. He owned traps, horses, sedan chairs, even an elephant! Yet here he was, forced to walk home in such inclement weather.

The orchard ended at a broad field, through which went a road. His house lay at one end of the road; at the other end, a few miles away, was the local cremation ground. A cremation ground named after Bhuteshwar Shiva.

As he stepped onto the field, he was reminded that his uncle had passed over this very road on his final journey, a mere fortnight ago. A faint smile flitted across his face. So he had wanted to make his peace with God, had he, by donating all his wealth to the Ramakrishna Mission? Well, the poor fellow never got the chance to do so, did he? Birinchi stopped for a moment and looked at the road. It went straight towards the cremation ground. Immediately he frowned. Why was the road so clearly visible, even in such pitch darkness? As though a giant white anaconda was crawling towards the cremation grounds. Most peculiar!

As soon as he got home, Gobinda started wailing loudly from the other end of the verandah. An old family retainer, Gobinda had recently become partially paralysed. After his stroke, he spent most of his time lying on the verandah. Kundanlal had been looking after the man's family. Birinchi came closer and saw that the man's wife was sitting next to him and weeping silently.

In a rough voice Birinchi enquired, 'Why didn't anyone come to receive me at the station? Where's that major-domo?'

Gobinda's wife said, 'He's resigned and left. He's not coming back.'

'Where's Ghisu, and Hariya?'

'They've left as well.'

Ghisu was the mahout and Hariya the syce.

'The sedan-chair bearers said that they were not coming back. So did the cowherd.'

'You mean that the animals haven't been fed all these days?'

'No, they freed them before they left. The animals are foraging.'

Birinchilal started screaming.

'What the hell are you doing here, then?'

'We're leaving as well. We don't wish to stay a minute longer than necessary. My son's arranging transport from the village.'

Gobinda's wife added, 'I cooked dinner for you. I've left it covered, in your bedroom.'

Stunned, Birinchilal stood there for a few moments. Then entered his room and switched on the lights. Immediately, his eyes fell on the portrait of Kundanlal. A big, rather round face and two eyes that seemed to be bulging out of their sockets. Birinchilal had never noticed it before but Kundanlal's expression seemed the very embodiment of silent astonishment. And underlying that, the hint of a smile. Birinchi frowned at the picture for a while. He would have the wretched object removed first thing tomorrow. Then he stretched out on an easy chair; he really was quite exhausted. Suddenly, he noticed that his clothes were covered with blood stains. It must have been the branch from the mango tree . . . Abruptly, he became rather preoccupied.

Footsteps outside—who was that? More than one person whispering, the faint light of lanterns—Birinchilal discovered that he had developed goose pimples. He stood with a start and came out to the verandah. A group of people were standing outside.

'Who's there?'

'We've come to fetch Gobinda . . .'

Birinchilal stood in silence.

They put Gobinda, a man who had worked for the family for who knows how long, on a cart, and left. Gobinda's wife followed them. Gobinda's wife—who had brought him up. But Birinchilal was unable to ask them to stay. An invisible hand seemed to take him by the throat; not a sound came out of his mouth. He suddenly became aware that a distant rumbling was coming from the sky. As though a lion was growling somewhere in the darkness. Then he became aware that he was hungry. He had last eaten early in the morning and walked nearly five miles not so long ago.

He entered his bedroom and started bolting his food down. No time to waste on any niceties!

What time was it? He looked at the wall clock. It had stopped. Yes, it had stopped but it was smiling. A strange glistening smile was radiating from that enormous clock face. Birinchilal had covered the portrait of his uncle with a towel because he could not stand its gaze any longer. Despite all the doors and windows being closed, there was a faint breeze in the room. The towel was swaying gently. Birinchi grew afraid. Was Kundanlal going to stare at him from behind that towel? All the three lights in the room were switched on, but the darkness had not been dispelled; indeed, it seemed to be thickening.

Sleep did not come to Birinchilal easily. He was reading the almanac lying next to his bed and hoping to fall asleep when he realized that it was a Saturday, and an amabasya, a new moon, at that. He sat up on his bed with a start. The whole world seemed to be reverberating with the sound of thunder. What on earth was going on? That loud rumbling sound, what was it? The horses were neighing loudly; perhaps it was the sound of their running. The sound was coming from the direction of the field. The door in the southern wall of the room overlooked the field. But he could not bring himself to open that door. The road that door overlooked led not only to the field but also to the cremation ground.

Another peal of thunder. And another. Then complete and total silence. A sudden shrill trumpeting, followed by the sound of something very heavy-footed, walking across the verandah. Again the shrill trumpeting. Was it the elephant . . . ? Then a loud blaring sound; it had to be the elephant. It tended to be very noisy when angry. Was it butting against the door? Yes, it was; very hard. One last violent butt. The door exploded inwards. A dumbfounded Birinchi saw the elephant standing outside. Then it turned and left, quietly. As though, having done its duty, there was no need to linger. It reached the bottom of the steps and then stood there, waving its trunk and looking around.

The road leading to the cremation ground came into Birinchilal's sight. A path of silver in the darkness. Then he noticed a light approaching. A torch. And behind it, four men bearing a pall. 'Bolo Hari Haribol, Bolo Hari Haribol', they were chanting rapidly. Birinchilal recognized them as they drew closer. The torchbearer was Kanchanmala, his aunt. The pallbearers were the four troll servants. Even the Alsatian was trotting behind. Birinchi started trembling violently. The elephant had knocked down a section of the wall along with the door. The group poured through the gap. The elephant raised its trunk in salute to its mistress. The Alsatian pounced on Birinchi as soon as it entered the room.

From behind the towel, Kundanlal ordered, 'Twist his neck until his head faces backwards.'

The four men jumped on Birinchi. In a flash, the order was carried out. Then they placed Birinchi's body on the pall and left. Left at great speed. The darkness pulsated with the cries of 'Bolo Hari Haribol, Bolo Hari Haribol'.

Birinchilal was found dead the next morning, lying face down on the floor.

The door was intact.

So was the wall.

Consort

Birendra-babu is a famous hunter.

The number of creatures that have died of a bullet from his gun is legion. Many a bird, pig, snake, tiger, bear, fox, porcupine, rabbit, deer, crocodile, monkey, etc., has given its life in order to prove that he is truly a skilled hunter. Everyone praises his ability. It is not merely a passion—from his childhood, he had received many opportunities in this field. Acquiring skills in hunting requires more than mere passion—it requires time and money too. The rich man's darling child Birendranath possessed both. But over and above this, he did have certain talents. He was not merely brave but extremely capable as well. And there was the strength of an ox in that tall, powerful frame.

Birendra-babu had married a few months earlier. His parents having died long ago, he had to organize everything himself. After scrutinizing more than a hundred prospective brides, he had chosen Minati. For reasons best known to himself. Because, one, she comes from a poor family; two, she is extremely sickly; and three, she is exceedingly timid. Perhaps her restless, startled eyes are what enchanted him.

Three months have passed since then.

Birendra-babu's zamindari is situated in a hilly and densely forested area of the Santhal Parganas. He has recently had this small two-storey house built at one end of the forest—for the convenience of hunting. This forest abounds with animals. A few days before his marriage, Biren had shot a huge python.

It is not late evening yet; just a little after sunset.

But the place is full of the sound of cicadas. There is a huge tamarind tree just behind the house, filled with nesting herons. The raucous cries and the fluttering of wings is disturb the darkness of the forest. The atmosphere seems sullen.

The howl of a jackal can be heard in the distance.

Minati began to feel afraid.

'Please, dearest,' she said in a frightened voice, to a Birendra already dressed for the hunt, 'Please don't go. I'm frightened.'

Tying a belt around his waist, a smiling Birendra answered, 'Are you mad? The machaan's been erected, the kill's in place, how can I not go?'

'What's a kill?'

'The kill is a baby buffalo tied to a spot. The tiger killed it last night. That's where I've had the machaan erected. The animal is definitely going to return to the spot tonight.'

Tying his belt tightly, he grinned. 'If it does, it's not going back.'

'But I'm so scared.'

'There's nothing to be frightened of. In any case, Phagua's going to be with you.'

'Please, don't go.'

'Now stop being silly!'

They fell silent for a while.

Minati said, 'What was in the parcel that arrived by bullock cart? Why've you hidden it? Why won't you let me see what's inside?'

Birendra stifled a laugh. 'Not tonight. I'll show you in the morning.'

Birendra left.

Minati was tossing and turning in bed; sleep eluded her. She had dozed off a little while ago but was woken by a horrid nightmare—a tiger was tearing her apart and drinking her blood. After much fretting, Minati finally sat up and started listening carefully to the night sounds. Was that the sound of a heron . . . ? Never. Sounded just like someone with a deep voice speaking from the treetop. Oh God! When would this horrid night turn into day? Suddenly she remembered the parcel that had arrived earlier. Here was the opportunity to examine it. At least it would kill some time. It was in the room upstairs. Minati slowly left the room, holding a lantern.

When Birendra returned home, dawn was just breaking.

Phagua, who was sleeping soundly, was woken up by the commotion. He sat up.

'The mistress wasn't frightened during the night, was she?'

According to Phagua, the mistress had locked her door after the master had left and not opened it since.

Birendra knocked loudly on the door.

No answer.

A few more knocks.

Still no answer.

An impatient Birendra kicked the door hard.

The door remained shut.

In the end, the door had to be broken.

The first thing Birendra noticed was the blood pooled near the door.

Blood from what? And where was Minati?

A long search proved unnecessary. Her body was lying under the stairs. Birendra bent down and saw that her skull had spilt open. The floor around her was wet because of bleeding from her nose. There were pools of blood. Birendra rushed up and saw that the stuffed python from Calcutta was lying coiled in one corner. The one he had kept secret from Minati, because he had planned on frightening her this morning.

No one would think the snake was dead. It was impossible to believe that it was stuffed with straw and cotton. Minati must have fallen down the stairs last night, fleeing the snake. She had had no idea that she was going to be greeted with such a sight. Birendra stared at the snake quizzically. Its artificial eyes seemed to be lit with a savage gleam. It was the same snake that Birendra had killed some days ago.

Birendra's hunt had not been in vain.

A little while later his retainers brought in the dead body of the fierce beast by bullock cart.

A huge tigress.

Birendra's uncanny shooting had shattered the tigress' skull.

The thought suddenly occurred to Birendra: Where was the tiger?

The Towel

The other day I found the material for a very short story in the bathroom. The face towel that I generally use to dry my hands suddenly spoke up.

'Aren't you ashamed of dirtying me every day?'

I was quite astonished.

Then I said, 'But I bought you to wipe myself with. What else do you expect me to do with you?'

'But I have an essence as well. Do you feel you ought to dirty it in such a fashion?'

'But I do send you off to be washed regularly.'

'Do you have any idea how painful it is to be put on the boil?'

'I do, but there's not a lot I can do about it. I need a towel and that is why I bought you from the shop . . .'

'I know you're my master, and that I'm a slave. That is why my pain is all the greater.'

'So what are you doing about it?'

'I'm gathering my strength, and praying to the creator . . .'

'And what is your prayer . . . ?'

'That I am sent as your master, and that you become my towel . . .'

A Slap in the Face

The patient who was meant to bring me the remainder of the fee he owed me did not turn up. I felt rather disappointed; it is difficult to recover fees, or drugs that are unpaid for. Persistent demands result in being called a skinflint. So one cannot even do that. Moreover, people who owe fees or the price of the medicines also have their self-respect; therefore, they tend to avoid one. If they come across me on the road, they pretend that they have not seen me or quickly duck into a side-lane. And when they need further medical treatment, they go to some other doctor. The ingratitude of certain people makes one bitter. I had visited this man twice a day for four days in succession, but he had not parted with a paisa. Today he had faithfully promised to pay what he owed, but there was no sign of him yet. It was nine in the evening, but not a word from him yet. What a country to be born into.

I was about to leave in disgust when Ganesh-da arrived. Ganesh-da is no longer in employment, having retired years ago. His wife is dead and his children have gone their own ways; therefore, he has nothing with which, or no one with whom, to occupy himself. Prying into other people's business, gossiping, collecting rumours and then passing them on—these are the sort of things he spends his time on. He has a number of pet ailments, including piles, gout and eczema. Whenever one of them flares up, Ganesh-da comes to me for medicine. Gratis, it goes without saying.

The moment he arrived, he said, 'You'd better stop practising medicine. Apparently, you can't diagnose illnesses properly, and you don't know the names of the latest drugs, I mean, why bother being a physician at all?' Then he burst out laughing.

'What was all that about . . . ?'

'Were you treating the Mitras' son?'

'Yes, for the past four days. Their man is supposed to come any minute, with the fees that are owed me.'

'I don't imagine he'll turn up. They've asked for the civil surgeon and they're telling anyone who'll listen that you can't even diagnose properly.'

'You're not serious?'

'Heard it with my own ears.'

I was absolutely burning with rage but I refused to show it. I merely smiled politely and said, 'Oh, well.'

After a while Ganesh-da said, 'My piles have been giving me a lot of trouble since yesterday. Do you think you could give me something for it?'

I remained silent for a few seconds before answering. 'Only if I'm paid my fees. I'm not keen to do anyone any favours right now.'

'Oh my, we are cross, aren't we? I'll try some home remedies and come back in the morning. Perhaps you'll have cooled off by then.'

Ganesh-da grinned once again and left.

I sat in sullen silence for a while.

I called the pharmacist. 'Can you tell me how much they owe?'

'About two hundred and fifty rupees, I think.'

'And did you send someone to them yesterday?'

'I did indeed.'

'And?'

'Not a paisa.'

'I'm going to file a complaint against them. The miserable, ungrateful, thieving . . .'

The pharmacist remained silent.

'Look, you hand over my bill personally to the Mitras tomorrow. The fees for four days' visits, which amount to thirty-two rupees, plus the bill for the medicines . . .'

'Right.'

'What a country to be born in! Not one decent person anywhere. They're all cheats, scoundrels and ingrates . . .'

And almost immediately, I received a slap in the face.

A young man appeared in the doorway. He was unfamiliar.

'Excuse me, is this Dr Samanta's dispensary?'

'Yes . . . ?'

'Is Dr Samanta in?'

'I'm Dr Samanta. What can I do for you?'

The young man hesitated; in fact he looked faintly embarrassed. Then, he entered the room and did a pranam.

'I'm from Ratandighi . . .'

After my medical studies, I had started my first practice in Ratandighi village. After a whole year doing virtually nothing, I had left. That was thirty- odd years ago. Who could this be?

'I'm afraid I don't seem to recognize you.'

The young man smiled faintly. 'There's no reason why you should. But you might remember my mother. Her name was Rasmani. I'm told that she was in great distress when I was conceived. If you hadn't been there, she would not have lived.'

A picture of a young village mother, her face distorted with birth pangs, instantly came to mind.

. . . Not that Rasmani had paid me a paisa either. 'I can never repay this debt, Doctor. But please believe me, I'll send you some money, no matter how long it takes.'

Hesitantly, the young man said, 'My mother's been dead these ten years. Before she died, she told me I must give you at least a hundred rupees out of my earnings. By the grace of God, I'm making a living these days, so I thought that I'd bring you this small token . . .'

He put a thousand-rupee note in my hand and in a very apologetic manner, said, 'It took me quite some time to trace you. Or I'd have come sooner.'

Native and Foreign

I used to work in a hospital those days.

I was attending a call in the country. The place was a village, quite a distance from the nearest town. Travelling about seven miles by bullock cart, I discovered that the patient was mortally ill.

A little child, ill with diphtheria. He was having trouble breathing because of a congested throat. I managed to ease that particular distress by means of a simple operation. But it was obvious that without diphtheria antitoxin, the child would not survive.

No antitoxin was to be found in a village such as this. The stocks in my hospital had long been exhausted. The pharmacies in town were not able to provide any either. In desperation, I was forced to send telegrams to Calcutta.

To begin with, I sent one to a famous Indian chemist firm. I said, 'Diphtheria antitoxin required immediately for mortally ill child. Please send as per return post.' I sent a telegram to an English one as well. I suddenly had the premonition that my telegram would not reach in time. In any case, receiving two lots of medicines would not matter; I would simply get the hospital to purchase whatever remained unused.

A man was kept waiting at the post office from the next day on. The parcel had to be picked up as soon as it arrived; no unnecessary delays were permitted under the circumstances.

After waiting all day, my man reported that no parcel had come.

I felt utterly distraught, particularly for the ill child. Poor fellow, he might have lived had the medicine arrived on time.

There was no alternative but to leave it in the hands of fate. I prayed for the child and left for my hospital.

A man was waiting for me.

'Excuse me, but are you Dr Mukherjee?'

'Yes, I am.'

'I have a letter and this medicine for you.'

The man had come from the well-known English pharmacist. The manager had written:

> *Dear Dr Mukherjee,*
>
> *By the time we received your telegram, it was far too late to send you the medicine through the post. Since you had informed us that the child was critically ill, I have sent a man with the medicine. I hope that you receive the medicine in good condition. I enclose the bill along with the medicine. If the patient's family can afford it, please arrange to have our employee reimbursed for his travelling expenses.*
>
> *Yours, etc.*

The supplies from the Indian firm did not reach the next day. Nor the day after that.

Seven days later, I received a letter from them.

They had written:

> *Sir,*
>
> *The price of diphtheria antitoxin has gone up according to the rates shown below. Please let us know if you wish to purchase it at the increased rates. We will act accordingly after receiving your reply.*
>
> *Yours, etc.*

Fortunately, I no longer had any reason to write to them. My patient had recovered.

Bhuvan Shome

I

Anil reached the wharf early, crossing one field after the other. His clothes were full of thistles; his feet, dusty. But the connecting train was absent and the steamer was running late. So he walked to the riverbank, and stared down the Ganges towards the east for a few moments. No, not a sign of the steamer, not even a wisp of smoke. But he carried on looking, because he had spotted a flight of geese. A flight of large geese, what in English were called bar-headed geese. He looked at them greedily, reminded that he had killed three geese, one after the other, last year. He was also suddenly reminded of Cricket. Cricket had been with him that day. Thin, with large, yellowing teeth, brownish hair and brown eyes, wearing a red-striped shirt, Cricket had eaten half the meat himself. Cricket was a great eater. Anil had invited him on another occasion, but he had not turned up; nor would he be coming either. The poor fellow had died in a road accident a few months ago. He was an open, friendly sort of man, Cricket. The sort of person who could never keep a secret, he had once even confessed to being a thief.

'It's Anil-babu, isn't it? How are you? How long have you been waiting here?'

Anil had not noticed that Sakhichand, the ticket collector, was quietly standing behind him.

'Only a few moments. Uncle Bhuvan's arriving by this steamer. I've come to receive him. But the boat seems to be rather late today . . .'

'Yes, very. By the way, I didn't know that you had an uncle? Where's he coming from?'

'From Sahebganj. Bhuvan Shome's not my uncle, really. But we've been very close for a long time. He's much closer to me than any uncle I might've had.'

'Bhuvan Shome? You don't mean the ATS Bhuvan Shome, do you?'

'Why yes, I do.'

Sakhichand's entire face, his eyes, mouth, brows, nose and chin, seemed to twist in a moue of distaste. At once, though, he looked a trifle abashed at letting his feelings show, and quickly controlled himself. 'I hadn't realized that Mr Shome was your uncle.'

'He is a hard nut, isn't he?' said Anil with a grin.

'I should say he is. Dismissed his own son, didn't he? You know about it, I imagine.'

Anil smiled gently, 'Yes, I'd heard.'

'Why's he coming here?'

'Bird hunting.'

'Keen hunter, is he?'

'He's certainly keen. Though he tends to miss more often than hit . . .'

'Well, I suppose the birds don't work for the Indian railways,' Sakhi-chand walked off with a bitter smile. After a few yards, he turned and said, 'You can't wait by the riverbank for ever. Come and wait in my house. The boat's not due for a long time yet. We can play a couple of rounds of chess in the meantime.'

'Good idea. The wife back?'

'My dear sir, of course not. In our society, there's a lot of jhunjhut associated with gaona.'

A proper Bengali would have pronounced the word jhunjhut differently. Though a fluent Bengali speaker, Sakhichand is a Bihari Gwala by birth. Which is why he used the expression gaona. Recently, members of his caste have started calling themselves 'Yadav' in order to raise their social standing; many have become educated as well.

Sakhichand hardly sounds like a Bihari. His in-laws live in a village a mere six or seven miles from the wharf. He had imagined that his transfer to this area meant that he would be able to bring his wife home. But the elders among his in-laws have announced rather officiously that there are no auspicious dates for the next three months. On top of this, Mr Bhuvan Shome had filed an official complaint about him. Not that he was not at fault, but everyone takes a backhander these days. That fat, dark little goods clerk, for instance; the man is positively rolling in money. All he had taken was a few rupees, that's all. The European officer would have given him a thorough ticking off and let him go. But Mr Shome (being a proper Bengali officer) had to write a lengthy report about him. Sakhichand has made enquiries at the office. The report has not reached the office yet; perhaps he has not sent it. But being what he is, a 'number one so-and-so', he will. Hearing about Anil-babu's relationship with Bhuvan Shome, Sakhichand saw a faint glimmer of hope—if only . . .

'When Mr Shome was here a month ago, he didn't visit you, did he?'

'No. Didn't have any leave, I suppose. He's specially taken leave for his hunting, this time.'

'Is he staying with you?'

'Where else could he live in these parts? Mind you, having said that, he doesn't like staying with people much. But he's always been close to us, you see. He used to call my father dada, respected him like an older brother. Always loved me like a son.'

The flames of Sakhichand's hopes flickered brighter. He said somewhat diffidently, 'Call him good or bad, he's a very hard man, that one. Look at the way he's reported me for a minor offence! Given the state of the job market, can you imagine where I'd be if I lost my job? I mean, people with BA and MA degrees had applied for my post. Do you think you could . . .'

Sakhichand stopped, hesitant, but Anil had no difficulty in understanding him.

'God, no, I wouldn't do that. And in any case, I'm sure it'll have the opposite effect. Recommendations tend to make him see red.'

'Is that right?'

But to himself, Sakhichand said, 'Bastard!'

They walked in silence for a while until they reached Sakhichand's residence—a thatched roof with walls of woven bamboo, and a small porch in front. Wan sunlight was falling on the porch.

'We might as well sit in the sun. It's become quite cold since yesterday.'

'Yes, that would be nice.'

There was a light wooden table at one end of the porch. Sakhichand dragged it over to the sunlight, went in and returned with two metal chairs, then went in once again. A few seconds later sounds started coming from the room.

'Anil-babu, could you come in for a moment?'

Anil entered to see Sakhichand tugging at the drawer of a table.

'The drawer's jammed. You're supposed to be very strong, see if you can get it open. I got it made from Sarban Badai. He charged me a large sum, and swore it was teak wood—but just look at its state now. How's my wife supposed to open this thing?'

'Do we have to open it immediately? I thought we were going to play chess.'

'My dear fellow, the chess pieces are inside that drawer.'

'Oh!'

Anil pulled at the drawer tentatively. It really was tight.

'It's jammed all right. Unseasoned mango wood, I think it is. Look, hold on tight to that end of the table. I'll pull on this end. See that the table doesn't move.'

'Hang on a minute while I move the table a bit. I'll be able to brace myself against the wall then.'

They did precisely that. Anil, a strong fellow, opened the drawer with one powerful heave. But a small accident occurred. Sakhichand's head struck a framed photograph, hanging on the wall behind the table. The glass shattered as it fell on the floor.

'Oh no, what've I done?'

The poor chap screamed.

Anil quickly went across.

'Have you hurt your head?'

'Not my head, my heart!' said Sakhichand with a grin. 'Do you know whose photograph that is? Here, take a look.'

He handed it to Anil, the photograph of a smiling young teenaged girl. The name was written under the photo, but in English: Mrs Vaidehi Yadav.

Sakhichand grinned. 'My wife. She's in primary school.'

'Does she speak Bengali as well as you do?'

'Much better, I'd say. Her mother comes from Pakur. Everyone speaks Bengali there.'

'Who took the picture?'

'My brother-in-law. He's been given a very expensive camera by his father-in-law and so he's running about taking pictures of everyone and everything. He's even taken my photograph. You'd better give that to me. I'll send it off to Sahebganj today itself, and get it repaired. It's a must.'

Sakhichand carefully wrapped the framed photograph in paper, and then tied the packet with a piece of string and kept it inside a trunk.

'Right, let's start our game, shall we?'

The two of them sat outside and started putting the pieces on the board.

If you have a relative, then there are no problems. Bhuvan Shome had no such advantage, so he had realized he was not going to get an extension of his employment. He had also realized that he must have committed a grave sin in his previous life, in punishment for which he was born in this country. Occasionally he felt that it might have been better being born in the jungles of Africa! He had been wounded in his social life as much as in his career. No one had ever considered his feelings—not his parents, siblings, children, relatives or friends; no one. When he was sixteen, his father departed for a far, far better place, leaving behind a vast family and a mountain of debts. Even now, Bhuvan Shome felt terrified at the very thought of those days. Not a paisa anywhere, and not a soul willing to extend credit. It had truly felt dark that day. He had not had the time to find out if the sun was up, or indeed whether it gave out heat and light any longer. Bhuvan Shome suddenly raised his hands in namaskar while in the middle of his reverie. The namaskar was in memory of his father's friend, Jogen Hazra. The man may have married thrice but he had been a true friend. He had supported them without any thought of gain after his father's death. The man worked in the DTS' office; the DTS himself used to favour him. He had used that influence to get Bhuvan Shome a job in the same office. His own son had passed the entrance examinations. But instead of him he had arranged a job for Bhuvan Shome. Not that he would have been able to do such a thing these days.

II

Dressed in Western clothes, Bhuvan Shome is sitting in an easy chair in a First Class cabin, lost in thoughts of his own life. He cannot stay in the present when he is on his own; he inevitably returns to the past. It is the past that he is considering at the moment.

Mr Shome's actual age is near enough to sixty, though his body has not aged accordingly. The hair has thinned somewhat, both front and sides, and a couple of teeth have been extracted, but his body remains strong. His official age is fifty-four but he looks younger. He will have to retire in about a year or so. Many people have been granted extensions after retirement, or been offered new jobs, but he has no such hopes. Despite his brilliant service record, he entertains no such ideas. His bosses are not pleased with him at all. Bhuvan

Shome is incapable of flattering people. He has battled all his life; battled, and been wounded; but he has never bowed his head to any one. The previous European bosses used to value his qualities; he had, therefore, risen from a lowly clerk to his present position of ATS. He would never have made it under these people. These people first ask a man about his caste, then whether he is a Harijan, and then whether he has been to prison for satyagraha. Suitability is about the last criterion. And in those cases where the first three qualities are present in sufficient quantities, suitability can be waived. Ministers are no longer meant to have Brahmin relatives. If they cannot flaunt true untouchables, they must at least be able to provide the odd barber or Gwala. Being a member of the upper castes is virtually a crime. Such are the wonders of gaining independence—an entire country changes into a den of thieves overnight! Ticket-collectors and guards conspire to ferry hordes of ticketless passengers for a paltry bribe. Large crates travel in the brake vans without anyone being the wiser. Even filing reports about people caught red-handed does no good whatever. Being some minister's cousin fifty times removed is sufficient to get them off scot-free. Independence means that scum can get ahead while gentlemen suffer.

Bhuvan Shome pulled on his pipe. He held the inhaled smoke for a while and let it out slowly, before going back to reminiscing. His entire life has been one long fight. His mother's only interest in life was an obsessional fault-finding. And despite all his attempts to satisfy her exacting requirements, he had never been able to please her. Following her husband's death, the woman had become convinced that her one reason for existence was to expiate her sins. And her greatest complaint was that she had been unable to marry her daughters off in the proper manner. Apparently her husband would have managed to marry those ugly sows to princes of royal blood!

Not that Bhuvan Shome had not tried his utmost. He had borrowed five thousand rupees, in addition to giving all his mother's jewellery as dowry. But, in spite of all this, Birinchilal and Jagannath were the only bridegrooms going; no one else was available. Of course this country has worse prospects than Birinchilal and Jagannath, and they seem to be leading perfectly happy married lives. But his two accomplished sisters were quite unable to manage this. They refused to go to their in-laws', saying they were not going to live in some back-woods village. His mother, it goes without saying, agreed with them. Between the malaria, the stinking ponds, snakes and what have you, who could live there? Not the two of them, certainly. They refused to leave home.

As a result, the two brothers-in-law arrived after a few weeks. And stayed on! Bhuvan Shome has had to look after his nephews and nieces ever since. He had managed to get Birinchi and Jagannath jobs after considerable effort. But they never showed the slightest inclination to leave. His mother refused to let them. And even after they started their jobs, neither of them helped by paying so much as a paisa. On the sly, however, they would buy expensive perfumes, or sweets. As though it was Bhuvan Shome's bound duty to take care of them.

And there were quite a number of them to take care of. Between his two sisters, they had managed to produce fourteen children. Children who had completely ruined Bhuvan Shome's life. He had built a garden with much labour; they had destroyed it. Not one flowering shrub left standing! He had found it impossible to get a decent night's sleep due to their incessant screaming and wailing. In the end, they had started pilfering things. They had always stolen money from his pockets; one fine day, his wife started missing bits of her jewellery. But because of his mother, it was never possible to punish them. His mother would protect them, to the extent of constantly lying for them.

Bhuvan Shome had always had to deny himself in order to feed that vast brood. He had always eaten the cheapest of foods. Day after day. Until the very thought of a good meal caused distress, to say nothing of indigestion. Only the other day he had been invited to a wedding party. All sorts of wonderful things, and not one had inter-ested him in the least. Despite owning a cow, he'd never had a drop of milk. Part of the milk was reduced and consumed by his mother who had an opium habit. The remainder would be diluted with water and distributed among the three or four younger children. There were always three or four younger children in the family. And he certainly had never considered the idea of depriving them for his own benefit.

But of course his body had not been bound by such niceties. One day, returning from office, he had a dizzy spell and fell unconscious. Dr Chandan arrived and said, 'Your blood pressure's very low. You've got to improve your diet.' He also left behind a long list—eggs, fish, milk, red meat, and god knows what else. His mother, of course, suggested that she would take a loan to buy whatever was necessary. But Bhuvan Shome knew that she had no intention of repaying any debts; that would be left to him. A couple of days later he met the doctor and told him, 'Look, doctor, I can't very well eat all those nice things by myself. And I can't afford the expense of buying such things for the entire family. Perhaps you could write me up a good tonic of some kind.' Dr Chandan generally tended to go along with his patients. Whatever his patients demanded, he would acquiesce to. He had been known to give diabetics permission to eat sugar if they pestered him long enough. He had one strict rule, however—he would never make out a false medical certificate. Dr Chandan's cheerful, white-moustached and white-browed face suddenly floated in front of his eyes. What was that tonic he had prescribed? He couldn't remember the name. The doctor had also prescribed chicken extract, old port, cod-liver oil in bottles. Buying them once had nearly bankrupted him. He had not tried them a second time.

. . . He got up suddenly. A biting cold wind was blowing. He fetched a balaclava cap out of his bag and put it on. It had become quite wintry; he felt much better with the cap on. His older daughter-in-law had made it for him. Very good for all this fancy stuff but not for plain cooking or pickling vegetables. The sort of people who would want to get their daily meals from a restaurant if they could afford it. Apparently pice hotels were opening in Calcutta. He thought: Dear God! Where is this country going? To perdition. And at breakneck speed, at that! I can't recognize it any longer. Then he stared at the sandbanks in the Ganges. There were sandbanks on both sides; he stared at them distractedly for a while. Not a single bird in sight. Yet Anil had written that hundreds of geese were nesting in the area. So where were they?

'Shall I move the chair to the other side, sir? It's very windy here.'

Bhuvan Shome came out of his reverie with a start. He turned his head and saw that a diffident ships' purser had arrived unnoticed behind him.

'I'm quite capable of moving it myself if it's necessary. Don't you have anything to do?'

The embarrassed young man started walking off.

'Just a minute.'

The lad returned.

'What's your name?'

'Bikashendu Gupta.'

'Your lot had better get rid of one idea from your heads: You shan't please me through flattery. Never. I belong to the old school. *Duty first, self last*, that's my motto. Perform your duties properly, and I'll be happy. Shirk, and God help you. And all the bowing and scraping in the world won't save you. Understand?'

'Yes sir.'

The lad left with a hang-dog look. Bhuvan Shome stared after him for a while. He suddenly felt rather warm about the young fellow. Not the usual brash Baidya boy.

He fished out his notebook and wrote the name down. He'd recommend him for a promotion if he got an opportunity. Bhuvan Shome filled his pipe once again and sat quietly, engrossed in his surroundings. A kingfisher was flying over the water; it swooped for a moment, rose with a small fish in its mouth and flew away. It was an enchanting scene. He pulled on his pipe and realized that he had not got around to lighting it. He gave up after a couple of attempts; it was far too windy on the deck. He went back to his cabin, lit the pipe expertly and returned to his deck chair. The kingfisher was nowhere in sight. He returned to his past.

. . . His two brothers had given him as much trouble as his sisters. Neither had bothered with their studies. Both had failed their examinations, three or four times per class. They had started sprouting moustaches while in Class Four. Bhuvan Shome had not given up, of course. However, Mahadeb-babu, the headmaster, was a strict man and he threw the boys out of school; he told Bhuvan Shome bluntly that he was not about to keep them in his school—they were teaching the younger children all sorts of bad habits. That was the end of their educational careers. His mother had wanted to send them to a boarding school in Calcutta, but he had not been able to afford the expense. His mother moaned and whinged about it for a few days, then gave up.

It had to be said, however, that his brothers had become quite successful despite their lack of education. Bipin, known as Bipnay, had shaved off his moustache and become famous for his 'female' roles. And Khokon, known as Khokna, had turned into a football player. One of the country's finest centre-forwards, as a matter of fact. Just as well that they had not bothered with their education; even with an MA degree, all they would have achieved would be a nine-to-five job. Not that they had not got jobs. They had good jobs at that. Bipnay got a job in a big engineering firm thanks to his acting. The head clerk of the firm was so taken by his 'Sita' that he was moved to tears. The very next day, he called Bipin to the office and organized a job for him. It was the same with Khokna; he was given a job because of his football-playing abilities. Mohun Bagan were playing a nondescript team that day and everyone had thought the strangers were due a proper hiding. On the contrary, the rank outsiders won, because they had Khokna playing centre-forward for them. The boss of Mackenzie Lyall was among the spectators. Khokna's prowess attracted his attention. The next thing you know, he had a job.

Puffing on his pipe, Bhuvan Shome thought, why, it seemed as though it had happened only yesterday. And yet . . . He stood up abruptly. There were hundreds of curlews nesting on a sandbar, entire flocks of them. He stared at the birds avidly. Would it be possible to reach the spot by boat? God only knew what arrangements Anil had made. He stared after the birds for as long as they remained visible.

Hunting was his sole hobby these days. And not just a hobby, it was also a form of release. All his life he had longed for a temporary respite from domestic strife. Unsuccessfully. For a while, he had tried his hand at painting. An Anglo-Indian guard had initiated him into watercolours. He had been a nice man, Mr Brown. Occasionally a bit the worse for wear due to drink, he was nonetheless a nice human being. Indeed, Bhuvan Shome had imbibed a drop or two himself, in Mr Brown's company. Any objections would be met with Brown saying, 'There's no difference between wine and water. It's all a matter of perspective.' He would then roar with laughter and add, 'And that explains the difference in prices. The one's free while the other costs ten rupees a bottle.' One could buy a bottle of decent Scotch for ten rupees those days. Brown had taught him how to draw. He had painted for a few days, or, to be more specific, attempted to paint. But with no results whatever. No one would allow him to settle down for a moment. The household chores would pile up on Sunday, his one day of rest in the week. Get the rice—we're running short of dal—the dhobi hasn't turned up, find out what's wrong—the children need new clothes, get the tailor—and so on. Despite the house being crammed with overweight louts who seemed to spend all their time eating, no one would raise a finger to help; nor would his wife let them, even if they did. Apparently, they were not capable of doing anything right. Thus, everything had to be attended to by Bhuvan Shome.

In the afternoon, having finished the chores, he would sit with his water-colours; and immediately, he would be surrounded by a flock of children, like a lamp surrounded by insects during the monsoon. They would fidget, get in the way, pull at things, overturn the water container; indeed, a nephew once threw his box of watercolours away. But of course, no one could be told a thing, because their mothers would sulk all day.

One day he returned from work to find that someone had daubed one of his watercolours with mud. His wife said in an indifferent manner, 'It's either Bilu or Nipu. They must fancy themselves as artists. Imitating their father, I expect. Not that I can blame them. Why, only yesterday Bilu was trying to smoke, using a twig for a cigarette.' He had felt like giving the two boys a real whipping, but, like all his other desires, he had suppressed this one as well. A few days later, the largest of his brushes vanished. His wife said, 'Must be the mice. I've been complaining about mice for months, but did you bother to do anything about it? Who cares about your silly brush, they've even managed to remove Lakshmi's aasan.' So he bought a mousetrap. No mice were caught, but one of his nephews cut his finger on it. That caused a real furore in the household. Doctors, medicines, injections—all in all, he was fifteen rupees out-of-pocket by the time it was over.

This had been the way of it all his life. And there was one more funny thing he had noticed—the women of the household seemed to have it in for whatever he enjoyed. Not that they opposed him openly; they would hardly do that. But he was aware that they were boiling inside. He had to give up painting because of his wife. Because the ambience of the house had to be conducive to painting. But his wife's attitude meant that it could never be a part of his home. Not that such a thing was impossible, mind. But she refused to let it happen. Bhuvan Shome had had to tolerate a lot from his mother for as long as she had been alive. But the one favour she had done him had been to keep that shrewish wife of his under control. As long as his mother had been alive, she had never opened her trap. The moment his mother died, the woman became like a bird let out of a cage . . .

Puffing on his pipe, Bhuvan Shome lost the thread of his thoughts. He stood and paced about for a bit, then sat down again.

Yes, he had had to sacrifice his desire to paint. After Mr Brown died, the urge had died down further. A strange and tragic death. After he retired, Mr Brown would disappear for days at a time. It was later discovered that he used to go to the forests and spend his time painting.

He was sitting on the railway tracks and painting in a spot where the tracks took a sharp bend. And a speeding train dismembered him. It was no fault of the driver's, he had not even been able to see Brown. By the time he had caught sight of him, putting the brakes on would have meant the train going off the tracks. Brown, who was painting a sunset, spattered the canvas red with his own blood.

Yes, Bhuvan Shome had given up painting. For quite some time he had done nothing. But that sort of inactivity was quite stifling too.

His next attempt at using his spare time for his pleasure had misfired as well, because he had miscalculated from the very start. Using your own time for pleasure ought to mean just that, adding anything to it can only end in ruining things. Something that would both entertain him as well as help the family—such a hybrid could neither be pleasurable nor last for any length of time. He found a book, in English full of recipes for pickles, jams and all sorts of condiments. He was struck by a sudden enthusiasm for jam-making, pickling and so on. He spent a small fortune purchasing various books in English and Bengali, quantities of ingredients, and even a clay oven which he had specially constructed, so that he could work standing up. Banishment to the labour camp was preferable to spending time crouched over a chulha in a dingy kitchen. He had wanted to have a similar chulha constructed for the women, but they had only laughed at him. They were a strange tribe, women. In any case, he had got a nice little chulha built for himself in one corner of the verandah. He would have bought an European cast-iron oven, but he could not afford it. He had already found himself in debt. Thus, one fine day, he started on his new venture. He had hoped, of course, that he would be able to keep himself entertained while bringing some benefits to his family. His wife, who had never helped in any of his projects, was no different on this occasion. She had passed just one comment, which still retained the power to sting. He had bought some ripe guavas for making jelly. His wife had taken one look at them and said, 'Well, you're such an expert in everything else, you had to try this as well. Oh, ye whitened sepulchres.' He had felt like the family's rubbish bin, with everybody dumping their rubbish in him. Not that he had let his wife's comment affect him; he had simply plowed on with twice the enthusiasm.

Every Sunday, from morning to evening, he spent his time engrossed in his hobby. The children had been very helpful this time. Indeed, they had been even more engrossed than he. It was the sort of work that tended to come to a dead halt without help. The children would wait eagerly to be able to offer help. A request, and off they would dash. What energy. They really had worked for those few days; nothing would have been achieved without them. True to form, the women in the family not only did nothing to help but also did every-thing in their power to create obstacles. His wife, who had never shown any interest in the children's studies, indeed it was doubtful that she even knew who was in which class, said one day, 'The chil-dren are supposed to be catching up on their work on Sundays, doing their homework and so on. And you're making them work like a bunch of slaves—get this, hold that, go there, do that.' He had been left burning with rage, but he had not said a word. After a few days, his wife's sarcasm no longer affected him. He had got used to it; like a familiar scab, or sore, one took no notice of it.

But his greatest problems started when he finished making the jams and so on. Entire rows of jams, jellies, pickles, jars of biscuits—who was going to eat any of it? He gave some to the younger children for a few days. The older ones refused to touch them, unless forced to by him. Even then, they would have a sly smile on their faces, as though it was part of some joke. His wife said, 'Why on earth are you forcing this rubbish on them? They're going to fall ill one of these days.' And of course, as soon as Bhona suffered a bout of diarrhoea, the entire household was up in arms. As though no one in the family had ever had an upset tummy before. They conveniently forgot the fact that the child had suffered from a weak stomach from birth. Kundu, that crippled physician, started screaming, 'I can see all the signs of food poisoning.' The man was a thoroughgoing scoundrel. He used to have his name on a shingle outside his home, which said,

Ghanashyam Kundu, MD, FDS. The FDS meant female-disease specialist. In case people failed to understand, he had it written in Bengali as well. He spent his time getting young women from poor families to sit opposite him while he asked them the most outrageous questions. Adi Kundu was the neighbourhood grocer and Ghana was his son; he had fallen while attempting to steal guavas from the Chakravartis' garden and broken his leg. Not that the incident had taught him a lesson. He used to hobble all over town, involved in some misbe- haviour or the other. That very Ghana hung up his shingle one fine day, proclaimed himself Dr Kundu, and started practising in front of old Dr Chandan's house, whom he would laugh at behind his back. And yet, without Dr Chandan, the man would not have lived . . .

God! Everything was possible in this country. He'd had to consult a well-known physician for Bhona. The man had said, 'No, it's not food poisoning, but I don't think that you ought to let the children eat those things.' That did it, of course. His wife immediately put a pad- lock on the cupboard which contained all the bottles of preserves, so that no one could even get a look at them. A distant aunt said, 'Your mango pickle is rather nice. I'll take them even if no one else does.' There were only four bottles of the mango pickle. But whatever was he going to do with the rest of the stuff?

In the end, he had to seek Keshta's help. His friend Bishtu Mitra's son Keshta ran a grocery shop. He asked him if he could help dispose of the preserves. Keshta was a decent enough fellow. He said, 'Uncle, I can put the goods on the shelves but I don't imagine anyone will want to buy them. There's been a rumour about food poisoning, you see.' No one kept track of any useful information but everyone knew the story about the food poisoning. What a country. Disgusting, absolutely disgusting!—

Bhuvan Shome stood up suddenly after pulling at his pipe. His pipe had gone out. He absentmindedly walked to his cabin, to light his pipe, but turned back from the door. It occurred to him that it was futile trying to light a pipe in such a stiff wind. It was going to go out anyway; perhaps he ought to light a cigar. He returned to the deck, fished out a cigar from his bag, bit off the end with his teeth and returned to his cabin. The cigar reminded him of an amusing incident. Not amusing at all really, sad; but he had been rather amused by the whole thing. He had given his nephew Hanu ten rupees to buy some cigars. The boy returned after a while to say that someone had picked his pocket in the crowded market, and that, consequently, he had bought the cigars on credit from Keshta. The market was in any case being plagued by pickpockets, so he had more or less taken his nephew at face value. But as they say, the truth will out; Hanu's younger brother Jambu produced the note from his pocket. Jambu had quickly rifled through his pockets when Hanu was taking a bath. Fortunately his wife had happened to be present, so they were caught with the goods as it were, otherwise Jambu would certainly have taken the money. Jambu was only eight years old but already an expert at going through people's pockets. His mother had certainly named her two grandsons appropriately—Hanuman and Jambuban.

Bhuvan Shome returned to his deck chair after lighting his cigar. The image of the bottles of preserve came to him once again. He'd had to distribute them but most people had been unwilling to take them. No one near his house had wanted them, nor had he attempted to give any of them a thing. That damned cripple would have screamed 'food poisoning' at the top of his voice if someone had fallen ill from his preserves. He had given them to people living far away instead; even then, it required considerable persuasion to get people to accept them. He would take the preserves with him and distribute them to people he met on tour. He would say in a diffident tone, 'I've made it myself. Tell me what you think of it.' He had never heard a 'Thank you' from any Bengali, much less any praise. Not that they had hesitated to be critical. He had given Mrigen Bhaduri a bottle of mango slices in vinegar. Some days later, the man told him, 'Couldn't eat it. Sorry. Tasted just like rice water that's gone off.' Possibly it was the first time in his life the man had eaten anything like it. Gupta said that the guava jelly was far too sour. Charan Mukherjee said, 'This biscuit's harder than cast iron.' But the foreman, Mr Smith, had praised his jam to the heavens. He was an European after all. The man had not only thanked him but also written him a long letter afterwards; the letter had contained a new recipe for jam.

They were a different race—polite, aware of what was appropriate and what was not; it was hardly surprising that they were still ruling the world. And fancy this sorry lot trying to take them on. How neatly they had created Pakistan on their way out. And why, Pakistan as well as Hindustan, both were in the same rotten state, with each man's hand raised against his neighbour's. Well, they could keep their independence. Mountbatten had told Mahatma Gandhi, 'Mr Gandhi, your Congress is now with me.' What the words meant was that the slightest taste of power, and your supporters were crowding round the trough. Well they killed Gandhi, didn't they. Though mind you, just as well; the way he was going, the old man would have made every member of the Congress Working Committee go to a mosque and recite the Koran. Thinking such thoughts made him feel guilty. He had always respected Gandhiji. There was no doubt that he had been an extraordinary man.

He remembered something that had happened a long time ago. Gandhi was still Mr M. K. Gandhi those days, not yet Mahatma Gandhi. Nor was Bhuvan Shome an ATS—just a petty clerk who got a pass for the Third Class compartment. He had boarded such a compartment at Barharoa Station; the coach was impossibly crowded but he had noticed a thin man wearing a huge turban and reading a paper in the corner. Next to him was a bearded old man. Of course, one came across so many different types on the trains that Bhuvan Shome had hardly been bothered about who the man in the turban was. But in the end, he had been forced to. The old man started coughing for a few moments, then expectorated inside the compartment itself. The man in the turban immediately said in Hindi, 'This is extremely wrong. You can't spit inside the train. Spit outside if you must.' It was a very measured protest. But the old man was a right so-and-so. To begin with, he refused to answer; he started gasping. After he had recovered from his bout of gasping, he revealed his true self. He glared and pointed out that he had a chest cold, and that if he stuck his head out of the window, his illness might worsen. Therefore he was going to spit on the floor; anyone who was upset could sit in another compartment. The coach was no one's personal property. The old man's attitude had made Bhuvan Shome grind his teeth in rage. But he had kept quiet, having learnt from hard experience not to interfere in other people's affairs. So he had not said a word. But what the thin man did was quite remarkable—he tore off a bit of the newspaper, wiped the spit off the floor and threw it out of the window. The old man glared once again but said nothing. But after the next fit of coughing, he again spat on the floor. The thin man simply tore off another bit of newspaper and threw the phlegm out again. The entire coach was enjoying this free entertainment. Watching things from a distance is our national pastime; even the slightest incident on a road draws a crowd of gawkers. The old man spat a third time; the thin man wiped it off and threw it out of the window a third time. The old man now looked at the turban-clad man with wide eyes and asked in Hindi, 'Please, what do you think you're doing?' The thin man simply smiled in answer—a smile of angelic sweetness. Bhuvan Shome had never seen such a smile before. The entire coach was waiting with bated breath for the next round of coughing. As though everyone was at some sort of a football match. In a few moments the next round of coughing duly occurred. But on this occasion, the old man leant out of the window and spat. The entire compartment roared with laughter.

Within the next few minutes the train arrived at a station. A number of gentlemen were waiting with garlands in their hands. As soon as the turbanned man got down, they garlanded him. It turned out that the thin turban-wearing man was the Africa-returned barrister, the all-conquering Mr M. K. Gandhi.

. . . Bhuvan Shome pulled on his cigar while tapping his legs. He'd had such a variety of experiences in his life. And now, his life was slowly coming to an end—an endless succession of mornings, evenings and nights. It seemed only the other day that he had started his job . . . What was that, a kingfisher? He stood up. No, not a kingfisher. He had seen that bird many times before but never found out what it was called. Was it some kind of duck? No, it didn't look like a duck. He turned to see a man observing the bird through a pair of binoculars. Bhuvan Shome went towards him; as soon as the gentleman put his binoculars down, their eyes met.

'Do you know what that bird is called?'

'It's called tern in English. Its Latin name is *Sterna aurantia Gray*. I'm not sure what they call it in Bengali. Some people call it a gull, but I think that's wrong.'

'Oh.'

Bhuvan Shome moved away instantly and went back to his deck chair. To himself he said, 'Oh my God! Not another specimen. I hope he doesn't start pursuing me with his fancy information. Who asked you for the bird's Latin name? Showing off, that's all.'

Following one unpleasant experience after the other, he no longer fancied the company of his fellow men overmuch. When he had started hunting, after his preserve phase, he used to invite a friend along for company. Not any longer. He found it impossible to tolerate their incessant chatter. The freedom that he was seeking from the conflicts of urban life would be missing.

Bhutnath spent all his time boasting about his own cleverness. How he had stunned his boss with his cleverness; why the big boss' wife kept asking for him; how his wife's copperplate meant that his son was a dab hand at calligraphy; how the headmaster had refused to promote him out of sheer partiality but how, as soon as Mr Godson saw his son's handwriting, he promptly offered him a job in his office; how his son-in-law was so rich that he would never travel without reserving an entire First Class compartment. An endless stream of stories. The man simply did not know how to stop; he would go on and on and on.

He took Dwijen with him instead of Bhutnath once. But he had never realized that the man's mind was such a cesspit. He would, on the sly, utter the odd obscenity in the office. But once away from the restraints of company, he seemed to give full vent to his not-inconsiderable talent in this direction. Bhuvan Shome had never heard such utterly foul language in his entire life. He listened in bemused wonderment. The man may have failed the departmental examinations thrice in a row, but he knew his Havelock Ellis, *Ananga Ranga* and *Kama Sutra* by heart. He regaled him with an endless succession of such tales. The man would tell one of his stories, roll his eyes and then burst out laughing. When his sides ached with laughter, he would bend and hold his stomach with his hands and say, 'Honestly, they'll be the death of me.' Once he laughed so loudly that all the birds on the lake flew away. Not one came within range. So Dwijen had to be dropped as well. One could not take a man like that to a quiet, deserted spot. Though he, of course, thought all along that he was discussing something suitably esoteric.

After Dwijen, it was the turn of Chhottu Sen. Now there was another specimen for you. The man wanted the entire credit, and pleasure, of the shoot for himself. He would run forward and start firing as soon as he clapped eyes on a bird. He would appropriate any birds that fell. If two birds were hit, he would take both, and say with a big smile, 'These two are hardly enough for my family. Won't even come to a piece per head. Let's see if we can get a few more.' But of course, there was no question of any birds remaining after two rounds had been fired. He had invited Chhottu Sen to a shoot twice, with the same result. Never after that.

He had also invited Kartik Mukherjee. But the man was an absolute Jonah. On every occasion that he had come along, they had never bagged a feather, much less a bird. Once they hit a lalshar, which fell. Bhuvan Shome managed to catch it but, just as he was about to hand the bird over to Anil, it slipped his grasp and flew away. After this incident, he never invited Kartik either.

He no longer invited anyone, not even Anil. Anil was a fine young man, no bad habits, but Bhuvan Shome always felt rather constrained about shooting in Anil's presence. The lad tended to get very irate at misses; he was himself a crack shot. But then Anil was twenty-five while Bhuvan Shome was getting on to sixty. But Anil tended to forget that. He would frown so terribly at a miss that it would be impossible to look at him for the next hour. Not that he would say anything; merely look sullen and glum—but that was even more uncomfortable. Which is why Bhuvan Shome goes shooting on his own these days, without any companions. Anil makes all the arrangements for him, nevertheless.

Being on one's own is a special kind of pleasure. The pleasure of total freedom, of doing whatever one wants, without advice, without obstructions, without listening to any idle chatter. Freedom from official responsibilities and neighbourhood irritations, from the tedious boredom of toothy smiles and empty words—total freedom. Just the sky above and earth below, with trees, forests, rivers, lakes and birds all around; and the freedom to do what one wanted in these surroundings. Do what you like, stay as long as you want, fire as often as you wish, kill as many birds as you can; whether you hit or miss, no one to laugh at you, no one to frown at you. It is true that he goes to hunt birds, indeed that he even tries to shoot birds, but killing birds is not his goal. With increasing age, he no longer cares for meat in any case. On the odd occasion that he manages to shoot a bird, he hands it over to Anil. Because there is no one left in his family.

No one left. This harsh truth suddenly assaulted him. His wife had died long ago, about a year after completing the Savitri-vrata. This qualified as a feat of some kind, since it was rare for women who had completed the Savitri-vrata to die before their husbands. His brothers were settled in their jobs, one in Calcutta, and the other in Allahabad. Birinchi and Jagannath were both dead. Birinchi used to eat like a pig, consuming nearly half a seer of rice and equivalent amounts of dal and vegetables each day. He had turned diabetic and gone blind towards the end. Jagannath, who also ate excessive amounts, had died of typhoid; he had contracted the illness at a dinner invitation in Rampurhat. His widowed sister Chhabi was dividing her time between her two sons, one in Liluah and the other in Jamalpur. Out of respect for him, the head of Bhuvan Shome's department had got the two boys jobs in the railways. Bhuvan Shome had not requested it, of course; he had never made such a request for anyone, ever. That is why the Europeans used to respect him. His older son Bilu was an England-returned big shot, his father-in-law having financed the UK trip. He lived in Delhi. Big shot only meant colossally selfish—he was only interested in himself and his family.

His younger son Nipu was the only one living with him. He had entered the railways after passing a competitive examination, and for a while done quite well. But in the end, he, too, changed. To begin with, he had not suspected anything. He first found out after returning from a bird shoot. On that occasion, he had bagged a large number of teal, nearly twenty or twenty-five of them. Even after distributing them to all and sundry, five or six of the birds were left. He brought them home, thinking that Nipu would cook them. A distant widowed aunt used to stay with him; but she had objections to cooking meat. Nipu used to cook the meat. His aunt looked at the birds and said, 'Oh dear, we're going to have problems. I don't think that Nipu'll be willing to cook meat any more. I tell you what, I'll put everything together for you, you can do the cooking yourself.' He was astonished by all this. What on earth did she mean, Nipu wouldn't touch the birds? His aunt explained, 'He's become a disciple of Jatababa's. He's been a vegetarian for the last few days and does the pranayam every morning.'

Nipu was not at home anyway, so he had to cook himself. When Nipu returned, he asked him, 'I believe you've become a vegetarian. What is this all about?' Nipu replied, 'It's part of my vows. My guru has given me a mantra and told me not to eat meat.' Bhuvan Shome immediately asked their young servant to go and fetch a bel leaf. There was a sagging bel tree next to the house. The bel leaf duly arrived. Bhuvan Shome told Nipu, 'Write your wretched mantra on this bel leaf and immerse it in the Ganges. You'll have said goodbye to your vows. Then you can eat your meat and rice. This sort of humbug won't do in this house.'

Nipu stood for a while with a sullen face, then left the room. Then one day, Nipu left home without warning. He had apparently not gone to work, nor taken any leave. Later, it became known that he had gone to Benaras, to attend his guru's birthday celebrations. This meant that he lost his job. Bhuvan Shome could not forgive even his own son for such a gross dereliction. In fact, he was even less inclined to be forgiving. Apparently, he was living in the guru's ashram these days, teaching at the attached religious school. A boy who had passed his IA exams in the third division after three attempts ends up a teacher! Fortunately, he had never thought of marrying the fellow off; his wife would have had a hell of a time.

It occurred to him once again that he was now quite alone in his house. There was just him and that distant aunt. After all the time, money, energy and hard work that building the house had required, the way he'd had to borrow in order to raise the money, the people he'd had to flatter, the place was slowly turning into a haunted house. There was not a single person he could call his own. Without his presence, it would soon turn into a mouldering pile of bricks . . .

Bhuvan Shome puffed on his cigar and kept tapping his legs. No, the birds meant nothing to him. It was not the shooting that he came for. It was to escape from the crowds, to breathe some fresh country air, to forget about himself and his life that he came. But this time, he would have to get a few birds, if at least to show Anil and that Chhottu Sen that he, too, could shoot straight. It was true that he frequently missed, that his hands shook every time he aimed at the target; but there was no doubt in his mind that he could shoot straight if he wanted to. He would have to prove it this time. Anil would want to go along, but he would not let anyone accompany him. The gentleman studying birds through his binoculars was, occasionally, looking at Bhuvan Shome as well.

What a strange man he was, constantly talking to himself.

III

The steamer finally docked. The port train had already arrived. The wharf, till a little while ago completely deserted, was now teeming with people. As if half the population of India had decided to arrive at the same time. All sorts of faces, all sorts of baggage, all sorts of apparel, all kinds of bad manners, many forms of politesse. Shouting passengers, screaming porters, the strange street-cries of the various vendors, beggars demanding alms, policemen ordering people about—the entire area was in an uproar. The passengers from the port train had already arrived; now, with the arrival of the steamer passengers, it seemed as though two rivers were meeting. Anil was standing in a somewhat less crowded area, on a suitably raised spot, staring carefully at the stream of descending passengers. Bhuvan Shome's pith helmet was the first thing he saw, followed by the cigar in his mouth. He went forward to meet him, and as soon as he was close enough, did a pranam.

'It's all right . . .'

But whatever he might have said, in his heart of hearts he was quite pleased. Young people seemed to have forgotten how to do pranam properly to their elders. Any sort of gesture would do as far as they were concerned. Some were imitating the Biharis and saying namaste, some others were saying 'Jai Hind'. He had not heard any-one saying 'Ram Ram' as yet. These young worthies felt it an insult to their prestige to have to touch their elders' feet while doing pranam. He had known friends' children who would drop in during Bijaya Dashami, eat the sweets offered but leave without doing pranam. But Anil was not like that. He came from a good background. After all, breeding must show.

'What's that in your hand?'

'Some dal I just bought for you. Harbans sells very high-quality dal in his shop.'

'Is there any asafoetida at home?'

'Yes.'

'Tell them to add a dash when they cook the dal. How's your wife?'

'She's well. But there's no one at home. They've all gone to her parents'.'

'I see. Who's doing the cooking?'

'We have a thakur.'

'A maithil, eh? That's all we need. What's he like as a cook?'

'Pretty good, really.'

'Let's go, shall we? Where's that porter? Hey you, bring it over here . . .'

He moved on towards the train, Anil behind him. There was an empty Second Class compartment waiting. Bhuvan Shome found a window seat for himself, lit his cigar, turned to Anil and said, 'I've brought good English cartridges with me.' He laughed and continued, 'Do you remember what happened last time? My word, what a stupid idea. Hardly the sort of work I'm cut out for. Talk about asking a boy to do a man's job. All I managed to do was to throw good money away.'

Anil was smiling as well. Last year, Bhuvan Shome had decided to load his own shells. The finished product looked all right, and made the requisite sound when fired. But the buckshot seemed unable to travel any great distance; its range was measured in a distance of yards. Not one pellet even touched a bird; they tended to fly away unscathed. He had tried to crawl closer to the birds in order to gain range, but all to no avail. He had not been able to touch a bird last year.

'What arrangements have you made this year? Are the birds around?'

'Lots of them on the sandbanks of the Ganges.'

'But how'll I get there?'

'I've arranged for a bullock cart. Well, it's mine actually. You'll have to go by bullock cart early in the morning, to Kishanpur. From there it's on foot for a while until the sandbanks are reached. They're absolutely crawling with birds—curlews, geese, teal, pintail—you name them. I've been once. If you want, I'll come with you.'

'No thank you. I'll manage on my own.'

Anil had been expecting this response. The subject may have been discussed further but Sakhichand Yadav chose this moment to arrive with a hubble-bubble. He bowed low to Bhuvan Shome and said to Anil, 'No hookahs in the entire area, I'm afraid. But Radhanath-babu bought this hubble-bubble yesterday. Its been lying untouched. I suggest that you take this along.'

'Very well.'

Sakhichand put the hubble-bubble down in one corner, bowed low once again and left the compartment with an ingratiating expression. Before leaving, he also returned the half-rupee coin Anil had given him for the hookah. Seeing Sakhichand reminded Bhuvan Shome that he had not filed his report about the man. He would have to send it off as soon as he went back to work. His memory was definitely worsening with advancing age.

He looked at the hubble-bubble and asked, 'Who is that for?'

'For you. The hookah I'd got for you from Katihar has broken. I'd given Sakhichand some money for a hookah, but he wasn't able to find one anywhere in the area.'

'Return the hubble-bubble. I'm not going to smoke from that.'

'But you invariably smoke a hubble-bubble after a meal. I've got some really nice tobacco for you.'

'Don't worry about all that. You return that hubble-bubble.'

Anil had to get off and return the thing.

It took about an hour for them to reach Anil's house. By the time they had freshened up and finished lunch, the afternoon was nearly over. Bhuvan Shome was very pleased with the maithil's cooking. 'Better cook than most women, isn't he? You'd better take care of the fellow, you certainly won't find too many like him.' Bhuvan Shome referred to people who pleased him as 'fellows'. If he disliked them, it was 'bloody fellows'.

Anil had collected all the appurtenances for smoking tobacco—fine fragrant tobacco, charcoal pieces, a chillum—everything. Only the hookah was missing.

Bhuvan Shome said, 'Tell you what. There're a lot of banana trees growing in your garden. Tell someone to cut a thick branch for me. I'll make my own hookah.'

And that is what they did. Smoking his makeshift hookah on the eastern verandah, Bhuvan Shome said to himself, 'There've been days when I've held the chillum in my hands and smoked tobacco. Now some half-grown kid's going to fix hookahs for me.' Inside, Anil was making the bed for him; he chuckled briefly. Bhuvan Shome had grown into the habit of speaking to himself. It almost sounded as though he was having a conversation with someone.

Anil came out and said, 'Uncle, I've made up your bed. Why don't you rest a bit?'

'I won't be able to sleep. Not used to sleeping during the day, you know. I'm either working or, during the holidays, hunting and fishing. But I will lie down for a bit.'

He went to bed with an English novel. He had long become used to reading a novel in bed. He had bought this one from Wheeler's at the start of his journey; he started frowning after the first two pages. There were two murders on the first page itself; a girl and her aunt, both shot. And not one revolver, but three. And all three found inside the room as well. This was a riveting affair indeed! He read a few pages with a frown, then closed the book with a bang. Utter drivel. Sleep would not come either. He stared for a while at the picture of Anil's father, hanging on the wall in front of him, then said, 'Just as well you're dead, brother. You'd have had to suffer if you'd been alive. Virtuous men like you have quick, clean deaths. God only knows what's in store for the likes of me.'

He got up from bed, opened the connecting door and cautiously peeked into the next room. There was no sign of Anil, but he could smell cigarette smoke. A faint smile dawned on his face; so the boy had started smoking. At least he was smoking out of sight of his elders. He felt pleased. Anil was really a decent boy. Not that he was surprised, considering the kind of father he'd had. One of those worthless young men of today would have blown smoke in his face. He wore his shoes and shirt and carefully descended. To see that plot of land. The plot to the south of Anil's house, on which he had hoped to build his own house one day. When his ancestral property was sold to meet his father's debts, he and his family would have been on the streets, but for Anil's father. He was a very kind person, Anil's father. It was he who had arranged that piece of land from the zamindar, for nominal rent and earnest money. 'Build something here for now. Later, when you have the money, you can buy a property in town.' They had even dug the foundations for the house; but his mother's constant whingeing and moaning had resulted in the whole thing being abandoned. Bhuvan Shome had to borrow money at extortionate rates of interest in order to build a house in town. But this piece of land still attracted him in a strange way. So many memories . . . of Buchkun their servant, Dulal, Tagar, Tuni and so many others . . . he always visited this piece of land when he was in the area. But today, he was not able to step on it. It had been fenced all around with coloured bamboo matting. Someone must have bought it. It had been lying empty till last year. He stood next to the fence for a while. He noticed that somewhere towards the centre of the plot—where he had hoped his living room would be—a little thatched structure had been put up. Inside the tiny room, two female labourers were grinding bricks in a huge mortar. One promptly covered her head decorously on seeing him, the other favoured him with a cheeky grin. 'Be damned,' said Bhuvan Shome and moved away. As soon as he returned, he met Anil.

'Hello, where have you been? The coffee's ready.'

'Coffee? Have you started drinking coffee as well?'

'No. I had some sent in for you, from Katihar. You can't even get decent tea here. I know that you drink coffee in the evenings.'

Bhuvan Shome looked at him for a few moments, and said, 'Since you've made a special effort about the coffee, I'll drink it, of course. But it was wrong of you, nevertheless.'

'Wrong of me? Why?'

'Because you're being formal. I'm a member of the family, I ought to be able to enjoy myself here with whatever's available at home. By making special arrangements for me, you're keeping me at a distance.'

'I don't know why you should say such a thing. After all, I used to bring lots of special things for Father as well. Kataribhog rice from Dinajpur, ghee from Calcutta, special moong dal, tobacco from Gaya, and who knows what else. Why, you yourself used to . . .'

'I think you've missed my point. But never mind. Tell me, how long has the coffee been percolating?'

'A couple of minutes.'

'Let it stand a few minutes more.'

They entered the house.

The coffee was drunk in due course. A few minutes later the maithil entered with a large timepiece in his hand.

Anil took it from him and asked, 'It's OK, is it? The last time, the man had ruined it.'

'Well, he said it was all right.'

'What is this all about? Whose clock is it?'

'Mine. The postmaster's son's sitting his exams, so he borrowed it from me. He wakes up early in the morning to study. Since we have to get up early ourselves tomorrow, I asked for it back.'

Bhuvan Shome commented, 'All this borrowing drives one crazy. It's just as well that our limbs and eyes can't be separated from our bodies. I'm sure people would've wanted to borrow those as well. Look at what happened to my gramophone because of repeated borrowings. Not one record intact, and the other day I noticed that someone had broken the spring as well. I'm happy, because no one's going to want it again. You'd better check the clock, one never can tell, it might not ring. When do we have to get up?'

'Around two. It'll be around three before one can start. We must get to the place before sunrise. I've asked the cart driver to sleep here tonight.'

'Good idea. Is the cart here as well?'

'Yes, it belongs to me. I purchased the pair of buffaloes recently.'

'But you used to have bullocks earlier. Why did you buy buffaloes? They're not nice animals, you know. Yama's mount and all that.'

'Only buffalo carts manage the local roads during the monsoons. The roads around the area are so bad that bullock carts can't cope. They're saying the roads are going to be improved. We're going to have motorable roads soon—apparently the central government's providing funds.'

'So I'm told. But I don't believe it'll ever get built. A few of these fellows are consummate actors. They can deliver stirring speeches from public platforms. You get the feeling that they're going to bring the moon down for you to use as a lamp. The remainder are petty crooks. The money may well be granted but it'll end up in sundry bank accounts. No decent road will be built. Don't hope for it, at least.'

Bhuvan Shome stretched his limbs in the easy chair and lit a cigar. After smoking silently for a while he said, 'I'll go to bed early tonight. Tell him to make something light for dinner.'

'I've told him to make soru-chakli for you. Isn't that what you like?'

'Will a maithil be able to make soru-chakli?'

'He can make anything. I've asked him to pack some food for you.'

'Good. I'm sure I'll be in difficulty if I start feeling hungry on the sandbanks. Nothing there but sand . . .'

'Oh, there's a village not far away. You can get milk there.'

'Milk! Good grief, I can hardly digest the stuff . . .'

IV

After mumbling a hasty prayer, Bhuvan Shome climbed aboard his buffalo-drawn chariot at precisely three in the morning. There was a thick mattress in the cart, with a bed made up, warm blankets, even a quilt.

'Get under the quilt and get some rest, Uncle. You'll get there by sunrise. I can come with you if you want. After all, you've never been there before.'

'No no, you don't have to come. Don't stand here in this cold, go back to bed.'

The cart moved off. After a while, Bhuvan Shome felt that if the buffaloes kept moving at this speed, not only would he not get any sleep but also his bones would come apart.

'What is your name, my man?'

'Bhutta.'

'Well, would you like to drive slowly?'

'Right you are, master.'

The cart went slowly for a while. Bhuvan Shome made himself comfortable under the quilt. The cart had a covered roof, and the mattress was quite thick and soft. So he dozed off comfortably. But his sleep was soon interrupted. The buffaloes were running once again. He rose on one elbow and peered outside. A thin crescent moon could be seen. And what he saw in that pale moonlight made him shudder. What Bhutta was doing would make elephants break into a dead run, much less a buffalo—he was extending his legs between the hind legs of the buffaloes, and tickling them. The man was going to kill them. Who knows what such huge-horned beasts were capable of if tickled in such a fashion?

'Bhutta, my dear fellow?'

'Yes, master?'

'I want you to squat on your haunches. Don't sit with your legs dangling.'

Bhutta looked at him in astonishment. He couldn't understand what the gentleman was saying.

'What, master? What's that you're saying?'

Bhuvan Shome was not able to see the look of bewilderment on the man's face; it was still quite dark. But he realized that the man had not understood the Bengali word for squatting. He did not know the Hindi expression for squatting. He hardly knew much Hindi, anyway. Nor had he ever bothered to learn the language; he usually spoke Bengali or English with the Biharis he met. Those who under-stood neither, he managed to communicate with using his pidgin Hindi. He had never considered that he might be in difficulty for not knowing the Hindi word for 'squat'. As the animals started running even faster, he banged his head against the roof of the cart. Anil had obviously entrusted him to the care of a raving lunatic. The man was merrily tickling the buffaloes. What would happen if they struck a ditch or a bad bump? At his age, it was unlikely that any broken bones would ever set. Old Chatterjee had died of a fractured bone; the man had suffered from gangrene in the end. Finally, he told Bhutta in his pidgin Hindi, 'Don't sit with your legs dangling.'

'How'll I drive the buffaloes then?'

'Well, don't tickle them so.'

'What's that again?'

Tickle was another word Bhuvan Shome did not know the Hindi equivalent of. This was turning out to be a major problem.

'Don't drive them so hard.'

'But we have a long way to go. The master told me to get there while it was still dark.'

'Never mind that. You just go slow.'

Bhuvan Shome managed to get the gist of the man's retort—the sun would rise and no birds would be found.

'That doesn't matter. Just go slow.'

Bhutta, however, paid not the slightest attention to him. He sim-ply whacked one of the buffaloes with a stick, and screamed at them in his own tongue. This time Bhuvan Shome understood every word that was said, 'Walking like a gentleman, you bloody crocodiles.' He felt rather amused. The law by which humans are abused as monkeys was the law that Bhutta was following; he had not said anything illegal. Nevertheless, it was the first time he had heard such an abuse.

'Please drive slowly—I'm not ready to die just yet.'

'You just lie yourself down, master. Nothing to worry about.'

Having said that, he promptly twisted the tail of one of the buffaloes and started making clicking noises with his mouth. Bhuvan Shome realized that ordering the man was not going to work. First, he did not have the language; second, Anil had obviously left strict instructions that he should reach before sunrise. The man was, equally obviously, not going to disobey those instructions. But at this rate, every joint in his body was liable to dislocate. He was hardly going to be able to hold the gun in his hands. He decided to adopt a different strategy. Perhaps if the man could be distracted, he might get some results. Because if the fellow concentrated on the buffaloes in such a singular manner, he was certainly doomed. But what could he start a conversation about? The chap did not understand politics, there was no question of gossiping with him about other people, railway administration and English novels were both arcane mysteries as far as he was concerned. Perhaps he could talk to him about farming but he knew nothing about such matters. He decided to start on personal matters.

'It's a lovely name, Bhutta. Who named you?'

'My aunt.'

'Your aunt, eh. That's wonderful.'

Bhutta started telling his life-story. Bhuvan Shome felt he was in the presence of a second Buddha. Bhutta was apparently born in the middle of a cornfield. His mother, about to conceive, was busy harvesting corn at the time. She died in the same cornfield, immediately after giving birth to her son. His aunt had then adopted and raised him. After his uncle died, his father had married the sister-in-law. It was true that the cornfield was not quite the royal gardens of Lumbini but the similarities did seem rather numerous. In any case, what Bhuvan Shome had hoped for happened. The cart started travelling slowly. But as soon as he had finished, Bhutta attacked the buffaloes with redoubled vigour while making a strange snorting noise. He also started twisting their tails as well as tickling them, all at the same time. As though he had to make amends, with interest, for the temporary loss of concentration that he had suffered. The two buffaloes started running for their lives.

'Slowly, slowly, let's go a little slowly.'

Bhutta turned and smiled at him. The sort of indulgent smile that adults reserve for scared children. It was light enough to see by now. The bloody fellow was smiling at him. He started shaking with rage. But this was not the time to express his anger; he had to use diplomacy.

He asked a further question. 'What sort of things d'you like to eat?'

'Gram sattu.'

'Gram sattu, eh? Well, I like that too.'

Bhutta turned his head and smiled.

'Is that with gur, or oil and chillies?'

'Both are nice.'

'Do you prefer rice, or roti?'

'Roti.'

'What about vegetables?'

'Karela.'

Bread and bitter gourds. What an extraordinary palate!

'What about other vegetables, potatoes and so on?'

'Those as well. But nothing like bitter gourd fried with onions, I say.'

The cart had slowed down considerably. Bhuvan Shome decided he had to carry on this conversation for a while. He tried to imagine what bitter gourds fried with onions would taste like with roti. The thought nearly made him retch! And yet this was the fellow's favourite food. Talk about barbarity. Something happened just then, however, that made any thought of food vanish—all the birds called out together. Bhuvan Shome was completely startled. For a few moments he said nothing, was able to say nothing. Birds called out first thing in the morning, they always had done, yet this commonplace occurrence seemed so unprecedented that he was totally dumbstruck. He sat up and looked about him in silence.

The buffaloes were no longer running; the road had improved, the cart was travelling at a normal speed. It seemed as though even the animals were enjoying the scenery. Bhuvan Shome observed that the eastern sky was slowly reddening with the colours of dawn. The city-dweller was overwhelmed. Bhutta seemed completely unaffected. He had seen such sights all his life. Water had no novelty for a fish; he might have been affected by a mill chimney. His only concern was to get the gentleman to his destination on time. He started forcing the animals to go faster once again. Bhuvan Shome no longer tried to stop him. It was very pleasant, anyway. In a little while it became light. By now Bhuvan Shome was no longer thinking about the buffaloes. He had spotted the green fields on both sides of the road, and was staring at them, fascinated. What were those plants? Rice? But no, they didn't grow rice in this area. He asked Bhutta. Bhutta mumbled something casually.

Wheat, barley and gram? But which was which? Bhuvan Shome suddenly felt embarrassed. He really did not know a thing. He had spent his life collecting worthless information. The eastern sky reddened further.

He suddenly noticed something very curious. A bird abruptly rose from the field, sang a song briefly in the air, then dived straight back into the field. Soon another rose, then another, until the skies filled with birdsong.

'Bhutta, what bird is that?'

'Bhartha . . .' Bhutta answered indifferently, as though he had not even heard the birdsong.

'Bhartha? What sort of a bird is that?'

Bhutta answered in his own tongue that the birds were building nests in the field, in which they would lay their eggs.

Bhuvan Shome was not able to understand a word. He would have understood if he had been told it was a lark, but bhartha he could not make head or tail of. Nor would he have understood bhardwaj, even though bhartha was merely a corruption of the former word. That they build their nests and lay eggs in fields was something that Bhutta knew, but he did not. He felt deeply embarrassed. But he was so fascinated that the feeling did not last too long.

The cart continued. They went a good distance. He noticed many other birds, both familiar and unfamiliar. He also noticed that Bhutta did not recognize a majority of the birds. He tended to call the unfamiliar ones 'wild birds'. The one or two he managed to name may well have been wrong. On one occasion he called a drongo a bluebreast. Bhuvan Shome was familiar with both species. He said, 'No, that's not a bluebreast.'

Bhutta seemed not the least bit put out. 'Perhaps it's some other bird then.'

Suddenly, something utterly unexpected happened.

'Ho, ho, ho . . .'

Bhutta jumped out of the cart. One of the buffaloes had thrown off its yoke; the cart had slumped to one side. Bhutta was not able to catch the buffalo, however. Bhuvan Shome was disconcerted. He had been about to light a cigar; he stopped. The second buffalo was also attempting to run away. Bhutta shouted out in a stricken voice, 'Oh no, a bihaniya.'

'What's a bihaniya ?'

'A bihaniya buffalo, master. Quickly, get down, get down . . .'

Bhuvan Shome jumped off the back of the cart. He was still not able to understand what was going on. But as soon as he was off the cart, he realized what was happening. Another buffalo was standing in the middle of a field, a little distance away. Its horns were covered with mud, it was a gleaming black in colour, it was making a soft bleating sound with its mouth, bending its head in a threatening manner. Its attitude was definitely not reassuring.

There was a silk-cotton tree nearby. Bhutta peremptorily indicated that he should climb the tree.

'Quick, quick, climb the tree, quick . . . this one's a bastard . . .'

He ran across, virtually bundled Bhuvan Shome off to the bottom of the tree, lifted him on his shoulder and said, 'Grab that branch, quickly now.' There was a branch within reach; Bhuvan Shome caught hold of it, then managed to clamber on to it with Bhutta's help. Then he observed that battle had broken out. The strange buffalo was furiously attacking the remaining cart buffalo while Bhutta started whacking the attacking animal with a pair of rope-covered bamboo sticks. Bhuvan Shome was amazed at Bhutta's bravery. Where had the man got the sticks from? He did not know that every cart driver kept such a pair of sticks, in order to stop the cart. They are called sipaha. Bhutta kept fighting with great valour. The first buffalo had long since run away. When the second buffalo also broke from the fight and ran, the stranger seemed to find no reason to linger—it ran off as well. It had come to defend its territory. He realized the entire significance of the episode later. Bhutta explained it to him. A bihaniya was a breeding buffalo; it would not allow another male buffalo in its territory. If it spotted any other male buffalo, it would promptly come forth to give battle. That soft bleating from its mouth could be translated as a 'no quarter given or taken'–type of signal. It would either chase its opponent away or go down fighting. The bihaniya that Bhuvan Shome had come across apparently had a ferocious reputation. No buffalo in the area had ever succeeded in defeating it. Indeed, it had killed the local doctor's buffalo.

Bhuvan Shome had managed to observe everything from the tree. After all the three beasts had left the scene, he was suddenly made aware of the intimate presence of yet another enemy. The tree was crawling with red ants. He was wondering what to do when he heard Bhutta say, 'You can come down now, master.'

Bhutta seemed utterly chagrined; this much was clear from his expression. As though he was personally responsible for the sudden appearance of the bihaniya. The poor fellow was sweating despite the winter cold and a finger on his right hand had been injured, but he was oblivious to such details. What was bothering him was that his master's guest had got into trouble because of him. He straightened the cart with the pair of sipaha sticks, and said in a subdued voice, 'Please get down, master.'

Bhuvan Shome was also in a fair hurry to get down. He had become very worried about the ants, particularly if they succeeded in entering his trousers. He jumped down without any assistance from Bhutta. As soon as he was down, it struck him: What now? Both the cart buffaloes had run away. Would it be sensible to proceed on foot? The bihaniya might have fled after the thrashing it had received from Bhutta, but what if it returned? This was far from unlikely, since the beast was hiding somewhere nearby; it had certainly not gone far. What were those large plants there? Bhutta had called them rahar, meaning arhar or pigeon pea. He had noticed from the tree that the animal had entered the arhar field.

But Bhutta was categoric that the bihaniya would not appear again. He suggested that they go to Mahendar Singh's dota which was not too far from the spot. Now what on earth was a dota? The small shelter that the well-off farmer built in the middle of his field was called a dota in this part of the country. Bhutta said that he wanted to take Bhuvan Shome, along with all his belongings, to the dota. They might well find another bullock cart at the spot. Mahendar Singh owned a bullock cart and had bought a pair of matched high-class oxen during the last fair. He held Anil-babu in great respect; he would therefore undoubtedly help any guest of his. And last, the sandbanks were not very far from the dota; the gentleman could walk to them if he so wanted. Indeed, walking might prove the quicker alternative; going by cart would mean taking a roundabout way and take longer.

Bhutta would escort him to the dota and then search for the two runaways.

It seemed an eminently reasonable, as well as practical solution, to Bhuvan Shome. Not that there was much choice. He agreed. Fortunately, the bihaniya had not charged the cart itself; otherwise his gun and cartridges would have been scattered who knows where. He was wearing European clothes; he had kept his chesterfield cape aside while lying down. He wore it now, filled his pockets with cartridges and shouldered his gun. Then he wore his hat and set out after Bhutta. Anil had sent a packed tiffin-carrier along. He handed this to Bhutta. A military-style canteen, slung over his shoulder, carried his drinking water. He had nothing else with him; nor did he need anything else.

Arriving at Mahendar Singh's dota, they found it deserted. Nothing but a thatched, single-room structure. Mud walls and a straw roof, with a high earthen verandah on all sides. There was a strong-looking bench on the verandah to the eastern side of the structure. The courtyard in front contained a well. There was nothing else. In the distance, a young man was cutting grass in a field. Bhutta put the tiffin-carrier down and went to speak to him. Bhuvan Shome sat on the bench and lit his pipe. He felt that his wits would need to be fumigated from the very beginning, otherwise there was no getting out of this mess

Bhutta returned to say that Mahendar Singh was no longer there. He had left on his cart to attend a marriage, in a village some twenty-five miles distant. No one knew when he would return; his major-domo was also not available—he was in police custody for his part in the recent Gwala versus Bhuihar clashes. The other servants had also run away for the same reason, namely, that the police would arrest them as soon as they were spotted. Bhutta added that he felt Mahendar Singh had fled for the same reason; the invitation was a mere excuse. The chap cutting the grass was Bhagiya. Though he was not one of Mahendar Singh's servants, he was looking after things for the moment. Apparently he was the major-domo's nephew. He assured Bhutta that he would help the gentleman in every way he could.

Bhutta also received some unfortunate news from Bhagiya: apparently, a group of bird hunters had arrived very early by boat. Bhuvan Shome was quite depressed by the news. He said to himself, 'So much for my ambitions. The best thing now would be to get out of here.' But of course there was no way of 'getting out' since both the buffaloes had fled.

'How long will it take for you to find the animals?'

'Who can tell? Who knows where they've run off to. I'll have to search.'

'Well, see how quickly you can find them, then. Meanwhile, I'll look around and see what I can spot.'

Bhuvan Shome noticed that Bhutta was a good fellow. Before setting out, he had filled a pitcher with water from the well. The well had a bamboo post with an iron-bucket arrangement for drawing water. Before going off to look for the animals, Bhutta said he would take them to Bhaggu Modal's place, east of the silk-cotton tree. He would leave them in Bhaggu's cow-shed, because it would not be safe to bring them through the bihaniya's territory, the border of which he felt was marked by the silk-cotton tree. He also gave Bhuvan Shome some interesting information on the topic: that the buffalo which fled first had realized that it had entered the territory of a bihaniya without permission. A bihaniya marked out its territory with dung. Other buffaloes, smelling the dung, realized that they were in the territory of an enemy and that further advance would lead to battle.

Once again, Bhuvan Shome realized how little he knew. He finished eating before Bhutta left. But his eyes popped out as soon as he opened the tiffin-carrier. Oh oh, what had the boy done—he had packed an omelette and mango pickles. Both were unlucky foods; no wonder the trip had gone so badly. Nevertheless, he ate them all. There were also a few puris and about four sweets. He was not hungry but he finished eating, mainly to get the job over with. Moreover, he realized that walking about with the tiffin-carrier was going to be a bother. Nor could he leave the thing here. Was that Bhagiya person trustworthy? Most probably not. Bhutta was planning to leave after washing the tiffin-carrier and filling his canteen with water. But Bhuvan Shome now felt that the canteen was also an unnecessary burden. It was winter and he was unlikely to feel thirsty; and if he did, the Ganges was nearby. He gave Bhutta the canteen as well.

. . . After Bhutta left, he lit his pipe. He looked in front of him and exclaimed, 'Magnificent, glorious.' The eastern sky was beginning to be lit by colours. Heavy clouds had gathered in the east, making the colours look all the more beautiful. The sun was attempting to peer over the horizon but the clouds were making it difficult for him to reveal his presence. But who was capable of stopping the sun? Bhuvan Shome was gently pulling on his pipe and enjoying the spectacle. The red started precisely where the horizon spanning green met the sky. The trees at the horizons' edge looked as though they had been drawn with sepia. Then the red; not just one kind of red but reds of many shades and tints. And where the reds ended, blue—bright, shining blue.

Bhuvan Shome used to paint at one time. He was truly enjoying the sight. The way one colour seemed to merge into the other, without any abrupt, jarring changes.

He was again reminded of Mr Brown, the guard. Occasionally, when drunk, he would utter great profundities. Once, he wagged his fingers in front of Bhuvan Shome's face and said, 'Babu, if you can truly lose yourself in the play of colours, you might find God. You don't have to go to church, or to a temple. God is colour.' As a Hindu, Bhuvan Shome had heard the phrase 'sabda brahma'. But that even colour was God, was a secret that Mr Brown had revealed to him. He could still see Mr Brown's face clearly. Blue eyes with bags beneath them, which seemed eternally watery. A head full of dishevelled silky hair. Thin red cheeks, with fine veins visible. He had the habit of staring in a pop-eyed manner; he would rarely blink when he looked at anything. His eyes would always seem to be full of tears. He used to wave his hands around when speaking; his fingers would shake all the time. The tips of his middle and index fingers were brown with nicotine stains. Brown had said, 'God is colour.'

He was suddenly reminded of his granddaughter Reba. She had sung a Tagore song for him once; a song about mingling one's colours with everyone else's. 'It's utter nonsense, you can't mingle your colour with everyone's,' he said out aloud. But the thought of his granddaughter kept recurring. He hadn't heard from them for a long while. She never even bothered to write a letter. And why should she? She did not need anything any more. He remembered that Reba had lost one eye because of a small-pox infection. A one-eyed girl would never get married. Her parents were teaching her music in the hope that she would have a means of supporting herself. But Bhuvan Shome knew it would not. A woman's only support was a man, just as man's only support was woman; it would not, could not be anything else. If it did, there would be problems. That is why a person like Vidyasagar wanted to even widows to be free to remarry.

He stood up abruptly. The sound of repeated gunfire could be heard.

'Damn, that'll get rid of the birds . . .'

He shouldered his gun and walked to where Bhagiya was cutting grass. 'Which is the road to the sandbanks?' The fellow did not bother to answer. Was he deaf? He had asked in Bengali; he now asked in Hindi.

'How do I get to the road which goes to the riverside?'

Bhagiya remained silent.

He carried on cutting the grass, oblivious to Bhuvan Shome's presence.

'Damn! Hey you, can't you speak?'

Bhagiya raised his eyes and looked at him once, but still made no answer.

'For goodness' sake, can't you tell me where the road to the river is?'

'No road.'

Whatever did the fellow mean? No road! He repeated his question. Bhagiya remained silent. But Bhuvan Shome was unrelenting; he fired question after question.

Finally, the gist of what the chap said in his own language turned out to be that the so-called river road did not exist. Anyone who wanted to walk to the river would have to go through the arhar field. Not that there was a road where the arhar field ended. Beyond the arhar field were wheat and barley fields. He would have to cross them by walking over the narrow ridge between the fields, because trampling on the crops would result in the owner, Bhikhan Gope, attacking him with a stick. Bhikhan was apparently hiding behind some bushes, waiting to ambush the unwary traveller. On the other hand, if the gentleman wanted to take the road, he would have to return to the silk-cotton tree which marked the bihaniya's territory. From there he would have to take the road going east; after walking that road for a good while, he would come across a mango tree in full blossom. The road to the river was next to the tree.

Bhuvan Shome was stunned.

Bhutta had abandoned him in the middle of a maze and cleared off. He said, 'My God!' then grew quiet. He remembered the next moment that he was a gentleman, and, therefore, helpless. It was 'their' time; 'they' could do as 'they' pleased; he would simply have to tolerate things. Since he had come this far, he would have to get to the sandbanks. He would have to appeal to this chap. But what could he do to satisfy the wretched little snake's ego? He thought for a while. Finally he decided on the ultimate incantation of the twentieth century, the one cantrip that satisfied all the gods, known and unknown.

In plain Bengali, he said, 'Take me to the river, sonny. I'll give you a nice tip. Look, here's something in advance.'

He took out a two-anna piece from his wallet and handed it over. Bhagiya took the coin and stuck it in his ear. The square two-anna coin seemed to fit his ear quite nicely. Bhuvan Shome noted that there was a biri stuck behind his ear as well. But the fellow showed no signs of getting up. He carried on as before, cutting the grass.

'Two annas not good enough. Right, here's two more. Now come on, son, get on with it.'

He produced another square two-anna coin and handed it over. Bhagiya immediately fitted it into his other ear and blandly carried on cutting grass. Bhuvan Shome started shaking with rage. And at once he realized that losing his temper would only ruin everything. He waited silently for a minute. The silence seemed to pay dividends. Bhagiya tied the bundle of grass, then stood upon it and tugged on the rope as hard as he could. He tied the bundle once again to his satisfaction, then tucked the sickle into the bundle. What he did after this was truly dramatic: he produced a five-rupee note and gave it to Bhuvan Shome. The money had dropped out of the master's purse when he was taking out the two-anna coin. He, Bhagiya, had covered the money with the grass, just to see what would happen. His eyes were twinkling with mirth but his face remained as bland as ever. Silently, and seemingly without any effort, he lifted the huge bundle of grass on to the top of his head and marched off towards the dota.

Bhuvan Shome was astonished by the fellow's behaviour. He followed him.

After reaching the dota, he put the bundle down, latched the door and said, 'We can go now, master.'

Bhuvan Shome was delighted. The man had finished the task in hand before considering anything else. Nor had money made the slightest difference. He was most probably indifferent to money, or the fellow would never have returned the five-rupee note. He had never seen such a thing. He was reminded of Hanu, his nephew.

Bhagiya returned at a run, to the spot where he had been cutting grass. He turned back once to look at Bhuvan Shome, and then entered the arhar field. Bhuvan Shome was not capable of running as fast as Bhagiya; nevertheless he reached the spot as quickly as possible. But he found it difficult to enter the arhar field with the gun shouldered, so he hung it by the strap and entered with some difficulty. But he could find no trace of Bhagiya. Where the devil was the fellow?

'Bhagiya, where're you?'

'Over here, master.'

He followed the sound of the voice for a distance. The sola topi started falling off every so often, and the gun kept getting stuck amid the plants. He finally tucked the hat under an arm.

'Bhagiya . . .'

'Yes, over here . . . this way . . .'

He was astounded to find Bhagiya standing in a clearing in the middle of the arhar field. It looked like a little compound, fenced all around by arhar plants. Nor was it any too small. Indeed, there was a little hut at one end of the clearing. He looked inquiringly at Bhagiya, who said that the field belonged to him and that he spent the nights in the hut guarding his property. Bhuvan Shome noticed that Bhagiya was an animal fancier as well. He was keeping a wild rabbit in a little hutch. He uprooted some grass from the arhar field and left it inside the hutch, then turned to Bhuvan Shome and said, 'Now we can go.'

'Where did you get the rabbit from?'

Bhagiya announced with pride that he had run the rabbit down on foot.

'Only eats grass, does it?'

'Milk and barley too . . .'

Bhagiya seemed disinclined to waste any time over words. He entered the arhar field once again and started off at a very brisk pace. As though the place was his living room. Bhuvan Shome was not capable of traversing even the cemented courtyard in front of his house at such speed. Bhagiya seemed less a man than a hare. He kept bounding on; Bhuvan Shome had to speed up. He tried his best to keep up but this was no easy task in that dense arhar field.

He had to endure this tribulation for about five minutes, when they crossed the arhar field and reached the wheat and barley field. This was a fairly large field of grain, with a small hut at one end. Inside the hut was the owner, Bhikhan Gope, whom Bhagiya had warned him about not a few minutes ago. The man's appearance was truly daunting—a huge head of curly black hair, and a face covered to the eyes with so tangled and matted a beard that the very nostrils could not be seen. Bhuvan Shome was walking on the ridge, carefully following Bhagiya's instructions, when something rather unexpected happened: Bhikhan Gope came out of his hut, ran across, bowed very low and smiled shyly. Bhuvan Shome noticed that the man had a sense of vanity—his two front teeth had small gold dots in them.

Bhuvan Shome had expected an enraged Bhikhan. He thus felt amused at the sight of this ultra-humble and obedient man. It was presumably the effect of his European clothes. Bhagiya seemed somewhat overjoyed at the sight of a benevolent Bhikhan Gope. He acted as though the sahib's presence in the field was entirely to his credit. Then, in his rough dialect, he explained to Bhikhan Gope why the sahib had come. Bhikhan Gope seemed to be entirely gratified and said that there was a boat moored at the ghat, his own boat, and that he would be quite honoured if the sahib made use of it.

'Is there a boatman to go with it?'

'Bhagiya can take you.'

'You mean Bhagiya knows how to use a boat?'

Bhagiya enthusiastically nodded yes.

Bhuvan Shome was having great difficulty walking on the narrow ridge between the fields. This made Bhikhan do something entirely unprecedented. He told Bhuvan Shome, 'Please walk through the field. After all, trampling the odd plant will hardly make a difference.'

Bhagiya was astounded. This was something he had never expected to hear.

Beyond the wheat and barley field was yet another arhar field, though much smaller. It required little effort to cross it. Immediately beyond it, they caught sight of water. Not the waters of the Ganges but floodwaters trapped between two high dunes during the monsoon, which had not dried out yet. As soon as they reached the water, a flock of wagtails flew past. They settled a little distance away and started wagging their tails. Bhuvan Shome was surprised to see a number of yellow ones. He had never seen the birds before. He looked at them for a while; they were magnificent.

'Those're dhobin birds.'

'Dhobin bird? No, no, they're wagtails.'

'No, they're dhobin birds.'

He realized that these people called the wagtail dhobin.

'Where's the boat?'

'Not far, master.'

By the time they had crossed the sandbanks to reach the riverside, the sun was up.

The sound of gunfire could be heard once more. He also heard the calling of geese. In the far distance, a flock of geese flew past.

'The other sahibs have come by phatphatiya-nao . . .'

Phatphatiya-nao meant motorboat. Who were these people who travelled by motorboat? Must be the magistrate; or a minister, perhaps. And these were the people who had turned Mahatma Gandhi into the 'Father of the Nation'.

He stared after the geese for a while. The fools would not even be able to scratch the birds, but that did not prevent them from scaring them away.

The motorboat could be seen going past, hugging the farther shore.

'The sahibs aren't going to come this way . . .'

Bhikhan Gope's boat was moored not far away. To begin with, he felt hesitant about getting into it. Ought he trust his life to Bhagiya's tender mercies? Bhagiya had obviously deduced his frame of mind from the expression on his face. He assured him that he would pole the boat slowly by the bank; there was no need to be worried. Moreover, they would find the geese after travelling a short while.

He muttered a prayer and climbed aboard. Lord, the boat was swaying. He had never hunted from a boat; he had always been on foot. Would he be able to aim correctly while standing on a boat? He remembered the Sanskrit *swadharme nidhanang shreyah, parodharme bhayavahah.*

He immediately thought of Father Tuntuni.

He had used the expression first.

. . . Bhagiya was gently poling the boat forward. Bhuvan Shome became preoccupied with thoughts of Father Tuntuni.

The crest of every wave was now gilded by the rays of the morning sun. Looking at the river, he was again reminded of Father Tuntuni's face.

He lit a cigar. Father Tuntuni was an ugly man, no doubt about that. Short, squat, swarthy, with a salt-and-pepper beard, wearing a priest's cap and robes. The man had done him an immense service: he had organized a letter from Reverend Ferguson to the agent. And immediately afterwards, he'd got a double promotion. Who could stop a man the agent himself was taking an interest in? They had godlike powers those days; cripples became capable of crossing mountains through their dispensations . . . he was truly indebted to Father Tuntuni. Yet their first meeting had been accidental and brief. In a railway waiting room. Then, Tuntuni had arrived at his house one day. He had apparently come to a nearby village to enquire about an ill person. Since he had some time to spare before the train, he had come to find out how Bhuvan Shome was doing. It was a Sunday; during the conversation it turned out that Tuntuni had not eaten anything all morning. He asked if there was a restaurant nearby. 'I'd have gone to the local Kellner's, but they're very expensive. Is there something a bit cheaper?' Bhuvan Shome had not eaten lunch; he insisted Father Tuntuni join him. After much persuasion, Father Tuntuni agreed. He said, 'Please spread a plantain leaf somewhere on this verandah, and ask them to give me something to eat. I know what a problem it is for an orthodox Hindu to invite a Christian to his home.' Bhuvan Shome retorted, 'What nonsense! We'll eat together. In any case, we have no such bigotry in this family. For us a guest is an object of veneration.' Father Tuntuni was quite gratified at this statement.

Not that he had arranged anything special for the man; there was not even a fish course that day. After the meal, Father Tuntuni remained silent for a while, then sighed and said, 'So many memories come to mind.' 'Memories of what?' asked Bhuvan Shome. 'Of my past life,' replied Father Tuntuni. 'Would you believe that I was born into a Brahmin family of the highest status? People used to throng our house, waiting to receive prasad and padodak.' Bhuvan Shome had been astonished to hear this. He had always imagined that people of the lowest caste tended to convert to Christianity. Why would a Brahmin want to convert? Had he fallen in love or something? What Father Tuntuni had told him in reply had been even more astounding. It was the sort of incident that could have formed the basis of a novel. He could still remember the entire story.

Tuntuni was travelling as a member of the wedding party of a boy from his village. They were going by bullock cart, in a caravan of four or five carts. It was midsummer, mid-June. After travelling a while, he started vomiting and developed diarrhoea. No one was left in any doubt that he had developed cholera. Since a person suffering from cholera was obviously not to be taken to a wedding feast, they left him under a convenient tree. Not even one of his fellow guests considered staying with him; they all left. Alone under a tree, in the middle of an empty field, he suffered the anguish of the damned in that midsummer heat. He was dying of thirst, but who would give him water? After a while, he fainted. He had no idea how long he was unconscious. When he regained consciousness, someone was carrying him on his shoulder. By now Tuntuni's entire body was covered in vomit and faeces. Was this a demon? It took him a while to realize that it was an angel. A tall, powerful, upright European—a Christian missionary. The man carried him to a hospital, arranged for proper treatment, and, essentially, gave him a new lease of life. Tuntuni never returned home after recovering. He converted to Christianity and spent all his energies proselytizing for the Christian Church. For the last twenty years he had spent his life thus. He had tramped from one village to the other in his attempt to convert men and women to Christianity.

He had been successful, as well. Having finished his story, Tuntuni had stared in silence at the skies for a while, before saying something that was so unexpected that it had truly startled Bhuvan Shome. Because, even though his behaviour was impeccably courteous, his feelings were anything but. Despite what Ramakrishna or Swami Vivekananda had said, he had no respect for Indian Christians as such. But what Tuntuni said then, made him start.

'Let me ask you: if I went through the appropriate purification rituals and reconverted to Hinduism, would you people take me back into the fold?'

'What made you say that?' asked Bhuvan Shome.

Tuntuni became silent once again, and ran his fingers through his beard for a while before answering. 'I "say" that because I've realized my mistake. The people who left me under the tree might've been cowardly, ignorant and superstitious, but they were not base. Nor were they responsible for their lowly condition. It was the result of their long subjection. The English wanted only to make clerks out of us, not human beings. Indeed, they had made every effort to ensure that we remained subhuman, so we could stay their slaves. I only got to know what they truly thought of us after I became a Christian, and had the opportunity to mix with them. Equality is only a convenient phrase for them. They like to tell us that they're spreading Christianity and Western civilization in order to benefit us, but in their heart of hearts, they don't even consider us human. I'm astounded at their baseness. We can't even share the same graveyard. No matter how able you might be, no matter how great a scholar you might be, your place is always below the white man's. Given what I've achieved for the Church, I should've been a bishop by now. If I haven't, it's because my skin's black. Of course, there're a few exceptions, there always are. But they alter nothing. If the people of this country have sunk into a dismal state, it's because they've been subjugated for so long, because they've been kept uneducated for so long. Despite all the pride in their civilization, you've no idea how base these people can be towards us. Sometimes I think that if I'd only spent a fraction of the energy that

I did for missionary activities, on ridding this country of ignorance, I'd have achieved something truly remarkable. Not that there's much scope for anything like that these days. They tend to send any and every right-thinking patriot to jail, or into exile, or even to the gallows. But there will come the day when the country will become independent, so I was thinking that perhaps . . .'

Father Tuntuni stopped in mid-sentence. Bhuvan Shome noticed that his eyes had filled with tears; he might easily have spoken for the Europeans, but seeing the tears, he held his peace. A month or so after Father Tuntuni left, Bhuvan Shome was unexpectedly promoted. He discovered that it was due to the confidential order of the agent himself. Some months later, a Christian Santhal arrived, carrying a basket of mangoes and a letter. The letter was from the Reverend Ferguson: 'We are deeply grateful to you for the courtesy with which you treated Father Antonio Ghoshal. Father Ghoshal had wanted to send you a basket of mangoes. He would have delivered them to you himself had he been alive, but Father Ghoshal died a few days ago of apoplexy. I was aware of his wish, and have thus taken the liberty of sending John Kacchap to you with the fruit.' Not that the mangoes were all that wonderful, being the sour variety growing on hillsides. But there was no doubt that Father Tuntuni had been a fine man. Later, he had been told that Reverend Ferguson was a great friend of the then agent's. He realized why he had been promoted. Obviously Tuntuni had put in a word with the good Reverend, and set things in motion. But he was prevented from thinking about Tuntuni any further. Bhagiya suddenly started screaming.

'Look master, a bird . . . a bird . . .'

Then he promptly jumped into the river. Bhuvan Shome saw a dead swan was floating past. Bhagiya started swimming in order to catch it. Bhuvan Shome was rather intrigued to begin with, but soon realized what had happened. Obviously, the previous party of hunters had brought the bird down, but had either not noticed that it had fallen or had not been able to retrieve it. Bhagiya was swimming desperately by now, and even Bhuvan Shome was standing up in a state of considerable agitation. In the meantime, something had been happening that he had not taken notice of—the boat had been caught in a current and was drifting away from Bhagiya at speed. What was one supposed to do under such circumstances? Bhuvan Shome tried poling the boat towards the bank; he failed. He also failed to keep his balance, and nearly fell into the river. 'Bhagiya . . . Oy, Bhagiya, the boat's drifting away.'

He couldn't tell whether Bhagiya heard or not; of course these people often pretended to be deaf. In any case, Bhagiya showed no signs of turning back; he was swimming expectantly towards the bird and had nearly reached mid-stream. Meanwhile, the wind speed seemed to be increasing.

'Bhagiya . . . hey you, Bhagiya . . .'

Bhagiya did not even deign to look back, continuing to swim ahead instead. The boat continued to drift towards mid-stream. Bhuvan Shome was quite frightened by now. What had he got himself into? All through accepting a ride in a boat! Was he going to die a helpless death? He suddenly noticed that the boat was drawing water from the bottom. He was reminded of Robinson Crusoe, and promptly started bailing water. He turned to see what Bhagiya was up to. No, no signs of turning whatsoever. The boat proceeded on its course with great rapidity.

'Bhagiyaaaaaa . . .'

It was still not possible to say whether the man had heard. He was still swimming straight towards the swan. Thank God, he had finally caught the bird. He showed him a handful of feathers and started on his return journey. But the boat was drifting away at great speed. Who knows where it was going to stop? There was little else to do but keep bailing. His expensive woollen trousers were covered with mud. It was going to cost five rupees to get it dry-cleaned from Suleman. The man was adept at doing salaam but refused to bring his price down by a paisa. Bhagiya suddenly started shouting, 'The boat's adrift, help, help.' He carried on shouting for a while, as though he was calling for aid. Were there no people in these desolate sand-banks, then? It soon turned out that there were. Three or four large and muscular individuals emerged out of the desolation; they may well have been working in the arhar field. Bhagiya started shouting even louder after he caught sight of them. The men promptly plunged into the river. The boat, however, had drifted a considerable distance by then, and it took the men a good fifteen minutes to catch the boat. Bhagiya arrived with the bird around the same time.

Bhuvan Shome noticed that it was a fairly large pintail. He was very annoyed and shouted, 'Couldn't you hear me calling you?'

Bhagiya nodded that he had heard.

'In that case, why didn't you return?'

Bhagiya was puzzled by the question. He explained that he had jumped into the river in order to recover the bird; so how could he return without completing his task?

Then he said, 'It's for you, anyway.' His expression seemed to say that the person he was stealing for was calling him a thief.

Bhuvan Shome said, 'I don't want it. I'll hunt my own birds. You keep that one.'

Bhagiya's face fell. He had hoped that the babu would praise him for his efforts.

One of the others said, 'Come on, we'll roast it and eat it.'

Bhagiya put the bird on the prow of the boat.

'Look out, a khokna will snatch it away.'

Bhagiya kept poling with a glum expression. He did not even bother to look at the bird. He was mortified by Bhuvan Shome's behaviour.

Bhuvan Shome asked, 'What's a khokna?'

One of the men explained that the khokna was a large hawk-like carrion bird that swooped on dead birds and snatched them away. They often tended to follow hunting parties. One of the men picked up the bird and put it inside the boat. The boat had oars; they started pulling on them.

'Which way shall we head, master?'

Bhuvan Shome answered that he no longer wished to go anywhere by boat. One trip had been more than enough.

In a little while they deposited him on the sandbanks. The boat went its way.

Bhuvan Shome started walking.

V

Bhuvan Shome had lost track of how long he had been walking. On three sides were empty sandbanks. On the fourth was the river—the Ganges. The banks were of varying heights, some high, some low, some others fairly even. They were so high at places that it felt as though he was climbing a small hill. After walking for a while, he started feeling a sense of excitement, as though his youth had returned. He started climbing even the higher sandbanks. After climbing them, he looked around to see if he could spot any birds. As far as he could see, there was no sign of a bird; nor could he hear the cry of a single bird. It was that damned motorboat that was responsible for this disaster. He climbed to the top of one sandbank after the other, then climbed down again.

This carried on for a while. Other than sand, the sandbanks also contained trees, mostly tamarisks. In the tamarisk trees were an unknown species of bird, small in size, buff-coloured, very much like a sparrow but with an unusually long tail—it almost gave the impression of being unbalanced. It had a very sweet call. Moreover, it was a restless little bird, calling continuously, first from one branch and then from another. It would fly from one tamarisk tree to the next and perch, only to fly off again. It was a species unknown to Bhuvan Shome. He had first thought it was a bagri, but then noticed that it was not; it was some other bird altogether. The young man with the binoculars would undoubtedly have told him the Latin name had he been here. There was something else Bhuvan Shome had noticed while walking through these desolate and unpopulated sandbanks:

there were large numbers of crows, yellow-beaked black birds, drongos and bluebreasts. In the distance he could even see a large kite, circling lazily. He noticed two or three different varieties of kingfisher. One small kind was particularly captivating, as bright as an exotic butterfly. He noticed a few pairs of bataan. This reminded him that he had shot a bataan once. No one had been able to eat it; it had too gamey a smell. But they were pleasant-looking birds, walked in a delicate manner, craned their necks to observe anything that approached, then made a little choking sound to fly away. Only to settle somewhere not too far. Suddenly, Bhuvan Shome was reminded that he was missing the 'real' birds—there was not a single goose or duck in sight. Was he going to return empty-handed? But no, he would have to get one bird at least, otherwise Anil would never let him live it down. He would surely find a few further ahead. And if he did not, he would stay in the area overnight, there was certain to be a village nearby. Indeed, Anil had said that there was. He looked at his watch; it was nearly eight o' clock. It was unlikely that he would find any birds at this hour. The birds had flown because of those imbeciles. But how long could they continue to fly, they would have to settle somewhere. He looked down and started walking in a determined manner. The sand was shining in the sun . . .

A little further ahead he noticed the remains of a tattered rope bed as well as the shards of a number of broken pitchers. As he came a little closer, he also noticed that there were some coals strewn around. Someone had obviously cremated a corpse at the spot.

He was suddenly reminded of his father's death. Then his mother's, and his wife's, his two nephews', Birinchilal's, Jagannath's. He had cremated them all and immersed the ashes in the waters of this same river, the Ganges. He had completed the rituals in a faultless manner in each case. But his own death was approaching. Who was going to take his body to the Ganges? Certainly there was no one at home capable of fulfilling this obligation. The lads of the neighbourhood Satkar Samiti would no doubt do the honours. That dyspeptic Nimai, the short-tempered Sridam, the fat Bhombol, the ganja-addict Haren, the alcoholic Fatik—he could suddenly see their faces. Were these the sort of people who would bear his pall? Would the foreign-returned Bilu and ascetic Nipu come as well? 'No they won't, not for me they won't. No one's worried over me. Better luck next time, I mean in the next birth cycle,' Bhuvan Shome muttered to himself, then started walking again.

An incident suddenly came to mind. A few days before his death, Birinchi had wanted to eat rosogollas. Instead of the rosogolla, he had given him a real ticking off. It occurred to him now that he had been wrong. What difference would it have made if he had got him the sweets? The man had died in a few days, anyway. Dr Chandan had agreed to his having the sweets; it was Bhuvan Shome who had refused.

He kept walking in a distracted manner. His pace slowed but he walked for a long time. His reverie was broken by bird calls. He looked up to see a flock of parrots fly past calling loudly, as though they were joking with him. Bhuvan Shome had the feeling that the birds had come for a morning stroll on the riverbank. They were not usual inhabitants of the Ganges banks.

He stopped walking after a while. How long was he going to wander like this? But there was no alternative, really; he had to keep walking. It was imperative that he return with a bird today. The birds had obviously been scared half to death, but surely they had to settle down somewhere. That is where he would go, where he would have to go.

He started walking once again; his legs were aching by now, but he would not stop. There was a huge sandhill in front. Nothing could be seen beyond it. He climbed up with some difficulty. And saw that not far away, a man was sitting on the bank, having cast a line.

He climbed down the sandhill and walked near the man. He noticed that the fellow was sitting with his head between his knees. He had never seen anyone with such long thighs. He looked like someone with his head on the chopping block.

He asked in his usual pidgin Hindi, 'Do you know where the birds nest in these parts?'

The fellow may not have heard him the first time. He repeated his question, in a loud voice. When the man removed his head from the chopping block and looked at him, his gaze suggested that he was a decent sort. He looked a trifle sheepish. When he answered in fluent Bengali, Bhuvan Shome was surprised.

'Keep going. You'll come to a little village after a while. Across the village, you'll find that the Ganges takes a slight bend. There're a lot of birds nesting near the bend. I've seen them myself not long ago.'

'Are you a Bengali?'

'Yes sir, I am. From Sheyakhala village, in Hooghly district. My grandfather left the place to settle in Birbhum. Now that is where we are, near Dubrajpur.'

By now, Bhuvan Shome had realized that he was in the presence of a garrulous fellow.

'What do you do here?'

'I'm a teacher in a minor school, about five miles from here. It's not a particularly wonderful job, but the climate's good. That's why I'm here. I've got dyspepsia you see . . .'

'I carry on straight, do I?'

'That's right, just carry on straight. You'll come to the village in a little while. They're nice fellows there.'

Bhuvan Shome refused to linger any longer and started walking. Hearing about the birds had given him fresh enthusiasm. After walking for a while he did come across a village; or rather, a collection of four or five small thatched huts, the smoke from the morning fires still visible. A little closer, and he could see a little girl collecting cowdung. But a little closer, and he came to a dead halt. Good Lord, there were buffaloes tethered here as well. He stopped for a while, then, maintaining a good distance from the beasts, moved on.

He had intended to rest a little while at the village before setting out in search of the birds. But he was obviously fated to be unlucky that day. He had just arrived near the village when someone shouted, 'Run, babu, run quickly.' He turned to see a buffalo charging straight at him. It was that damned bihaniya. What a disaster! He started running as fast as possible, but how could he outstrip a charging buffalo? Another moment, and he would be gored to death. But the girl collecting cowdung suddenly screamed, 'Subodh, stop where you are.' It worked like a charm. The buffalo stopped dead in its tracks.

Bhuvan Shome was gasping for breath not far away. He saw the girl approaching. She went up to the buffalo and tweaked its ear, 'You naughty creature. Forgotten the last thrashing that I gave you, haven't you, you shameless thing.'

The buffalo took this scolding with a bowed head, then looked at Bhuvan Shome once again. His rage had not yet been mollified. Bhuvan Shome now noticed that there was a rag tied just under the horns. He thought to himself that the beast must have murdered some poor unfortunate, and the rag had no doubt stuck to the horns during the incident.

He was surprised to hear the girl speak Bengali. Was she the daughter of that teacher fellow? And wandering around in this manner, gathering cowdung?

The buffalo was again attempting to advance towards him. The girl said sharply, 'Subodh, heel.'

The buffalo stopped immediately but waved its tail furiously.

'Let's go. I'm going to tie you up, you're far too naughty . . .'

She climbed on to its back without any visible effort. It was difficult to imagine even an expert horse-rider mounting a horse with such little effort.

Bhuvan Shome continued to watch with amazement. That this demonic beast should be called Subodh! And what an amazing young woman. He had read of Mahishasuramardini, but this was the first time he had seen her. What was going on here? The girl was lying on the buffalo's back with her arms around its neck. The beast slowly took her to the village, swaying from side to side.

He began to feel tired. He noticed a raised area not too far away and went and sat on top of it. It was turning into a singularly unlucky morning; he must have started out at a particularly unpropitious moment. It must have been the eggs; they were unlucky things, most unlucky. He'd had a similar experience with eggs once before, in Rajmahal. Had it occurred to him, he would certainly have warned Anil. These modern young people neither knew nor accepted such conventions, but the omelette was still making its presence felt. As long as he could not digest it, his luck would not change.

He sat there staring at the Ganges. A kingfisher was flying around. After staring at the flowing current for a while, he began to feel more peaceful. He also began to feel rested.

'Please sit on the khatiya, master . . .'

Bhuvan Shome turned and saw a towering, mighty-limbed and elderly man respectfully addressing him. The face resembled that of Michael Madhusudan Dutt—or, at least, the beard was similar. Bare-bodied, with a dhoti up to his knees and a dirty sacred thread around his neck. He had not noticed that the man had dragged a frayed khatiya into the middle of the field and covered it with a coloured chador.

The man folded his hands and said, 'Please sit, sir.'

His address was in the honorific mode. The expression on his face seemed equally respectful. Bhuvan Shome came down from the raised spot. The man bowed when doing a namaskar. After returning the greeting, Bhuvan Shome asked 'What is your name?'

'Chaturbhuj Gope.'

A milkman, but with a sacred thread around his neck. Everybody was being initiated into the sacred-thread ceremony these days; which was probably why Brahmins were giving it up in droves. What was the world coming to?

He sat on the khatiya.

Then, he said, in Bengali, 'I've come for bird shooting. I was told that there're ducks nesting here.'

'There're plenty of birds all right . . .' the man replied in his local language.

'Where?'

'By Nawalkishore's field. Straight east . . .'

Bhuvan Shome rose from the khatiya. It was already very late, it would not do to waste any more time. Since he had finally found out where they were, it made sense to see for himself. His tiredness seemed to be miraculously dispelled at this news. Speaking in the language of Ballia, Chaturbhuj Gope suggested that he rest on the bed for a while before starting. The birds stayed at the spot all day. But Bhuvan Shome was in no mood to heed such requests. He lit his cigar, shouldered his gun and set off.

A narrow lane went through the village. He took the lane. The bihaniya was tied to a stout stake by means of a strong metal chain. It was sitting, but rose with fire in its eyes as soon as it caught sight of him. He strode past rapidly. Beyond the village there were more sandbanks, but fairly even ones. He had no difficulty negotiating them. As soon as he climbed down, he could see a green field. It had to be Nawalkishore's. The ducks were somewhere nearby, according to Chaturbhuj Gope. He started forward with redoubled enthusiasm. As he came near the field, he noticed a number of men cutting grass while a few others were uprooting something.

'Are there any birds here?'

'Yes, master. Just a little further on.'

Bhuvan Shome felt curious. What were those people uprooting?

He found out that they were chickpea plants. But why? Because they were growing too close together and needed to be thinned out. The uprooted plants would not be wasted. The greens were eaten by people and also used as animal feed. The entire plant could be roasted to make odha. It was delicious to eat.

'Go straight, shall I?'

'Yes, master. But you'd better throw your smoke away, or the birds will fly from the smell.'

He had just lit the cigar. It was still almost whole; but he threw it away.

There was a narrow lane through the field. After going down the road for a while, he could see the bend of the river. And hear the call of geese. And of curlews. After going forward a bit, he was left neither here nor there. There was indeed a flock of geese nesting at the place. And a flock of curlews. He started advancing most cautiously. He had to come within range; he certainly ought not to fire until he could see the feathers on the geese clearly. He had a double-barrelled gun. He loaded both barrels, then slowly advanced, holding the gun concealed behind him. He looked like a giant comma creeping on the ground. After proceeding like this for a while, he squatted at one spot. Then *boom boom*, he unloaded both barrels, one after the other. The geese flew away with much cackling. He stood up and looked around him with great hope, but no, not one bird had fallen. He felt enormously disappointed. And immediately there was loud female laughter behind him. He turned to see that it was the same young woman, the one who had ridden the buffalo. She had covered her mouth with a corner of her dress, and was laughing merrily behind it.

What a bad-mannered young woman! Of course, everyone was bad-mannered these days! He was reminded of the time he had slipped on a banana peel, much to the amusement of his nephew Gobu. He had given the boy a tight smack on the face; of course, he had only been able to do that because the boy was his nephew. He certainly would not be able to smack this girl. So he pretended that he had not heard the mocking laughter and carried on staring at the flying birds. He went forward a little, and decided to lie in wait for the birds. Once the birds returned, which they no doubt would do, he would try once again. He had to take at least one bird with him. He would lose face for ever, otherwise.

'Excuse me . . .'

It was the wretched girl. She was following him.

'What is it?'

The girl came a little closer.

'Why're you shooting at those perfectly innocent birds? They've not harmed you, have they?'

What an opinionated little monster! And smiling cheekily as well.

'You don't eat meat, I suppose?' she asked.

'No.'

'But you do eat vegetables, don't you?'

'Yes, of course I do.'

'Well, what harm have they done, that they should be cut into little pieces and be eaten? They're alive as well, they feel pain when you cut them.'

'Do they? I didn't know that.'

She started wrapping the cloth around her index finger.

'But vegetables and birds aren't the same, are they? Vegetables don't bleed when they're cut, they don't scream in pain, either. But if you kill birds, they bleed, and scream.'

She pressed her lips together and made an expression which suggested that she had demonstrated some irrefutable logic.

Little Miss Know-All, aren't you? thought Bhuvan Shome to himself.

The girl started again.

'You like bird meat, do you?'

'I used to once, but not any more.'

'In that case, why've you come to kill the poor things?'

No rational answer came to his mind.

He carried on without answering. But the girl kept following him; she was not one to let go.

'Since you don't eat, why don't you stop killing them? Let them go.'

'I have to kill at least one bird today. Otherwise I'll lose a wager, and lose face as well.'

'Oh, you've made a wager, have you?'

It was as though she had finally found a logical reason for his behaviour. She remained quiet for a few minutes, with a thoughtful expression on her face. Then she said, 'But the way you're going about it, you'll not get a single bird. You're sure to lose your bet.'

Bhuvan Shome was experiencing precisely the same anxiety.

'So what do you think I should do about it?'

'Will you do exactly as I tell you to?'

'Tell me what it is I have to do.'

'You can come with me for a start.'

To begin with, Bhuvan Shome could not make up his mind whether he ought to follow or not. Ought he to waste his time on the fibs of an impertinent chit of a girl? What did she know about bird shooting? Who knows what trouble he would land in this time, the eggs not yet having been digested?

'Come along.'

There seemed no alternative but to go with this stubborn creature. One would have to wait and see what happened. All one would lose would be a bit of time, anyway.

The girl turned back towards the village; Bhuvan Shome followed her. He had not experienced any difficulty climbing down the shallow slope of the sandbank. On his way up, he felt slightly short of breath. Oblivious to all this, the girl went up skipping. And occasionally looked back with a faint grin, brushing her masses of curly hair away from her face. He was reminded of Togor; Togor was much like this.

They became acquainted en route.

'Are you the teacher's daughter?'

'Teacher, which teacher . . .?'

'The one who's fishing there.'

'No. Why should I be his daughter? My father's name is Chaturbhuj Gope, the one who brought you the khatiya.'

My word! To imagine that hirsute fellow's daughter could speak such excellent Bengali.

'But how did you manage to learn Bengali?'

'I was brought up by my maternal uncles who live in Pakur. I was also taught Bengali after I came here, by the man who's fishing, as a matter of fact. He's a very good teacher, if a trifle deaf . . .'

That he might be talking to Vaidehi, the young teenaged wife of Sakhi-chand, the man he planned to file a report against, was a possibility that never occurred to Bhuvan Shome. Nor was there any reason for it.

He started talking about something else

'That buffalo would've killed me if you hadn't been there today. He certainly obeys you, doesn't he? He stopped immediately.'

'Well, of course he does. I've brought him up from when he was a baby. As long as he was a child, he was very gentle. He used to spend most of his time sleeping. That's why I'd named him Subodh. But the older he's getting, the more aggressive he's becoming. He's been out this morning and got into a fight. He's got a big cut on his forehead. I've had to put tincture of iodine on it and bandage it.'

Bhuvan Shome realized that the injury was the result of one of Bhutta's blows. But he kept quiet about it.

'Tincture of iodine will help the healing, won't it?'

'Yes, it will.'

'Are you a Bengali?'

'Yes.'

'Then why're you wearing Western clothes?'

'Impertinent little so-and-so,' said Bhuvan Shome to himself. To the girl he said, 'It's easier to walk in Western clothes.'

'Could you keep pace with my father? He gets up at three every morning, and walks to Hansbar, only to return in the afternoon. He leaves again after his noon meal, and returns at ten in the evening. Hansbar is five miles from here.'

'Why does he go there?'

'We have some land there.'

'I notice that he hadn't gone there today.'

'No. He had some work here.'

Just then someone could be heard shouting at a distance, 'Bidiya . . . hey, Bidiyaaaaa . . .'

'Father's calling. He'd sent me to look for you. Please don't complain about me. Instead, tell him his daughter Bidiya is like Lakshmi. All right?'

Without waiting for an answer, Bidiya started running.

Bhuvan Shome looked at the sky once again. He could no longer see the geese. They must have settled somewhere. He noticed that a small white cloud was floating in the sky like a duck. As though the sky was a blue lake. He stared at it for a while. One of the people working in the field suddenly piped up—

'Return after an hour or so, master. They'll be hiding somewhere for a while.'

There was no shortage of people doling out unwanted advice. As though he was unaware that he would have to wait.

He started walking towards Bidiya's village. After going a short distance, he met Bidiya returning.

'Why're you walking so slowly? Come quickly. I've just had a quite unnecessary ticking off from father because of you. He said to me, "What did you come running for, leaving him behind?" Come along now . . .'

Bhuvan Shome walked a little faster. As he reached Chaturbhuj Gope's house, the man came out. He greeted him respectfully once again, and requested him to sit on the khatiya. The substance of what he said, in the Ballia dialect, was as follows. He had heard the sound of gunfire. Random shooting was not going to help Bhuvan Shome.

This was not the way to hunt birds in this area. He would have to use other techniques. He should eat something, and rest for a while. Later on, Bidiya would arrange things for him. She knew all about such matters. The girl might be young, but she was very bright, even though a touch naughty. Her gaona was due in a few months' time, but at the moment she had no sense of worldly matters. She had no idea how to talk to people, or indeed, how to walk decorously. She was just running around like an unruly heifer.

Bidiya started gesticulating from behind her father.

In his demotic Hindi, Bhuvan Shome said, 'Your daughter is a veritable Lakshmi.' He had rarely lied so outrageously in his life.

Chaturbhuj's leonine face lit up with joy, his eyes closed. After being overwhelmed for a while, he said, 'It's all because of your blessings . . .'

Then he turned to Bidiya and said, 'Get some dahi-chiwda. Give the master something to eat.'

Bhuvan Shome immediately felt apprehensive. He explained he had eaten a little while ago and no longer felt hungry. From behind, Bidiya said sharply, 'But you must eat something, for the sake of my father's feelings. He feels hurt if a guest leaves our home without eating.'

Bhuvan Shome looked at Chaturbhuj, to see that the man was standing with folded hands. He was not saying anything, but the expression on his face made his feelings clear. Bhuvan Shome was unable to refuse.

Bidiya brought a shining, high-rimmed brass dish, heaped with thick reddish-coloured chiwda.

'Well, she's really acting like Lakshmi, isn't she?' he said to himself.

Then she brought a clay cup filled with yoghurt, and a few lumps of molasses. And a bunch of plantains.

Chaturbhuj remained standing with folded hands.

Bhuvan Shome asked, 'Do you have any shops nearby?'

'No, everything's home-made.'

'Really? That's wonderful. Why don't you give your father some as well? We could eat together.'

'He won't eat until you've finished.'

Chaturbhuj smiled and nodded his head to signify that what Bidiya was saying was right. He was feeling quite overwhelmed in any case. That his little girl should be conversing fluently in Bengali with an elderly Bengali gentleman had transported him to seventh heaven. He was unable to say a word.

Bhuvan Shome ate as much as he could. After he had finished, Chatur-bhuj sat down to eat. Bhuvan Shome was astonished by the amounts the man managed to consume. At least half a seer of the chiwda, with at least a seer of yoghurt, a quarter seer of molasses and six plantains seemed to vanish into his maw, with no difficulties whatsoever. He drank down a pitcher of water without once touching it to his lips, then burped.

After washing his mouth, Chaturbhuj said that the babu should rest for a bit. He was off to his field now. Bidiya would arrange things for him in a while.

Bhuvan Shome was stunned into silence. Was the man really planning to walk five miles after such a gargantuan meal?

In a short while, after putting on a pair of thick buffalo-hide sandals—they were stuck between the roof slats outside—and carrying a huge, well-oiled bamboo stick, Chaturbhuj Gope set off. Before leaving, he reassured Bhuvan Shome many times—everything was going to be fine, he ought to rest for a little while.

Bidiya turned up to say, 'Please lie down for a while. I'm just going out for a minute.'

'But aren't you going to eat something?'

'I've eaten at ten o' clock. I still maintain my schoolday habits, I'm afraid.'

Bidiya started mixing sattu with water in a small dish.

'Who's that for?'

'It's for Sari. It worries me. I don't know who'll feed her when I've gone to my in-laws'.'

'But who is Sari? Your sister?'

'Why should she be my sister? It's my pet bird.'

'Oh. Where is it?'

'It's wandering around at the moment. But it'll be back soon. And if it doesn't find its food, it'll make a great racket . . .'

Bidiya brought out an empty cage. She put the little dish containing the food inside the cage, and hung it outside.

Then she said, 'Can you see that palm tree there? Come a little this way, you can see it from here. She was born in that palm tree last Baisakh. One day I noticed that she had fallen from the tree. Luckily I was around, so I picked her up and put her in the cage and fed her. Her mother used to feed her insects and things. I fed her on sattu. Then one day, when she was able to fly, I saw that she had left the cage and was flying about. I was very pleased, I can tell you. I mean, I wasn't looking forward to taking care of her for the rest of her life. But would you believe it, the next day she was back in her cage. And she had ruffled her feathers and was chirping away at me, as if to say, give me my food, give me my food. So I did. Since then she comes every day . . .'

Bhuvan Shome was fascinated.

'When does she come?'

'There's no fixed time. And it's not as though I wait for her arrival. I leave her food in the cage and go about my business. When I return, I find that she has finished her food and gone. She might not come if she sees you here. My brother was visiting once, with a camera. He wanted to take her picture, but she wouldn't settle even for an instant. Lie down for a while. I'll dress Subodh's wound with some more tincture of iodine. Let's take the bed indoors. You shan't be able to sleep if the light falls on your eyes, and Sari won't turn up either. Hold that end of the bed, will you? I can't lift it by myself.'

Bhuvan Shome had no desire to enter the house. But he had realized that it was not going to be possible to disobey her. Just like Togor, and as stubborn.

They managed to drag the bed in between the two of them.

'Lie down for an hour or so.'

'I'm not used to sleeping during daytime.'

'Lie down with your eyes shut for a while. I'm just coming . . .'

She left with a small bottle of tincture of iodine. Bhuvan Shome noticed that one of the shelves in the room was covered with various medicine bottles. He lay down reluctantly. But he had to get up almost immediately. Whose picture was that? It seemed a most familiar face. He rose and went near the photograph. It was that Sakhichand Yadav. How did that scoundrel's photograph come to be here?

'You're not lying down yet.'

Bidiya had returned.

'Subodh's head has a really nasty gash. I noticed it was still oozing blood. The tincture will stop it, won't it? I had sent word to Bibhuti-babu, the doctor in Bairiya. He sent the iodine across. It'll do the trick, won't it?'

'Yes, it will. But don't put too much of it. I'm told that if you apply it more than once a day, the wound becomes worse instead of healing. Now tell me, whose photograph is this?'

Bidiya turned her face and blushed.

Then she said in a soft voice, 'No one's.'

'It's someone's, certainly. Who is he to you?'

'My husband.'

Bidiya left the room at a run.

Sakhichand Yadav was Bidiya's husband!

What a strange coincidence!

He sat down on the khatiya. There was no sign of Bidiya for nearly ten minutes. After that, a bird's chirping could be heard from the verandah. Bidiya entered from a back door, as silently as a ghost and said, 'Sari's here. Come and see.'

As soon as Bhuvan Shome arrived on the verandah, the bird flew away . . .

'It was frightened of you.'

Bhuvan Shome returned to the room.

Bidiya came in as well.

'I know your husband, Sakhichand Yadav.'

'You do?'

'Yes. He's a very naughty fellow.'

'You're quite right. Do you know what he writes to me? That I should write him one letter a day. He's sent me coloured writing paper and a fountain pen. But how am I supposed to send him a letter each day? The post office is five miles from here—who's going to take the letter each day? I managed to persuade Makkhu to post one once, but he can hardly be expected to go every day . . .'

'You're right, of course. Who is this Makkhu person?'

'He's our charvaha, our herdsman.'

'Oh.'

'How did you meet him? Where did you meet him?'

'I work in the railways as well.'

'Is that so? You know, I've heard that one of your senior bosses is called Shome Sahib. He spends all his time making reports about people. My husband's written to me to say that he's been reported as well. Has he ever filed a report about you?'

'No.'

Bhuvan Shome's condition was indescribable.

'He says that this Shome Sahib is a nasty piece of goods. He even dismissed his own son. Just like my bihaniya—all he can do is gore people.'

She burst into laughter.

Bhuvan Shome said, 'Yes, he's a hard man. Sakhichand was taking bribes . . .'

Bidiya turned like a tigress defending her young.

'Why're you calling it "bribe"? Just call it an "extra". He helps the passengers out and they pay him something to show their gratitude. This Shome Sahib's just a dog in the manger. He's upset that some-one's making a few paisas, and reports him.'

Bhuvan Shome considered it politic to keep quiet.

'Do you know this Bhuvan Shome? Please, explain to him that if he loses his job, I'll never be able to go to my in-laws'.'

'I'll tell him.'

Bhuvan Shome was utterly embarrassed. But he knew well what he was going to do. He would have to send the report. He was never willingly going to be derelict in his duty. Only yesterday he had told the lad on the steamer, 'We're members of the old school, our motto is *duty first, self last.*'

'Aren't you going to sleep?'

'I can't sleep during the day.'

'In that case, why don't we make preparations for the hunt?'

Bidiya soon returned with two grimy, tattered pieces of clothing.

'Change your clothes, and wear these instead.'

'Wear these clothes? What d'you mean?'

'The geese will run away as soon as they see a gentleman wearing clean, washed clothes. But even if you get very close to them in these clothes, they won't run away. They'll think you're just another peasant. Let me tell you what I've decided. Load your gun and give it to me. I'll take it and hide in the field. They wouldn't fly away seeing me under normal circumstances, but they might if they see the gun. So I'll go as surreptitiously as possible and give you a signal when I'm really close. Put on this cloth turban, and when you see me signal, come straight to me carrying a bundle of chickpea plants on your head. You'll see, they won't fly away, because they'll think you're one more labourer. Then you can fire, and win your bet. How much did you bet? You'll give me a share, won't you?'

Bidiya started smiling mischievously.

'It wasn't a bet for money. It was a bet on my pride. They think that I can't shoot straight. I want to show them that I can shoot birds as well as they can.'

'Have you been here before?'

'No. I've been to places like Dilarpur, Baghadhbil, Kataha, Fasiyatal and so on. But this is the first time I've come here. Now I feel I shouldn't have bothered.'

Bidiya sounded like a mother coaxing a small child.

'There're loads of birds here. I'm sure you'll be able to get one. Now change out of those clothes and wear the stuff I've got for you. And load the gun and hand it to me. I'll get myself into place.'

'But why don't I come with you? If you can creep about, so can I.'

'No you can't. You're far too tall. Just do as I tell you.'

'But those clothes are filthy.'

'But that's precisely what we need. They're not scared of people wearing dirty clothes. It's people wearing clean, washed clothes, they're scared of. Of course, there's one more thing you could try. Do you think you could pretend to be a tree? But you'll have to stand for a long while.'

'How's that?'

'I'll cut some tamarisk branches and tie them all over you. From a distance you'll look exactly like a tamarisk tree. The gun'll have to be hidden inside the branches as well. Then you walk forward very slowly. Just a little, and then stop. Then forward once again . . .'

Bidiya demonstrated how he was to move.

'When you get very close to them, you can fire. If you can go very slowly towards them, they'll think you're a tamarisk tree, and won't fly away. Now tell me which idea you prefer and I'll make the necessary preparations.'

'Isn't there any other way?'

'No. Of course one could always do like that other lot, this morning. But you don't have a motorboat. They frightened the birds into flight, then all of them started shooting the birds on the wing. As a result, a few birds fell into the water. But you can't manage that. You haven't got a boat, and you're alone as well. Just do as I tell you and I'm sure you'll get your bird. The zamindar of Nawabgunj's son, Chhabila-babu, hunts birds in this manner. I learnt the trick from him. He was a labourer once, and a tamarisk tree the other time. He killed scores of birds.'

Bhuvan Shome had suddenly become rather undecided about what to do. From time to time, he had kept saying to himself: Never mind the birds, go home. But he kept seeing Chhottu Sen, Kartik and Anil's—particularly Anil's—faces, and changed his mind. He would have to take at least one bird back, if he wanted to salvage some pride.

'I think you ought to try dressing like a labourer to start with. If that doesn't work, you can try being a tree. Load the gun and give it to me . . .'

Bhuvan Shome made up his mind. One could but try. He loaded his gun and handed it over to her. He locked it. The girl was so restless and cheeky, she might cause an accident.

'Change your clothes quickly and come. I'll go quietly through the arhar field. I'll let the labourers working in the Nawalkishore field know. They'll give you a bundle of chickpea plants. I'll be somewhere near the place where you fired your first shots. I'll sit down wherever I spot the geese. When I give you the signal, come over. All right?'

Bidiya left with the gun. Bhuvan Shome climbed out of his clothes and wore Makkhu's clothes instead. God, what a smell. He'd obviously never washed them. It reminded him of Chuluha. Many years ago, he had had a servant named Chuluha. The man was a giant. But he had a fancy for tight vests. He would deliberately choose round-necked vests a few sizes too small for him. Three or four people would be required to get the thing on him. The vests tended to be so tight that, for a few hours after first wearing them, the man would not be able to bring his arms down. And once he wore the vest—that was it. He would never take it off. It would simply fall off him in tatters. These people never washed their clothes if they could help it.

When he came out clad in filthy knee-length clothes, his feet and upper body bare, and with a piece of filthy cloth wrapped around his head as a turban, Bhuvan Shome looked a sight for sore eyes. His chest and back were covered with hair and these had not been in such intimate contact with light and air for a long time. It was truly a hair-raising situation. Even though it was nearly noon, and the sun had come out, he could feel the nip in the air. However, Nawalkishore's field was only a brisk walk away. He was not feeling as uncomfortable as he had thought he would. In fact he felt as though he had been born again, as though a form of childish excitement had returned. He reached Nawalkishore's field at a very brisk pace indeed, almost at a run.

The labourers were still working in the field. They grinned when they saw him.

A young labourer bared a mouthful of teeth. 'The master's turned into a labourer in his greed for birds.'

At another time Bhuvan Shome would have got annoyed at the comment. Now, however, he laughed and sat down next to them. 'Not greed, obstinacy. I have to bag a bird today. Where's Bidiya?'

A labourer came out of the field. Bhuvan Shome followed the man. When they reached the spot where he had previously fired from, he noticed that there was neither any sign of birds nor of Bidiya.

'Hey, Bidiya . . . Hey hey . . .'

The labourer started shouting with his hand on one ear.

'Don't shout so loudly. All the birds'll fly away.'

The man smiled and explained that the birds would not be frightened off by their shouting. They constantly shouted in this manner; the birds remained where they were. He then shouted once again, with his hand on one ear. There was no response from Bidiya.

Bhuvan Shome asked the man to bring him a bundle of chickpea plants. He had decided to go up to the river, carrying the bundle on his head.

The fellow returned with a bundle, and said with a toothy grin, 'How 'bout one of those fat smokes, master?'

He was asking for a cigar.

'Haven't got one with me at the moment. They're all at Bidiya's place. I'll give you one later.'

He was walking with the bundle on his head. But where were the birds? He couldn't see any, other than terns, kingfishers and the sparrow-like birds on the tamarisk trees. After walking for a long time, he finally heard the call of geese. And caught sight of Bidiya. He was stunned to see her. The girl had knotted her sari around her waist, tied the gun to her back and was crawling up a sandbank like a reptile. She climbed up the sandbank and looked downwards. The Ganges was right below. She was a brave young woman; if the fragile sand-bank collapsed, she would fall straight into the river and to her death.

Bhuvan Shome watched with bated breath. Nothing untoward happened. Bidiya came down from the sandbank. Not by walking down, but by holding the gun high above her head and sliding. Like children using a slide in a park. She started looking around when she reached the bottom, until she spotted Bhuvan Shome. When she started beckoning him with rapid hand signals, he moved towards her. He had heard the geese calling earlier; as he came closer, he could hear them more clearly. Then, he could see them. He went very close to them but they refused to fly away. Bidiya demonstrated how to walk: 'Walk bent over.' He promptly walked bent over. As soon as he came near Bidiya, she handed him the gun and whispered, 'Lots of large ducks there, just beneath the sandbank. Climb to the top, and you can fire lying down. They're just underneath. Give me the gun. I'll hold it while you crawl up. I'll give it to you when you reach the top.'

Bhuvan started climbing just as he had seen Bidiya doing. Bidiya climbed up behind him, holding the gun. After reaching the top, he peered over carefully. The spot was full of ducks, geese, teal and so on. All within fifty yards' range.

Bidiya carefully handed him the gun.

He fired both barrels, *bang . . . bang*, after aiming for a long time. The birds scattered with loud cries. Bidiya ran down.

So did he.

Not one bird had fallen.

VI

Nearly an hour has passed. Bhuvan Shome is sitting on the sandbank; his appearance is extremely strange. Bare-torsoed, with a tattered filthy cloth up to his knees and a filthy cloth wrapped round his head. His chest, back, moustache, all sand-bespattered. Bidiya has gone to fetch tamarisk branches. She has assured him that he will definitely be successful if he pretends to be a tamarisk tree. Definitely, certainly successful. Bhuvan Shome is waiting, and hoping. Something inside him tells him that this is true. The birds will return to this same spot. He is also wondering about something else, something that still amazes him. Why had he burst into tears like that? He had never cried in his life; not at the death of his father, or mother, or wife, or even Togor—he had never cried at anyone's death. When the Marwari trader, Bishnudas, had their house seized because of debts, and the entire family had been turned out on the streets, he had not cried a single tear. But what had gone wrong with him today? Just because he had not been able to bring a bird down? Because his hands shook due to age? Were these reasons to cry? After all, ageing was a natural process. And of all the things, to cry in front of that little slip of a girl! Even though he had told her that the sand had got into his eyes, one look at her face had convinced him that she had realized the truth. She had understood all right, but she had not said a single word. Just stared at him with a look of incredulity in her eyes. Before leaving, she had told him, 'Please sit here. I'll be back with the branches. The geese will return very soon. I'm sure you'll get one this time.'

He would have to get one. He was not going to leave this spot without a bird; even if he had to stay here all night.

He stared at the sandbank in silence. Suddenly, he felt that his life was exactly like the sandbank—utterly empty. No one anywhere, nothing to see in any direction. At least the sandbank by the river had birds nesting on it, boats mooring, peasants working, people like Bidiya building homes nearby. His life was an unmitigated desert, not a mere sandbank. A desert without either oases or mirages. 'Never mind, better luck next time.' Meaning in the next birth. 'May I not be born in this country in my next birth.' He fell silent as soon as he said it. No, there was no point in blaming the country. The people that he had met since the morning—Bhutta, Bhagiya, Bhikhan, Chaturbhuj, Bidiya—were hardly bad people. Were the people in other countries any better than them? No, it was not the fault of the country—it was just his miserable luck.

Bidiya arrived, dragging a bundle of tamarisk branches behind her, along with some rope. She was gasping.

'Come on, let's get these tied on you quickly. I noticed a pair of curlews in that direction. They haven't settled anywhere yet, but they will, very soon. Somewhere close by.'

She started tying the branches all over Bhuvan Shome.

'Hide the gun among the branches in front. Have you loaded it?'

'Yes.'

'The curlews are going to settle here. Stand still. Don't move at all. I'll be inside the arhar field.'

A tamarisk-covered Bhuvan Shome stood silently. Five, ten, then fifteen minutes passed. He was looking at his watch from time to time. Another five minutes passed. He waited, motionless. They would definitely come; since Bidiya had said so, they would most definitely come.

'Caaw . . . aaaaaa, caaaaw . . . aaaaaaa.'

There they were. A shiver of anticipation passed over his body. But why had they become silent after one cry? Why weren't they calling any more? Where had they gone? He wanted to turn around and see, but did not dare. Because Bidiya had warned him against it. She was watching his every move from the arhar field. He waited silently.

'Caaw . . . aaaaaaa, caaaaw . . . aaaaaa.'

How many? Sounded like a lot. He held his breath and waited.

'Cawaa . . . aaaa, caaaw . . . aaaaaaa.'

A pair of curlews came and sat right in front of him. Very close to him. I'll let them settle down for a bit, before I fire, thought Bhuvan Shome. He waited for a minute, then fired.

Both the birds flew away.

Bhuvan Shome stood there, thunderstruck.

'It's fallen. One's fallen . . .'

Bidiya ran down screaming.

Fallen? Where? He had seen both the birds fly away. Quickly, he got rid of the tamarisk branches. He could not see Bidiya anywhere. Where had she rushed off to? Then he noticed she was bringing a live curlew with her.

'Here you are. The shot grazed its foot. It fell out of sheer fright. You can take it back alive. Just as well it isn't dead. You've won your bet, and the bird's alive. You can keep it as a pet if you want to. Do you think it can become a pet?'

Bhuvan Shome was speechless.

The labourers came running from the field. They tied the bird's wings and legs with rope so that it would not be able to fly away. They even made a little noose arrangement so that he could hang it from his hand. It was a large curlew. One of them looked at the neck and said that it was a male.

Bhuvan Shome returned to Chaturbhuj Gope's home with the bird in hand.

Bidiya followed him.

'Are you leaving just now?'

'Yes. I must be going, it's nearly two o' clock.'

'Won't you have something to eat?'

'No.'

He changed out of Makkhu's clothes and back into his own, then washed his face and hands. His entire body felt gritty with sand. After some hesitation he produced a five-rupee note from his wallet—the same note that Bhagiya had picked up.

'Here, take this. Buy some sweets from me.'

'Take money from you? Why should I do that?'

'Give it to your labourers.'

'No, you don't have to give anything to anybody. We don't take money from guests.'

What could he say to that? He stood there for an awkward moment or two, then shouldered his gun and said, 'Well, I'll be off then. By the way, give these cigars to the labourers. I'd promised them. Goodbye, then.'

'Yes, goodbye.'

Suddenly, Bidiya bent low and did a pranam.

'Please come again.'

'I will.'

Bhuvan Shome had walked some distance.

'Please, please . . .'

He turned to see Bidiya running after him.

'If you meet Shome Sahib, do have a word with him, please. If he's dismissed . . .'

'I'll tell him. But if he's taken a bribe, there's nothing Shome Sahib can do. After all, he's got a job too, you know.'

'I know. But please, tell him all the same.'

Bidiya left.

Bhuvan Shome was walking, the gun on his shoulder, the bird dangling from his hand. He was not even aware of where it was he was going. He was just walking on the road next to the Ganges. He was very tired but unaware of that as well. He was simply walking mechanically. 'Caaw . . . aaaaaa.'

He started. Was it this one?

'Caaaww . . . aaaaaaaa.'

He could see it now. Another curlew was flying overhead. Was it this one's companion?

He travelled a bit further.

'Caaw . . . aaaaaa, caaaw . . . aaaaaaa.'

It was flying ahead of him, just overhead.

'Let's get this one as well.'

He put the trussed bird down and loaded his gun. It was flying overhead but seemed to come down a bit. He fired, he missed. The curlew kept circling. He frowned at it for a while. Was it trying to run away? He fired again. Missed again. 'The hell with it.'

He picked up the tied bird and started walking once more. After a while he could hear it again, 'Caaw . . . aaaa.' The bird in his hand started struggling. Bhuvan Shome started walking rapidly. He was practically running by now. After a while he was gasping. He found a spot and sat down.

'Caaw . . . aaaaaa, caw . . . aaaaa, caaaaw . . . aaaaaaa.'

The curlew was keeping pace with him. As soon as he sat down, it started circling overhead. He put his hand in his pocket and discovered that there were two cartridges remaining. But he no longer had any desire to shoot. The curlew kept calling while circling overhead. He could see Bhikhan Gope's boat moored at a distance. There was no one nearby. He did not feel like walking to Mahendar Singh's dota. He would rather walk all the way to the ghat.

'Caaw . . . aaaa, caaaw . . . aaaaaaa.'

The curlew was staying with him. What a nuisance! Was the creature going to accompany him home? He kept walking without looking upwards, as briskly as possible. But the bird was persistent; it stayed with him.

'Caaw . . . aaaaa, caaaaw . . . aaaaaaa.'

This carried on for half an hour. Then something rather extraordinary happened. He was no poet, but a strange fantasy took shape in his mind. He felt as though the male bird, the one he had injured and tied, was Sakhi-chand, and the one flying overhead was Bidiya. He thought that behind the 'caaw . . . aaaaaa' he could perceive someone saying 'Please, let him go. If he's dismissed, I won't be able to go to my in-laws'.'

The bird kept struggling in his grasp.

The sun was lowering in the western horizon. Bhuvan Shome was walking through the sandbanks. The bird was circling overhead, still calling out piteously. He was holding on to the bird grimly. After walking a bit further, he came to a green field. His eyes felt soothed; it was as if someone had spread a deep green carpet there. A man was working in the field. Bhuvan Shome walked towards him. The man came as soon as he was called.

'Cut the ropes from the bird.'

The man had a sickle in his hand. He cut the ropes with ease. Bhuvan Shome set the bird free. In a flash it had flown to its companion. The birds flew off, calling to each other.

Bhuvan Shome stared after them for as long as they were visible.

VII

The boat was late that evening as well.

Sakhichand Yadav was sitting in his room, reading *Durgesh Nandini*. He was unable to decide who was more like Vaidehi, Tilottama or Ayesha. He was surprised to hear the pointsman Vasdeo's voice.

'Sakhichand, the babusahib's here.'

Sahib? Now which sahib might this be? He came out and saw, to his astonishment, that it was none other than the great Mr Bhuvan Shome himself.

Bhuvan Shome turned to Vasdeo and said, 'You can go now.'

Bhuvan Shome asked Sakhichand a peculiar question.

'Is there a tulsi plant in this house?'

'A tulsi plant? Why no, sir.'

'I want a few tulsi leaves.'

'The Boses have one. Shall I get some?'

'Do that.'

Sakhichand left quickly. Bhuvan Shome sat on the chair and started idly moving his foot. Sakhichand returned in about ten minutes, with a handful of tulsi leaves.

'Shall I wrap them in a piece of paper?'

'No. Where's the water in that pitcher from?'

'From the Ganges, sir.'

'Pour it in a bucket.'

Sakhichand was more and more astonished. But he simply did not have the gumption to ask questions. He poured a quantity in a bucket.

'Throw the leaves into it. And throw this coin in as well.'

He pulled out a copper paisa coin from his wallet.

'Now swear by copper, tulsi and Ganga water that you'll never take a bribe again. That's right. Hold all three things in hand, and say loudly—I will not take a bribe again. Say it loudly.'

Sakhichand had no option but to say it.

'Now keep this in mind. I'm letting you go this time. In the future, think about your promise. And one more thing. Let Anil know that I've left by this boat. Can you make sure he gets the message tonight?'

'I'll go myself, sir, as soon as my duty's over.'

'Let him know that I'd got a curlew.'

'Yes, sir.'

Bhuvan Shome rose and left the room.

As soon as Sakhichand tried to follow him with the lantern, he said, 'I don't need the light.' And strode off.

It is not possible to publish the detailed letter contained in the pink envelope that Jhaksu the peon handed over to Mrs Vaidehi Yadav, from her husband Sakhichand Yadav, some fifteen days later. I am only quoting the bit that is pertinent to this story. Sakhichand had written as a postscript, 'Beloved, there is a bit of good news. Bhuvan Shome did not file a report in my name, after all. I'm told that I am being transferred to Sahebganj. It's a very good station, that. Lots of extras . . .'

Not A Demon

A head of scruffy hair and bright but sunken dark eyes. Wearing tight trousers and a shortsleeved shirt, both frayed. A pair of worn sandals on his feet, and a cheap plywood box under his arm. The box is almost swathed in rope. He might well have been fair at one time, but now his complexion is sallow. The gaunt cheeks are covered by a scraggly beard. The expression on his face is best described as truculent.

It is evening. He enters a narrow alley. A few yards in and to the left—an even narrower lane. He enters this alley and stops in front of a dilapidated house.

'Daamu . . . Daamu . . .'

It has become necessary to shout, because the door has neither a knocker nor a bolt. It looks frail enough to be knocked down with a push.

Daamu comes out.

He is wearing only a tattered lungi.

'It's Biltu, isn't it? How are . . . ?'

'Lost my job. They put me in the clink for ten days. Not a jot of evidence, but they insisted that I was a Naxalite. Only God knows how many people I had had to beg, to say nothing of bribe, in order to get that job. But they threw me out—just like that.'

'Hadn't I warned you not to hang around with that Keshto? He's a Naxal all right, no doubt about it.'

'I've no idea whether he's a Naxalite or not. But I do know that he's been my friend since childhood, and that he's been there whenever I've needed help. So what do you mean, I shouldn't hang around with him?'

'You know exactly what I mean. Lost your job, haven't you? By the way, what's that under your arm?' Without answering, Biltu said, 'Let's go to the riverside.'

'You can go on your own, can't you? Why drag me along?'

''Cause I'm flat broke, and you can pay the bus fare.'

'What makes you think I've got money? I'm unemployed as well, you know. And I can't go on borrowing from my uncle, can I? I mean, he's always good for it, but damn it all, I feel so embarrassed.'

'Your uncle's a gent. Borrow five rupees, there's a good chap.'

'Five rupees? Whatever for?'

'I want to take a boat ride.'

'Take a boat ride? You're crazy.'

'Just feeling low, that's all. A boat ride on the river might cheer me up. The roads're crowded, the parks're jampacked, and as for the cinema halls, the less said of them, the better. You know, I used to sit on the wide rawk of that house in front. But the owners don't let you sit there any longer.'

'Who is it . . . Biltu?'

Daamu's uncle came out of the house.

'How are you?'

'Not too well, I'm afraid. Lost my job today. They suspected I was a Naxalite—simply dismissed me.'

'My God! Here, come inside . . .'

'Not now, thanks. Daamu and I are going out for a while.'

Daamu came out wearing a shortsleeved shirt.

After going a short distance, he said, 'Let's walk to the river. Once we get to the Ganges, we can hire a dinghy. I'll tap Bimal-babu down the road.'

'He'll give you the money, will he?'

'He most certainly will. Because he thinks I'm a suitable prospect for that dark girl of his. He visits my uncle frequently, you know. He's told him he'll even wangle a job for me at his place of work, if I marry the girl.'

'Take the money if you can get it. But I wouldn't marry if I were you . . .'

'But why not?'

'Take a good look at me, and you'll know why not. You'll marry because of pressure from your uncle, right? Well, I married because of my father. And now look at me. Father's paralysed due to a stroke, not one of my three sisters are married, both my boys died due to lack of treatment. We don't get two square meals a day, and now I'm unemployed.'

As soon as they neared Bimal-babu's house, Daamu said, 'Hang on. I'll ask him for the money.'

He returned in about five minutes.

'I've got the money. In fact, he gave me more than I wanted.'

'Good. But don't you get trapped into marriage.'

They walked in silence for a while. Biltu suddenly said, 'It's all father's fault—he's the one that's responsible. Driven by lust as he was, he kept producing one child after the other. We're three brothers and three sisters. My brothers have ve turned into criminals. And as for my sisters—whores, the lot of them. My father married me off when I was still young. When I hadn't even started shaving properly. And naturally, I followed in his footsteps, producing child after child. But when it came to keeping them alive, I wasn't nearly as successful. One boy died of diphtheria, the other of typhoid fever. Didn't have the money to afford a proper physician, you know. Had to rely on that quack homoeopath. But I'll tell you something; I'm grateful to the fellow. He never charged a paisa.'

After walking a further distance, they reached a bar.

'How much did you manage to borrow . . . ?'

'Ten rupees.'

'Then let's go to that bar. We can have a drink.'

'Drink? But I don't drink.'

'Well, you can buy me one, then. Please, I'm really feeling rotten.'
Daamu had to buy him the drink. Biltu was not willing to budge,
otherwise.

They hired a small dinghy from one of the ghats of the Ganges.

Biltu told the boatmen, 'Take the boat mid-river.'

When the boat reached mid-river, Biltu suddenly threw the plywood box overboard.

'What did you do that for?'

'I'd given my other two children to the Ganges. Now I've done
the same to this one.'

'What? You mean your child was in that box?'

'Yes, he was born today. A beautiful boy. I strangled him. A lovely
child like that had no chance in a hell like this . . . !'

'For God's sake, what're you saying? What about your wife?'

'Finished her off as well. And my father, for good measure—'

Biltu leapt overboard and disappeared into the river with a splash.

His body was never recovered.

A Refined Joke

A number of things exist—such as the Himalayas, for instance—that are impossible to resist. I likewise find it impossible to resist my dear friend Parimal's requests. It is at his request that I am penning this tale of a refined joke, for your delectation.

It was not very long ago. There was a beautiful south wind blowing that day. Having very little to do, I'd had a pleasant siesta, and then decided to go out for a stroll. I had just sat down on a bench in College Square and lit my cigarette when the man appeared. Rather handsome and elegantly dressed. He had on a fine, crisply ironed shirt, gleaming patent-leather shoes, a ring with a large stone on his little finger. He looked at me once while chewing paan, then, inclining his head gracefully, spat out the betel juice and stood in front of me with a smile.

'Could you help me, sir? Just five rupees would do. I'm in considerable distress . . .'

And this is where the story begins.

Very gravely, I said, 'I'm sorry, but you'll have to excuse me.'

'You mean that you don't have five rupees in your pocket?'

'I do all right, but I'm not giving it to you. Frankly, you don't look particularly poor to me.'

'These are all the signs of my previous riches. But please don't judge me by my external appearance, sir. I am truly poor now.'

'But what evidence do I have that you're not telling lies?'

'Well, why don't you visit my home and see for yourself?'

'And where do you live?'

'In Metiabruz.'

Suddenly, I started feeling rather bloody-minded.

'All right. Give me your address and wait for me at my boarding house. If I find that you're genuinely distressed, I shall most certainly help you.'

'A return journey to Metiabruz will take a long time, sir. How long do you expect me to wait for you? Why don't I come with you?'

He quickly realized, from my answer, that he was dealing with a sharp character.

'For all I know, you might be a criminal. And once you've got me where you want me, who knows what you might do! Nothing doing. You'll have to wait at my flat.'

'But it's such a long journey . . .'

'I'll take a taxi. It shouldn't take me long at all.'

After a while, the taxi would not go any further. Because it could not go any further. Lanes, bylanes and, finally, an impossibly narrow alley. No taxi could have entered. I was forced to get off and walk through that dark and serpentine path. Finally, I realized that even I was not going to get any further. A closed door was barring my way. A few sharp raps opened the door for me, however. An elderly man came out holding a lantern.

'Yes? What d'you want?'

'Could you tell me which one number 144/13 is, please?'

'You mean Mukteshwar's house?'

'That's the one.'

'Do you see that narrow alley running between those two houses? If you follow that, you'll come to a lumber yard. His house is the one behind that.'

I was about to set off, following the old gentleman's directions, when he abruptly said, 'You can drop in on your way back, if you're so inclined.'

I had no idea what he meant, but I said that I would.

I must confess that I felt quite helpless in the pitch darkness around that lumber yard.

'Mukteshwar-babu . . . Mukteshwar-babu . . . anyone there . . . ?'

A few shouts produced the desired effect. The rear of the lumber yard was suddenly illuminated. Then, a scrawny, half-naked boy emerged, holding a kerosene lamp.

'Who're you looking for?'

'Mukteshwar-babu.'

'He isn't in.'

'Oh. Where's he gone?'

'What do you mean? Why?'

'Because of his creditors.'

(You think you see the joke, don't you?)

'What did you want to see him for, anyway?'

I couldn't answer him; I was feeling quite flustered by now. Suddenly I noticed that there was a woman standing behind the boy. She was holding a gamchha in front of her, possibly to cover herself. Her clothes were in absolute tatters.

'He's not in any danger, is he?'

Her quavering voice and her question, both embarrassed me terribly.

'Oh no, not at all. We were acquaintances once. I just thought I'd drop in to find out how he was.'

'Please, won't you come in?'

Perhaps I should not have gone in. All in all, it cost me a hundred rupees. A house full of children, each one of them hungry. Not one had a single decent article of clothing. Two were in bed, with high fever. I began to feel rather helpless, to say nothing of faintly penitent. If only I had given the man his five rupees!

If you have not yet found it very funny, please listen to this.

After I came out of that alley, I met the elderly gent as I had promised. 'My god! It's a living hell!'

The old man just said, 'It's all show.'

'What on earth do you mean?'

'People are smart these days, you know. They don't give anything to beggars, so the beggars have had to get smart as well. The occasional person with a conscience, like you, only gives something after making enquiries. So Mukteshwar's given shelter to a few refugees behind his timber yard, and told them if anyone should come asking for him, they're to say he's disappeared to avoid his creditors.'

'You're not serious?'

He was a rather taciturn old gent; he just said one word more: 'Cocaine.'

Then he politely shut the door on my face.

Perhaps you still do not find it funny. In that case, let me tell you what really happened. The story, from the point where I started it, is just that—a story. It really happened this way. When the man saw that I was not willing to help, he produced a very expensive Sheaffer pen from his pocket and said, 'In that case, please keep this pen and give me five rupees.'

I realized that he must have stolen it from somewhere. But I did not call the police. I merely thanked my lucky stars and decided that I had got out of the right side of the bed that morning.

It is truly a very fine pen.

I use it these days to write scathing denunciations of the trade in stolen goods.

Professor Sujit Sen

Professor Sujit Sen was reading a newspaper, when his imagination caught fire.

Deep night. A bitter, cold wind is blowing across the vast desert. The myriad stars in the sky are looking down at the Bedouin, Wajid. Mounted on his horse, Wajid is waiting impatiently, for Noor. Noor—the beautiful daughter of the Bedouin chief, Jabbar Khan. Wajid is not the scion of an important family. Which is why Jabbar Khan is unwilling to let Wajid mary his daughter. But Wajid and Noor love each other. And so they have decided to elope. A line of tents can be seen in the far distance; by now, even Wajid's horse has become impatient. It is pawing and rearing. Noor had promised that she would come as soon as the North Star had risen. But the North Star has risen a long time ago—why has Noor not arrived? Is Abid with her? Abid is Wajid's rival, the Chief's choice for Noor's hand.

Suddenly, the desert sands seem to gain a voice: 'Wajid . . . Wajid . . . I have come . . .'

Astounded, Wajid sees Noor crawling across the desert sands.

'I had to travel this way because Abid is coming after me. He would have seen me otherwise.'

Wajid leaps down from his horse and scoops Noor up. He climbs on his horse; Noor sits behind him and holds him tight.

Through the dark, the horse gallops on.

A little while later, another horse emerges—Abid's horse. This horse starts galloping as well.

They are still galloping. Galloping for ever, against the background of history.

However, their forms change.

For example, the Prithviraj who escaped with Sanjukta on horse-back while being pursued by the soldiers of Jaichand—that Prithviraj and the Bedouin Wajid differ only in their external attributes. Their internal motivations are similar. Wajid's fate is not known, but what happened to Prithviraj is written in history. Jaichand invited Mohammed Ghori to invade, not just once but twice. Prithviraj for-feited his life in the name of love. He died in battle with Mohammed Ghori.

Such thoughts had risen in the mind of Sujit Sen, professor of history, after reading an item in a newspaper. A boy had eloped to Bombay with his girlfriend. The girl's father had taken the first flight out and arrived in Bombay the very next day. Then shot his daughter dead.

Many similar stories came to his mind.

The love story of Salim and Anarkali. Salim's father, Akbar, had supposedly been his rival for Anarkali. She had been walled up alive. He thought of the story of Jehangir, Noor Jehan and Sher Afghan. He thought of Radha's trysts, of Ayaan Ghosh's mute rage, and many other such tales from history, mythology and even ordinary, day-to-day life. Why, only the other day, didn't the girl from the house oppo-site run away with the chauffeur? They were all the tale of Wajid and Noor. With just a tiny difference. They had all ended in tragedy, in unremitting tragedy.

In the middle of all this, the doorbell rang. He came to with a start and hurriedly opened the door.

'Why Sumita! What're you doing here, love? Why've you returned from Calcutta? And who . . . ?'

Pointing to the salwaar-kameez-clad man standing behind her, she said, 'This is my husband. We were married a week ago.'

'Husband!'

'Yes, sir,' said the man with a courtly adaab, 'I'm your son-in-law.'

Sujit Sen stared in stunned silence. He could never have imagined that Sumita would do such a thing. Indeed, no father likes to imagine such a thing of his daughter. After he had gathered his wits, he said, in Bengali, 'You didn't tell me your name.'

'My name's Usman Khan,' the man said, 'I'm a Pathan.'

Once more, Professor Sujit Sen stared in silence.

He has written many articles on the topic, lectured all over the country for this cause. But he is not happy at the thought of his daughter marrying a Muslim. He looks at his daughter. She is standing in front of him, with downcast eyes, but there is a faint smile on her face.

He leaves the room abruptly and returns a few moments later, holding a revolver.

Handing it over to his daughter, he says, 'It is customary to give dowry in marriage. Take this. The road you've chosen is full of dangers and this may be of use when you're in trouble.'

He turns and leaves the room.

He goes up to the terrace on the third floor. From the terrace, he can see that a motorcycle is parked below. After a few moments, Usman Khan comes out and climbs on; his daughter climbs up behind him.

Professor Sujit Sen is once again reminded that Sanjukta, too, had climbed up behind Prithviraj on his horse. Immediately, another thought comes to mind—Prithviraj and Sanjukta had belonged to the same race.

It was so difficult to purge oneself of the feelings of race.

The motorcycle starts suddenly with a roar, then growls away.

Notes

'Necessity'

PAGE 3, Hindu hotel: A restaurant serving traditional Bengali food. It was common among conservative upper-caste Hindus to believe that food touched by Muslims or Christians would render it 'impure'. Restaurants would be called 'Hindu' hotels to signal that their staff were all Hindu and that it was 'safe' for Hindus to eat there.

PAGE 3, matric: Matriculation or the final school-leaving examination.

'Jogen Pandit'

PAGE 5 moshla: Mixture of cumin, cardamom, clove, betel nut and other spices, chewed on as a mouth freshener and/or a digestive.

'Nawab Sahib'

PAGE 10, khazanchi: Accountant.

PAGE 12, shingara, nimki, kochuri: Different kinds of savoury snacks.

PAGE 13, adaab: North Indian Muslim salutation. The word is derived from Urdu, through the Arabic word *adaab*, meaning etiquette.

PAGE 14, khaasi: The neutered goat, favoured among Bengalis for its tender meat; often sacrificed during the worship of Goddess Kali.

PAGE 14, zarda pulao: Pulao flavoured and coloured with saffron which gives it a yellow colour.

PAGE 16, paan: A popular Indian preparation combining betel leaf with areca nut, slaked lime and, sometimes, tobacco, chewed for its digestive and/or stimulant effects.

'A Puja Story'

PAGE 23, The Pujas: Durga Puja, the most important religious festival in Bengal that lasts for ten days in autumn and celebrates the battle of goddess Durga with the shape-shifting, deceptive and powerful buffalo demon Mahishasura. Popular mythology—and thus the idols worshipped during this festival—depicts her as a married woman returning to her parents' home for a four-five day holiday, along with her children— Ganesha (lord of prosperity), Lakshmi (goddess of wealth), Saraswati (goddess of learning) and Kartik (lord of war).

'The Human Mind'

PAGE 29, combined hand (in English in the original): Old-fashioned term for a male servant.

PAGE 30, *Ka Tava Kanta*: A Sanskrit phrase meaning 'who is your beloved'.

PAGE 31, kaviraj: A physician who practises according to ancient Indian medical systems such as Ayurveda.

PAGE 31 Tarakeshwar: A town 60 kilometres north of Calcutta, site of a temple to Shiva, a omajor pilgrimage in West Bengal with a reputation for miracle cures.

'A Moment's Glory'

PAGE 33, zamindar: A landowner, especially one who leases his land to tenant farmers.

'Vidyasagar'

PAGE 38, Ishwarchandra Vidyasagar: Born Ishwarchandra Bandyopadhyay (1820–91), Bengali polymath, writer, educator, social reformer and a key figure of the nineteenth-century Bengal Renaissance. The title Vidyasagar literally means 'ocean of knowledge', and he continues to revered by Bengalis as the epitome of the educated intellectual.

PAGE 39, muni: A hermit.

PAGE 39, nara: Man.

'Yesterday's Rai-Bahadur'

PAGE 49, Rai-Bahadur: One of the various degrees of titular order introduced by the British in India.

PAGE 50, swaraj: Literally, 'self-rule', the word usually refers to Mahatma Gandhi's concept for independence from foreign domination. It was a rallying cry during the Indian Independence Movement.

PAGE 50, Vande Mataram, Inquilab Zindabad: Popular rallying cries during the Indian Independence Movement. Vande Mataram means 'Hail

Mother' while Inquilab Zindabad means 'Long Live the Revolution'. The two slogans may be said to represent the religio-nationalist and radical-nationalist currents, respectively, of the freedom struggle.

'As It Happened'

PAGE 52, IAS: Indian Administrative Service, the premier civil service of India.

PAGE 53, Bouma: In Bengali, a term for 'daughter-in-law'.

'Under the Same Verandah'

PAGE 59, aap: In Hindi and Urdu, the honorific version of 'you'.

'Wildfire'

PAGE 63, Bom Mahadev: A rallying cry used by Shiva worshippers.

PAGE 64, gamchha: A thin, cotton towel, occasionally also used as a scarf.

PAGE 64, Kaamdhenu: A cow in Hindu mythology, famed for its capacity to grant any wish or desire.

PAGE 64, kheer: Sweet pudding made by boiling rice with milk and sugar.

PAGE 64, Vishwakarma: In Hindu mythology, the divine engineer of the world, the god of crafts and industry.

'Two Disciples'

PAGE 80, Aurobindo Ghose (1872–1950): Yogi, seer, philosopher, poet and Indian nationalist who propounded a philosophy of divine life on earth through spiritual evolution. From 1902 to 1910 Aurobindo partook in the struggle to free India from the British raj. As a result of his political activities, he was imprisoned in 1908. Two years later he fled and found refuge in the French colony of Pondicherry in southeastern India, where he spent the rest of his life developing his 'integral' yoga, characterized by its holistic approach and its aim of a fulfilled and spiritually trans-formed life on earth.

PAGE 80, sadhana: A word with a range of meanings, and includes both the process of achieving a goal as well as the goal itself. It can also mean a vow or a request.

PAGE 81, Tantra: In Hinduism. any of several books of esoteric doctrine regarding rituals, disciplines, meditation, etc., composed in the form of dialogues between Shiva and his consort. Also refers to the philosophy or doctrine of these books—the changing, visible world is the creative dance or play of the Divine Mother, and enlightenment is the realization of the essential oneness of the self and of the visible world with Shiva-Shakti, the Godhead.

PAGE 82, kamandal: A small metal urn used by mendicants to carry water.

PAGE 82, pakora: A very popular snack, consisting of small pieces of vegetable dipped in gram flour paste and deep fried.

PAGE 83, chandan: Sandalwood.

PAGE 83, guggul: Aromatics often burnt as incense.

PAGE 83, purohit: Priest officiating at a Hindu ritual.

'During the Riots'

PAGE 86, ashwattha: Sacred peepal tree.

PAGE 86, Gwala: A pastoral, cow-rearing community in different parts of northern and western India.

'Discovered the Next Day'

PAGE 91, Divakar: One of the Sanskrit words for the Sun.

'Afzal'

PAGE 93, jagirdar: The owner of land given in return for services to the throne; a hereditary title.

PAGE 93, Santhal Parganas: An area comprising portions of the present-day states of Jharkhand, Bihar and West Bengal, which is home to the indigenous Santhal people.

PAGE 94, majhi: Boatman.

PAGE 94, qurnish: A form of salutation performed by Muslims.

PAGE 96, baiji: A courtesan with singing skills.

'The Ultimate Dance'

PAGE 102, rambhoru: A woman with well-shaped thighs, specifically thighs like the trunk of a banana tree.

PAGE 103, ghungroo: Little bells on a strap worn on the ankles by dancers.

'Ramsevak'

PAGE 105, Harinaam: The name of Hari, or God.

'Another Day'

PAGE, 109 Bhumihar: A caste of landowners, chiefly in Bihar.

PAGE, 109 Kayastha: One of higher castes who, alongside Brahmins, comprise the upper layer of Bengali Hindu society.

PAGE 110, pav: One quarter of a seer.

PAGE 110, potol: Pointed gourd, a green vegetable available especially during the summer months.

PAGE 112, laal shaak: Red spinach. Both laal shaak and potolare inexpensive vegetables and part of the common man's diet.

'A Mere Ten Rupees'

PAGE 115, jatra: A traditional form of stage performance from eastern India marked by a melodramatic and theatrical acting style, music and song.

'Paired Dreams'

PAGE 120, dhobani: Washerwoman.

PAGE 120, matha and mundu: Both mean 'head' in Bengali.

'Bourgeois–Proletariat'

PAGE 122, maund: Traditional measure of weight. Approx. 40 kilograms.

'Punishment'

PAGE 126, daroga: An inspector or sub-inspector in the Indian Police.

PAGE 127, bel: A tree whose leaves are a special offering for Shiva idols.

PAGE 128, Bhuteshwar Shiva: Shiva as the Lord of Ghosts. Temples dedicated to this avatar of Shiva are often found adjacent to cremation grounds.

PAGE 130, amabasya: In most Indian languages, this refers to the moonless night of the dark lunar quarter.

PAGE 131, Bolo Hari Haribol: 'Call God's name!' This is chanted by pallbearers in Bengal while carrying a body to the cremation ground.

'Consort'

PAGE 133, machaan: A platform or dais built on trees from where hunters wait for their prey.

'Bhuvan Shome'

PAGE 143, gaona: The ceremony of taking a Hindu bride to her husband's home for the first time after the wedding and the obligatory visit to her paternal home.

PAGE 143, jhunjhut: Minor troubles, problems, irritations, etc.

PAGE 144, dada: Grandfather in Hindi; older brother in Bengali.

PAGE 148, Harijan: Literally 'Hari's people' or the Lord's people. Coined by Mahatma Gandhi as a substitute for 'untouchable'.

PAGE 148, satyagraha: Loosely translated as 'insistence on truth' or 'loyalty to the truth', a form of nonviolent civil resistance initiated and developed by Mahatma Gandhi.

PAGE 150, pice hotel: A restaurant serving traditional, wholesome Bengali food only for one paisa or 'pice'.

PAGE 151, Baidya: One of the three upper castes in Bengal. Also a practitioner of traditional Hindu medicine.

PAGE 152, Mohun Bagan: The oldest existing football club in India, founded in 1889. Its rivalry with East Bengal Club (founded in 1920) is legendary among football lovers in Bengal.

PAGE 153, dhobi: Washerman.

PAGE 154, aasan: Mat or seat (including a king's throne), or one of the postures in yoga.

PAGE 155, chulha: Primitive stove that uses coal, wood or cow-dung cake as fuel.

PAGE 158, Hanuman and Jambuban: Hanuman is the generic name in North India for the grey langur monkey. Also one of the central characters in the epic Ramayana, Hanuman is worshipped widely across the subcontinent as a symbol of strength. Jambuban, or Jambavana, the King of Bears, is an Asiatic or sloth bear and another significant character in the Ramayana (though he is also described as a monkey in other scriptures). In the story, Bhuvan Shome interprets the names pejoratively, by focusing on their 'monkey' (i.e. wild) origins.

PAGE 162, *Ananga Ranga*: An Indian sex manual written by Kalyana Malla in the fifteenth or sixteenth century.

PAGE 163, Savitri-vrata: A vow kept by married Hindu women in honour of Savitri, a potent symbol of spousal devotion in Hindu mythology, in which they pray for their husband to have a long life.

PAGE 163, seer: A traditional Indian measure of weight, equivalent to about 1.25 kilograms.

PAGE 166, Bijaya Dashami: The last day of Durga Puja in Bengal. On this day and over the following two weeks, Bengalis traditionally visit their relatives and seek blessings from their elders. Younger family members show their respect by touching elders' feet and are, in turn, offered sweets.

PAGE 167, maithil: A person from Mithila, northern Bihar.

PAGE 167, thakur: A Brahmin cook.

PAGE 168, hubble-bubble: Rudimentary form of hookah, in which the smoke passes through water, causing a bubbling sound.

PAGE 171, kataribhog: A type of fine rice.

PAGE 172, soru-chakli: A traditional Bengali sweet dish.

PAGE 172, Yama: The Hindu god of the underworld and the dead, usually depicted as riding a buffalo.

PAGE 176, gur: Jaggery, or cane sugar.

PAGE 180, arhar: A variety of pulses.

PAGE 181, Bhuihar: A caste of landowners, chiefly in Bihar.

PAGE 183, sabda brahma: In Sanskrit, 'The Word as God', also Om or Aum, the original sound at the creation of the universe.

PAGE 190, *swadharme nidhanang shreyah, parodharme bhayavahah*: Bengali for 'to die for one's own faith is preferable; for another's, terrible.'

PAGE 191, padodak: Water which has washed the feet of a holy man or woman, or even a temple or household idol. Consumed by devoted Hindus who consider it a blessing.

PAGE 191, prasad: Food items offered to the gods, then redistributed among the devout at the end of a puja.

PAGE 197, Satkar Samiti: Organizations which arrange funerals for destitute Hindus.

PAGE 200, Mahishasurmardini: The Goddess Durga, generally depicted as the slayer of a demon who had taken the form of a *mahish* or buffalo.

PAGE 200, ubodh: Literally, 'someone with good sense or prudence', also means 'docile'. In popular Bengali good boy–bad boy morality tales for children, the good boy is often described as *subodh*.

PAGE 201, khatiya: Charpoy, a cot made of wood and rope, popular in rural India.

PAGE 201, Michael Madhusudan Dutt (1824–73): Popular Bengali poet and a pioneer of Bengali drama, Dutt was known for his distinctive look, in particular his nineteenth-century Western-style beard and curly locks.

PAGE 208, dahi-chiwda: Yoghurt and flattened rice, a common snack among rural people in Eastern India.

PAGE 209, sattu: Flour consisting of a mixture of ground pulses and cereals, popular especially in Bihar.

PAGE 210, Baisakh: A month in the traditional Indian lunar calendar, also the month of summer.

PAGE 223, *Durgesh Nandini*: Literally, 'the beloved of the lord of the fort'. Also the title of a Bengali historical romance novel by Bankim Chandra Chattopadhyay in 1865.

PAGE 224, tulsi: The basil plant, an object of veneration for Hindus.

'Not A Demon'

PAGE 226, Naxal/ite: A far-left radical communist, supportive of Maoist political sentiment and ideology. The term Naxal derives from the name of the village Naxalbari in West Bengal, where the armed movement had its origin in 1967.

PAGE 227, rawk: A small balcony on the ground floor of a house, often on or facing the street.